THE LAST CROSSING

Brian McGilloway

THE
DOME
PRESS

Published by The Dome Press, 2020
Copyright © Brian McGilloway 2020
The moral right of Brian McGilloway to be recognised as the author
of this work has been asserted in accordance with the
Copyright, Designs and Patents Act 1988.

This is a work of fiction. All characters, organisations and events portrayed in
this novel are either products of the author's imagination or are used
fictitiously.

A CIP catalogue record for this book is available from the British Library

ISBN: 9781912534340

The Dome Press

Printe   ).A.

08/20
War

THE LAST CROSSING

In loving memory of my father, Laurence

'And may there be no sadness of farewell,
When I embark'

Alfred Lord Tennyson

THE FIRST CROSSING

CHAPTER ONE

Martin Kelly cried for his mother before he died.

His face was glazed with tears, his mouth a grotesque O as first he pleaded for his life and, when it became clear that they would not listen to him, called for his mother. Stripped naked, he knelt in the grave they had already dug for him. The light of the torch Tony held caught the shiny skin of the scar on his lower abdomen where he'd had his appendix out, standing out against the lividity of the bruising he carried there, his phallus shrivelled amongst the dark of his pubis at the outer edges of the glare.

Tony had wanted to cover him up, give him his coat to offer him some dignity, but Hugh had refused. He was aware of Karen next to him, her breathing quick and shallow as she watched, the black plastic bag of Martin's clothes, which they had stripped from him, twisted in her grip.

Martin held out his bound hands in supplication, looking from one face to the next. 'It wasn't me,' he said. 'I didn't do it.'

'You're a liar,' Hugh spat.

'I'm not,' Martin sobbed. 'I swear on me mother, I'm not.'

'And you knew what would happen.'

It was then that Martin broke down, his body wracked with sobs that turned to retching. He vomited onto himself, half choking on it, the bile and saliva hanging in a lace from his chin to his chest. He made no effort to wipe it away.

'Fuck this,' Hugh said, moving forward, raising his pistol.

'Tell me mother–'

The shot reverberated through the trees, which came instantly alive, cacophonous as a murder of crows took wing against the evening sky.

Martin twisted with the shot, his body thudding against the edge of the grave they had dug. Hugh moved across and, with his toe, pushed him down into the gaping space, before firing three more shots in quick succession, each one momentarily illuminating the still white body where it lay, the red wounds flowering as the blood unfurled with each shot.

'Get those clothes burned,' Hugh ordered, glancing at Karen. 'You,' he added, looking at Tony, 'grab a spade and get shovelling.'

It took them twenty minutes to fill in the grave, Hugh and Tony quickly shifting into an alternating rhythm while, in the distance, through the uniform ranks of the spruce trees, they could see Karen, her face illuminated by the flickering flames, burning Martin's clothes. The air, acrid with the smell of the fabric as it burnt, splintered with the crackle and hiss of the needles Karen had gathered up from the forest floor to kindle the blaze. When she was finished, they saw her dance on the embers, which sparked once more at her feet as she put the fire out and kicked a covering of leaves over the scorching.

In the distance, a low rumbling resolved itself into the roar of a plane taking off from Glasgow Airport and traversing the sky overhead, just above the clouds; the whine of its jet engines rising in pitch as the aircraft rose, building to a crescendo, before dissipating slowly into silence.

Tony wondered if any of those on board, glancing down, might see them about their business in the gloom. He felt his pulse throbbing in his ears, felt his own stomach twist and churn at the thought of what they had just done.

'Are you sure–?' he started, the first words either of them had spoken since taking up the shovels.

'We never talk of this again,' Hugh said. 'We never come back here again.'

Tony motioned to protest, but Hugh raised the spade in front of him. 'I'll fucking cleave your head in two if you don't stop. We did what we had to do. I'm no happier than you are about it, but he got what he deserved.'

As they gathered their stuff and left the clearing, Tony looked back once at the spot, the slight rise of the earth just visible, in the dying light of Hugh's retreating torch beam, through the fork of an oak, twisted with ivy. It took them almost an hour to pick their way back to the car, the journey through the trees made in silence.

Only once, as they crossed a stream that ran down through the woodland, bridged by a fallen tree trunk, did Tony stop and reach out a hand for Karen to help her across. She took his hand in hers, squeezed it a little in reassurance, held it a second longer than necessary after she reached the other bank.

They drove back to Glasgow that evening and dropped Hugh at the train station.

'I'll be in touch,' he said, as he left them. 'Go home and forget about the whole bloody business.'

They watched him shuffle his way into the station, sticking a hand in his pocket and pawing out a few coins to pass to the young fella squatted at the station entrance, a paper coffee cup his begging bowl.

'Where do you want me to leave you?' Tony asked.

'How about we get a bottle of something?' Karen suggested. 'There's an offie across the street.'

She arrived back with a bottle of Southern Comfort and two litres of Diet Coke. They drove to Karen's flat in Paisley. Once inside, they stripped off their clothes as Hugh had instructed and put them in a hot wash. They sat in front of the fire, wrapped in bed sheets, and drank half the Southern Comfort before Karen moved across and straddled Tony, her mouth sweet, her tongue cold in his mouth as she kissed him with an urgency, a hunger, which surprised him, even as she pulled the sheet off him and pushed him back onto the floor.

They made love there. Tony had the sense he was discovering her body anew in that moment, as if their proximity to death had somehow enflamed their desire to live, to breath, to feel. He tried to dispel from his mind the vision of Martin Kelly, kneeling in his grave, the thought that his body was cooling beneath the earth even as theirs blazed in a moment of climax.

They lay together, Tony's head resting on her chest, his hand on her stomach. He could hear the rapid beating of her heart begin to slow, and felt his own breathing synchronise with its rhythm. He imagined himself happy, imagined them together like this, somewhere at home, a Donegal winter wind blowing outside.

That was what he would remember in years to come, when he was both alone and lonely. This last time together. The heat of her body, the scent of her perfume, of her skin, the gentle lift and fall of her breast beneath him with each breath, the saltiness in his mouth as he raised his own head and kissed her, the light of the flames dancing across her flesh.

CHAPTER TWO

'Sins of the flesh,' he muttered, as if trying out the phrase, his tongue struggling with the words. Such an archaic formulation, he thought: sins of the flesh. How else to describe it? Even alone now, did that still qualify as a sin of the flesh, when that flesh was his own?

He ran through the shopping list of his sins, a habit since childhood, as he waited for Father O'Brien to shunt back the wooden slide of the confessional box. He could hear the low murmurs of the conversation being conducted to the other side of the confessional, alternating between the modulated timbre of the priest's deeper, softer tones and the hushed sibilant whisper of the lady who occupied the other box.

The confessional was dark and close, rich with the heady sweetness of the wood polish which he himself had used just the previous morning on the kneeling boards and frame when he'd done the weekly clean of the church.

He was surprised by the thud of the wooden slat sliding back into place; he'd not heard the muted rhythmic Act of Contrition from the other side.

'Bless me, Father, for I have sinned,' he began and, saw again, unbidden, Martin's white body, the red flowering of his wounds, the narrowness of his grave, itself as dark as a confessional. He stopped.

'Go on, Tony,' the priest urged softly.

'I have sinned,' he repeated. 'It's been a month since my last confession. I've offended God by…'

The laundry list failed him now. Spoken unkindly of someone? Watched porn a few times? They seemed infantile somehow.

'Are you OK?'

'I'm, ah, I'm away for the day, tomorrow,' he managed, his mouth suddenly dry, the walls of the confessional nearer to him than he'd realised, the edge of the kneeling board digging into his knee.

'Very good,' O'Brien said, a little quizzically. 'Do you want to confess before you go?'

'I was going to… I'm meeting a few friends from way back.'

He could see the silhouette of the priest through the mesh that separated them, his head nodding, bowed as he read from his breviary by the weak light that leaked through the curtains of the box.

'Very good,' the priest repeated. 'I can get someone to cover the funeral on Thursday, if you like.'

'No, it's grand,' Tony said. 'I'll be home tomorrow night. I'm on the last crossing back.'

'Crossing? Are you headed to Scotland?'

Tony cursed silently, then realised the irony of doing so in his current situation.

'Some old school friends?' O'Brien guessed.

'That's it,' Tony said. 'I'll be here for Thursday.'

'It'll do you good,' O'Brien said, raising his head now. 'What with everything over the past few months.'

Tony nodded.

'Do you want to confess anything?' O'Brien asked.

'I've done... I've done things I'm not proud of,' Tony said. 'That's as best I can put it.'

'Loneliness can do that to a man,' O'Brien began. 'We're social animals; we're not made to be alone.'

Afterwards, he walked up to his wife's grave. He'd visited it each day since her death. 283 days. The roses he'd brought for her birthday the previous week were wilted now, the stems soft, the heads hanging heavy, as if in prayer over her grave.

He hunkered at the edge, pulled an early weed from the soil above her, felt a sad satisfaction as he felt the roots tauten and give.

'I'll miss you tomorrow, Ann,' he said. He stood, laid his hand on the cold marble of the headstone. 'We're heading back.' He felt a tightening in his chest at the thought, and he placed his hand on the gravestone for support.

'Love you, Ann,' he concluded, once he'd caught his breath, his words barely a murmur. The stone beneath his hand was cold and unyielding and he felt shame at his thoughts, for they were not, he realised, of his wife.

He wondered how Karen had changed. Her hair had been long then, shoulder-length and brown. She'd be fifty-one now, maybe fifty-two. Did she think of him as he thought of her? Did she try to recreate, in her mind's eye, his touch? His taste and smell? Did she feel, for a moment, the pressure of his head on her chest, his hand on her body? And did she awake at night, Martin's final cries for his mother still audible in her ears, the smell of his burning clothes clinging to her hair?

And, more than that, he wondered if she turned to someone next to her in that bed and lied about what had disturbed her dreams. Or had she found someone to whom she could tell the truth? Or was her bed cold and wide and lonely, as his was now. As cold and lonely as Martin Kelly, where he lay beneath the earth.

CHAPTER THREE

The earth clattering across his brother's coffin heralded a scream of agony from his father such as he had never heard before. The man, tall, solidly built, proud, seemed to crumple, as if the wail had taken something of substance with it as it left him. Tony gripped his arm, tried to hold him upright, while the priest looked at him with a mixture of pity and embarrassment and his mother began sobbing once more into the clump of damp tissues she gripped.

Tony felt the shuddering of his father next to him and wondered at his own detachment. He felt a quiet guilt that he wasn't weeping too, wondered what the absence of emotions said about him.

To his rear, two of the group of men who had walked behind them up through the cemetery in a loose formation moved forward. 'It's all right, son,' one of them said. 'We've got him.'

His father recoiled at their touch, his hand scrabbling for Tony's to help him stand again. The men, seeming to understand, stepped back, respectful, heads bowed.

After the burial, the men, dressed uniformly in white, open-necked shirts and black trousers, spoke in soft earnest terms to his mother, passed his father with a nod and a grimace of shared loss but offered their hands to Tony to shake. The last one to pass him, one of those who had moved forward to help his father, cupped Tony's shoulder in one hand as he shook the other, his grip firm and warm.

'Sorry for your loss, son,' he said. He was small, heavy-set, brown-haired, with a thick moustache. He spoke with a slight stutter, as if his breath caught with every few words.

'Thank you,' Tony said. 'Thanks for your help there.'

'Your father's still raw,' the man said. 'Anything we can do to help, just let me know. Anything at all.'

Tony nodded, uncertain who the man was. He'd been at university in Belfast for the past few years, had lost track of his parents' neighbours and friends.

'They'll not get away with what they did to your Danny,' the man said, his gaze level and unyielding.

Tony nodded once more, muttered agreement, not entirely sure what else he was meant to say. He did, at least, know who 'they' were.

His brother, Danny, two years his junior, had been walking home from watching a football match in the Brandywell. The evening was cold, so he'd had his Derry City scarf pulled up over his nose and mouth. He'd cut up through the alleyways and out onto Bligh's Lane when an army Land Rover, racing away from a riot happening at the top of the lane, had careened down towards him. A petrol bomb had caught the wire mesh on the windscreen and the flames and smoke had, it was reported afterwards, made it almost impossible for the driver to see. He'd mounted the kerb just as Danny appeared, as if from nowhere, he claimed, and the boy went under the wheels.

If he'd survived for long after the impact, they could not say; the Land Rover had not stopped, for fear of an ambush. Whatever of that, the boy was dead by the time the people living in Nualamont Drive came out to see what had happened.

'What did Mullan want?' his father asked, later that evening. They were sitting in the kitchen, his father with an untouched mug of tea in front of him.

They'd invited all the funeral guests back to the local community centre for tea and sandwiches and hung round till the last of them departed.

Tony shrugged quizzically.

'Sean Mullan,' his father said, as if that clarified things. 'He spoke to you at the grave,' he added. 'The fat guy with the moustache.'

Tony was surprised at the personal nature of his father's comment. 'He said if we needed help–'

'Not from the likes of him,' his dad snapped. 'You didn't agree to anything, did you?'

Tony considered whether murmuring agreement to the comment that whoever had killed his brother should be held to account was something he should mention. In the end he simply shook his head. 'I don't even know who he is.'

'*Trouble*'s who he is,' his dad said. 'Looking to jump on the back of Danny's death.'

'How?'

'Mullan's high up with that crowd of hoods. He'll be claiming Danny's death was political.'

'It *was* political,' Tony said, feeling the first flames of his anger build – the first stirring of any emotion, in fact, since Danny's death. Comforted by its presence after days of numbness, he clung to it. 'The fucking army ran him over.'

'It was an accident,' his father said, lifting the spoon out of his mug and, with it, the film settling on the surface of his drink.

'Accident my arse. They drove over him, like a dog.'

His father lifted his head, gazed at him, his eyes brimming, and Tony regretted the insensitivity of the words. 'The guy who was driving is nineteen. Younger than you. It was his first week here.'

'Is that what they told you?' He kindled his own rage, even as he wondered why he was directing it at his father

The older man inhaled, sharply, then held the breath, as if reluctant to let it go for fear of what might happen. 'And what did Mullan tell you? That they'd get them back?'

Tony kept his expression neutral. 'Maybe someone should.'

His father nodded. 'And what good would that do? Would it mean Danny would be back home with us?'

'Someone should pay.'

'Why? Will that balance things out, if there's some other father sitt–' He paused, his breath a suspiration. 'Sitting stirring his cold fucking mug of tea the day he buries his boy. Will that make things better?'

Tony felt the urge to move to his father, to encircle him in his arms, but the distance between them seemed greater than ever. 'It'll not make them worse,' he said.

'Yes, it will,' the old man said, his expression drawn. 'You don't diminish your own grief by creating it for someone else.' He raised his chin, already trembling, but it did not stop the tears.

Tony sat for a moment as his father sobbed, hoping propinquity was its own support. Then, embarrassed, he moved into the living room.

After nine, father, mother and son, sitting in the silence of their home, exhausted by the day's events, heard the clatter of gunfire down the estate. The late evening news confirmed that a policeman had been shot on patrol.

At one in the morning, their front door was rammed open and six soldiers forced their way into the house. Tony was in his bed, sleeping only in his underwear. They were in his room before he even had a chance to grab something to cover him. His father was already being pulled down the stairs by the time they got Tony to release his grip on the bedpost; one of them raised his boot and ground Tony's fingers against it until he had to let go. Two of them dragged him after his father, ignoring his mother's screams.

He was down in seconds and out on to the street, illuminated by the strobing of blue lights from the police Land Rovers which were parked at the end of the row, keeping back the straggle of protesters who'd already emerged from their houses.

The bench in the rear of the Land Rover was cold, the cushion padding long since torn away. He thought for a moment that one of the soldiers, who he'd seen lifting his clothes off the chair beside his bed, would hand them to him, but the heavy doors swung shut and he sat in his pants, his father opposite in stripped pyjamas, his mouth moving wordlessly.

'Here, son.' The man next to Tony peeled off his shirt and handed it to him. 'Better half-dressed than buck naked,' Hugh Duggan said. 'Smoke.'

Tony shook his head.

'First time?'

'Aye.'

'They'll try all sorts,' Hugh said. 'Whatever they do, say nothing. But don't be surprised if they threaten to shoot your ma, or stitch up your da here. Fuck 'em. Tell 'em nothing. But they're a shower of dirty bastards. Whatever dirty trick they pull, you be ready.'

CHAPTER FOUR

'Be ready for 8.30,' the text had said. In fact, the car pulled up at the bus stop five minutes early. The youth who opened the passenger door for Tony was in his early twenties at most, his hair thick and curled.

'Tony Canning?' he asked.

Tony nodded. He'd been instructed to bring an overnight bag with a change of clothes. The only one he'd been able to find that morning was the small tartan travel bag he'd bought for Ann when first she went into the hospital. She only used it for a few days before it became clear her stay would necessitate more than two days change of underwear. Even with so little use, the bag had still smelt of the hospital when he'd opened it.

As he'd packed it for his own journey that morning, he'd found a pen lying at the bottom of it. He'd brought it in with her Sudoku book, to keep her entertained. He'd held it between his finger and thumb, as if it was a talisman from his dead wife. He'd contemplated bringing it with him, pretended to forget it on the dressing table after he left the house and felt embarrassed at such a poor attempt at self-delusion.

He wanted to ask where he could put the bag, but the young man made no effort to open the boot for him, so he set it in the footwell and then sat twisting slightly to one side.

'Richard Barr,' the driver offered, his hand held out. As Tony shook it, he noticed a sleeve tattoo of a Celtic design. Looking at Barr now, he saw the edge of a similar design hemming the neckline of his T-shirt and he wondered absently if it extended the whole way from his neck to his wrist.

The half hour drive from Derry to Dungiven passed in platitudes. They trailed behind a learner driver doing 40mph and Barr swerved lightly in and out behind her, one hand on the wheel, the other tapping some unheard beat on his knee before he finally pulled out and sped past her on the chevrons at a right turn junction. Tony instinctively gripped the dashboard in front of him, even as he glanced in the wing mirror, half expecting to see the blue lights of a police car spark into life behind them. It seemed foolhardy, doing anything that might draw attention to them, considering what they were going to do. But then what were they going to do? Visit Scotland? Three old friends and their younger driver.

Barr seemed to note Tony's discomfort, for he straightened himself a little in his seat, flexing his arm muscles as he gripped the wheel tighter with one hand, tapping out the beat of his own thoughts with renewed vigour.

'When did you last see Hughie?' the youth asked.

'Thirty years ago, too,' Tony replied. Hughie. He'd never called him Hughie. It was the name a friend would use. And they had never been friends.

For a moment, Tony didn't recognise Hugh Duggan, despite him being the only person at the bus stop just outside the town. When he stood, the wind caught and twisted his trouser legs, plastering the material against his frame, accentuating his thinness. His neck was narrow and jowly, the skin loose. His hair was shorn tight, little more than grey stubble. His skin was sallow where once it had been florid.

They pulled up alongside him and Barr got out of the car. He moved around the back and opened the boot, then approached Hugh, his hand outstretched. 'Mr Duggan,' he said. 'It's a real honour.'

Duggan muttered something, his gaze sliding from the youth's face towards Tony. He raised his chin a little, interrogatively, his expression not softening.

Tony opened the door and got out, using the stop as an opportunity to put his own bag in the boot of the car to afford him more leg room.

'Hugh,' he said, nodding. 'Long time.'

'Long time,' Duggan agreed.

'I'll get your bag,' Barr said, lifting Duggan's bag before the man could protest and taking it around to the boot.

'Was this your fucking idea?' Duggan asked, moving closer to Tony, the funk of his breath sharp as it rattled in his throat.

'I thought it was yours,' Tony said.

Duggan looked at him askance. 'Why would I? It must have been her. I knew she'd go soft.'

Tony followed Barr around to the back of the car to put his own bag away. He had to shift Duggan's a little to make space for his own. When he closed the rear door, he saw that Duggan had already taken his seat in the front, though he'd not noticed the car shift with the man's weight as it now did when Barr climbed into the driver's seat and started the engine again.

Tony took the back seat. He was glad in a way. He could tune out of the murmured conversation happening in front of him. It also meant that Karen would be sitting beside him, in the back. He reached across, brushed a few crumbs of dirt off the seat.

Barr was filling the silence with chatter. 'My da talked about you all the time,' he said. 'You and him did time together.'

'He was a good fella,' Duggan muttered. 'God rest him.'

Barr laughed, seemingly having not heard the prayer offered for his dead father. 'He told me this one time that the screws were bringing you across the courtyard because they thought you were passing messages through the wings and you took the piss out of them, pretending to hide things, and this screw was running from one side of the yard to the other, having to check every fucking hole in the walls. He said they even had to go down the drains, cause you pretended to drop something.'

His face lit up at this shared memory he had not even witnessed. A prison yard joke, passed between the generations, now mythologized.

'What—' Tony began, about to ask why Hugh had served time, but the question was pointless and he realised he did not care to hear the answer. He could guess; the specifics would change nothing.

'Do you remember that?' Barr asked, smiling open-mouthed across at his passenger.

'Do you mind just driving the fucking car,' Duggan said. 'What's that saying? The past's another country? Well, that's another country.'

The smile faltered a little on Barr's lips, as he processed the man's response. Somehow, he found a way to rationalise it to his own satisfaction, for he nodded earnestly and turned his attention to the road.

CHAPTER FIVE

The glare of the fluorescent light in the holding cell, buzzing behind a protective mesh cage, coupled with the heat of the room, had left Tony's eyes dry and reddened. He was aware of Hugh Duggan, the man with whom he was sharing the cell, studying him and wondered if he thought he'd been crying.

'That fucking light,' he said.

'They do it deliberately,' Duggan said. 'And it's either far too hot or far too cold. They don't want you getting comfortable.'

When they'd first arrived and were being processed, they'd had their cheeks and hands swabbed, prints taken and Tony's had been offered a Tyvek suit to wear in the cell. Tony had watched the insouciance with which Duggan had dealt with each element, the familiarity with which he opened his mouth for the cotton swab, didn't gag when they pushed it too close to the back of his throat. He'd clearly been through it all before.

Duggan had stretched out on the bench attached to the opposite wall, his legs crossed at the ankles, his hands behind his head as a makeshift pillow.

'Get some sleep, wee man,' he said. 'It'll be a long night.'

Tony had wondered at his calmness, his ability to shut out the shouts, the banging of doors, the whistles that echoed down the hall outside. He moved across to the heavy iron door and thumped on it, using his fist at first, but then open palmed when it had hurt too much.

'You're wasting your time, wee man,' Duggan said. 'They won't open that until they're good and ready. Or they think you're not.'

'I didn't do anything,' Tony said. 'My da, Jesus, what could he do?'

'You're the brother of the lad got run down, isn't that right, wee man?'

Tony nodded lightly, bristling at the appended 'wee man'. He studied Duggan more closely now. He was, perhaps in his late twenties, florid-faced, black hair shorn close, already peppered with grey. He was certainly no more than ten years his senior, though carried the air of one much older.

'Sorry for your loss. I heard they didn't even stop to see if he was hurt. Fucking terrible thing.'

Tony moved back to his own bench and sat. 'Bastards,' he muttered, then stood again, his anger boiling over once more. The strength of the feeling surprised him, consoled him. He could not bring Danny back, just as his father had said, but he could let anger honour his memory, raging against those who had killed him. 'Bastards!' he shouted.

Duggan chuckled to himself, lightly. 'Were you watching the game earlier?'

Tony stared at him, blankly. He didn't remember there being a match on and, for a moment, wondered if he was commenting on the match after which Danny had been killed.

'It was one-nil to them. Then our side got a wee late one,' Duggan added.

Tony sat again, nodding his head although he had no idea what the man was talking about. He began to wonder whether it was a ruse; perhaps Duggan knew that they'd be listening in to the cell and was moving the conversation on to something innocuous, trivial. It was only after an interminable description of the minutiae of someone's playing style, a discussion to which Tony could offer nothing, never having heard of the player in question, that he began to reassess the purpose of Duggan's choice of topic.

'Yeah. Don't be worrying. We got a late one; the balance sheet's even now, anyway, eh?' the man had said and winked at Tony.

Tony nodded. 'Thank—' He stopped himself. If the cells were being monitored, he reasoned he'd be safest saying nothing that could be contrived as dangerous. 'Thanks,' he said. 'I didn't see it.'

'Shame,' Duggan said. 'You'd have loved it. Great goal. A header.'

Ten minutes later, the door grated back on protesting hinges as two police officers came in.

'Duggan. You're with us.'

Duggan stood and stretched, as if twisting a crick out his neck. He padded past Tony, winking once. 'See you again, wee man. Keep her lit.'

The door slammed behind them, both officers ignoring Tony's questions about the whereabouts and well-being of his father.

Around 6am, one of the two men who had taken Duggan away arrived back at the cell with a cup of weak tea in a polystyrene cup which he handed to Tony.

'Wasn't sure if you took milk or sugar, so there's a bit of both,' he said. He was young, maybe only a year or two older than Tony himself. His hair was sandy, his moustache neatly trimmed. His eyes were bloodshot, shadowed with bags which suggested he'd had as little sleep as Tony. He moved across and sat on the bench on which Duggan had been lying.

'Where's my father?'

'He's fine,' the man said. 'I've a few questions and then you'll be done.'

Tony straightened, sceptical. He put the tea to one side.

'Where were you last night?'

'At home,' Tony said. 'I buried my fucking brother yesterday, where would I be?'

The officer raised his hand. 'Take it easy, big lad,' he said. 'I'm only asking. Was your father at home?'

Tony nodded.

'What were youse doing?'

Tony tried to remember. He wondered if they had already questioned his father and were looking for him to corroborate his father's statement.

'Watching TV,' Tony said.

'What was on?'

'I don't know. I wasn't paying any attention to it. The news at some stage, 'cause we heard about the cop being shot.' He'd used the term defiantly, stopping himself from self-correcting to 'policeman'.

The policeman nodded. It took a moment for Tony to realise he wasn't even writing anything down.

'You were talking to Sean Mullan at your brother's funeral, is that right?'

Tony nodded, quizzically. 'I didn't even know who he was till after, when my dad told me.'

'Your dad knows Mullan?'

'He knows of him,' Tony said, careful now. 'That's not the same thing.'

'And what did Mullan say to you?'

Tony studied the man's face. He returned the gaze without guile. Did they already know? Had they been listening in at the funeral? If he said nothing, would they have him because they'd know he'd lied?

'He expressed his condolences over the death of Danny. That's all I remember.'

The officer nodded, smiling mildly as if this was what he'd been expecting to hear. 'That's fine. I'm sorry for your loss, too. It was a dreadful thing to happen. We'll let you get home.'

He stood as Tony watched him open-mouthed. 'What?'

'Someone will bring you in some clothes. Your father will be ready in a few minutes. Thanks for your help.'

A weak winter dawn was breaking when Tony and his father stepped out of the station. Several others who had been lifted the previous evening spilled out, bleary eyed into the grey light of morning. But not Hugh Duggan.

'Are you OK?' his father asked him, touching his arm as if to assure himself that Tony was actually there.

'Grand. Are you?'

'Did they do anything?'

'Nothing. Asked me a couple of questions and that was it. What about you?'

'The usual,' his father muttered distractedly.

It was the following day before Tony began to suspect that he'd only been in the cell in the hope he might make Duggan talk. And it was the day after that when his parents told him that they had arranged with his uncle in Paisley that he was going to get out of the North and go and work in Scotland.

'We've lost one son,' his father said. 'We're not losing another one.'

25

CHAPTER SIX

'Another one,' the steward called, gesturing that they should continue up the slipway into the belly of the ferry. He walked backwards, facing them as he waved with one hand, the other holding a walkie-talkie to his ear. Tony reckoned he was about eighteen and wondered absently if it was his first day on the job, he did it with such earnest concentration.

Barr shifted the car into first to make the incline, over-accelerating while still holding the clutch so that, when the car did finally move, it shunted suddenly forwards and cut out. The youth cursed under his breath, his movements as he tried to shift the gear back into neutral agitated and imprecise, as if embarrassed to have made the mistake under Duggan's glare.

Tony twisted his head and looked back out across Belfast port and towards Black Mountain and Cavehill, looming above the grey city, the upper peaks wrapped in a mist which here, lower down, had dissolved into a miasma of rain that smeared the windscreens.

The last time he'd headed across, he'd left from Larne and the ferry had been slower. He craned his neck to see down to the departure area. Karen was getting on as a foot passenger and meeting them on the boat; he wondered if he might catch a glimpse of her, though he realised that now, thirty years on, he might not even recognise her. He didn't want to admit to himself that his real curiosity was whether or not someone would bring her to the boat; a husband or a child perhaps.

Below him, he could see people embracing: a younger man sending off an older couple. He embraced each of them for so long, Tony wondered what was behind their parting.

The ferry was quiet, those choosing to travel mid-week mostly middle-aged women taking a mini booze cruise across to Scotland. They'd not even disembark on the either side, but sit in the bar all day, have breakfast, lunch and dinner on board and be back home before midnight. Tony glanced across at one group, all women in their sixties, and, momentarily, he envied them their freedom.

They'd taken a seat at the front of the ship, by the window. Barr was speaking earnestly about their plans for the next two days, but Tony wasn't listening. He thought Karen would already be here, had found himself scanning the faces of every woman he passed on the way from the car, on the off-chance she was already waiting.

He'd announced he didn't think she was coming, to which Barr had replied that she still had twenty minutes to embark. Duggan seemed to have stopped listening to the youth too.

Finally, as if aware that the older men had lost interest in him, Barr lowered his voice a little and gathered his hands in front of him, as if to signify something important was to be discussed.

'The party appreciates what you're doing, gents.'

Duggan glanced at him askance. 'Sean Mullan tell you that? That he *appreciates*?'

Barr smiled, patiently. 'We know some of you are a little resistant–'

27

Duggan laughed derisively. 'Time was, you put some fucker in the ground, you left him there. Not anymore.'

'People like Martin are a source of embarrassment now. Our own that we stopped having a proper burial.'

'A source of embarrassment?' Duggan repeated. 'Is that what we are?'

Barr hesitated a moment, as if trying to find an appropriate angle from which to rephrase his comment.

'That's not what I meant, Mr Duggan,' he said. 'But someone like Martin, dead thirty years and his family never getting a chance to bury him; it doesn't work well for the party.'

'Doesn't work well for the party?' Duggan echoed, incredulous.

'The optics aren't good for us,' Barr started, already flustered.

'The only fucking optics you should be worried about are those ones behind that bar,' Duggan snapped. 'Get in a few whiskeys,' he added, 'and spare us all your bullshit about *the party*.'

Barr nodded, took a moment to spare his own dignity, then got up and headed across to the service area, Duggan chuckling at his willingness to do as he was told.

'So it isn't you I have to thank for making me sit here listening to this crap?' he asked.

Tony shook his head. 'Like I said, I thought it was you,' he said.

Duggan raised an eyebrow sceptically. 'Why would I want that?'

'Maybe it was Karen?'

Duggan shrugged. 'Who contacted you?'

Tony nodded to where Barr stood, placing his order. 'The young fella. You?'

'Sean Mullan,' Duggan said.

Tony nodded. He'd not spoken to any of them in thirty years; had seen Mullan only once since Martin Kelly's death and that had been

28

a coincidence; Mullan had been canvassing during one of the elections and had called at his door, looking for his vote. It had been Ann who'd answered. She'd given him fairly short shift. Tony had heard the disagreement and had come to the door, tea towel over his shoulder from the dishes he'd been drying.

Mullan had glanced at him, then looked a second time, more closely. Tony could see he was trying to work out how he recognised him, where he had last seen him. Then the expression softened, as he must have placed the younger man. He'd nodded lightly at Tony, thanked Ann for her time and headed back down the drive and on to the next house.

'Do you know him?' Ann had asked.

'From years ago,' Tony had said. 'He came to Danny's funeral.'

'He gives me the creeps,' Ann said. 'All softly spoken and polite, wearing loafers.'

Tony had laughed at the time. 'I didn't even notice what he was wearing. What have loafers to do with it?'

Ann considered the question, her eyes wrinkling at the corners as she smiled at her own comment. 'It just seems wrong. A man like him wearing something as ordinary as loafers, like a regular person.'

Tony frowned quizzically.

'A man who orders other people dead. You'd think he'd be recognisably different from the rest of us.'

Tony had straightened a little, did so even now as he thought of the conversation.

'That idea that you could be talking to someone and not even know that they'd once killed another person. That gives me the creeps.'

She smiled, satisfied that she'd rationalised her thoughts to herself, then padded back into the kitchen. Tony followed slowly behind.

'He's Mullan's nephew,' Duggan explained now, nodding at Barr.

Tony nodded his head a little, as if indifferent to the information. 'I guess Mullan himself is a little too important to be wandering around woodlands in the middle of Scotland.'

'He was always too important. That's why he had the likes of me,' he said, then added after a slight pause. 'And you.'

Tony smiled mildly, more at the pause than the comment. 'How have you been?'

'I'm still above ground and breathing,' Duggan muttered. 'What more can you want?'

Tony nodded. He wondered whether the man was married, had children, grandchildren. But he also realised that he didn't really care enough to ask and, more importantly, wasn't sure Hugh Duggan would even want to tell him.

'When did you come back home?'

'A few years after you,' Duggan said. 'Once the heat over the guy done in retaliation for your brother had passed.'

In all the time they had spent in each other's company, all those years past, Duggan had rarely mentioned Danny or the policeman shot on the day of his funeral. Tony was surprised that he did so now, as if inviting him to question it further.

'What have you been doing?'

'I was building for a while until the recession killed it all off. You?'

Tony folded his arms. 'I taught for another few years, then my wife took sick and I had to leave altogether.'

'How is she now?'

'She's a ... She passed away,' Tony said, simply.

Duggan nodded. 'You're lucky. My two ex-wives are both still alive and bleeding me for every fucking penny they can get.' He cleared his throat, sitting back in the seat, his arm stretched across the back of it and the seat next to him.

Tony regarded the man, trying to find some redeeming feature. His lack of empathy over Ann's death was unsurprising, but nonetheless hurtful. He remembered why, by the time he left Scotland thirty years ago, he'd despised the man.

'Tell me this,' Duggan said, leaning forward suddenly. 'After the whole thing with Kelly, did anyone ever come after you? Were you ever questioned?'

Tony was a little shaken by Duggan's earnestness, could sense there was something else at play here which he could not yet grasp.

'No,' he said. 'Never.'

'Never?'

Tony shook his head. 'You?'

'Not for any of what happened,' he said. 'They got me for something else when I came back, but nothing over Kelly.'

Tony nodded vaguely.

'Do you not think that's a bit strange?' Duggan asked, leaning back in his seat, as if his point should now be evident.

'Strange?' Tony asked, but the question remained unanswered, for Duggan's attention had shifted.

'Here we go. You keep it in your pants, big man,' Duggan added, nodding indicatively towards the entrance to the lounge where a slim figure stood, surveying the room.

Despite his expectation of her arrival, seeing her still took him a little by surprise so that, instinctively, he exclaimed, 'Karen!'

CHAPTER SEVEN

'Karen,' someone called. Tony watched as the girl in question twisted, raising her wine glass to indicate to her friend, who'd been standing in the doorway of the kitchenette, what drink she wanted.

The room, which might comfortably have seated eight, throbbed with the heat of over thirty bodies crammed together, those standing bouncing in rhythm with 'Pump Up the Volume' which blared from a pair of tinny speakers on the flat's windowsill.

She noticed Tony and returned his gaze, once, for a second or two longer than necessary, before looking back at the girl next to her, who was in full flow of conversation. Tony felt his stomach twist a little, felt a tingling deep inside him at her glance.

'Strange we both ended up here, eh?'

Tony's attention was drawn away from the girl, Karen, and back to Hugh Duggan who sat opposite him at the breakfast bar.

'In Scotland?'

'Aye, I suppose. And at this party,' Duggan said.

Tony had been across over two months. His father had arranged for him to live with his uncle and aunt in Paisley, just outside Glasgow. He'd headed into a bar in the Barras for a night out and met someone from Derry, who'd invited him back to a house party.

'I guess.'

'What brought you across?' Duggan asked.

'My ma and da didn't want me staying in Derry. I think they thought either the cops would keep at me, or else that I'd do something stupid and get involved or something.'

Duggan smiled. 'And would you have?'

Tony frowned, the conversation moving faster than he could quite follow.

'Would I have what?'

'Got involved.'

Tony glanced back at the girl again, hoping he might catch her eye. She was sipping from her wine glass, watching her friend intently. But she seemed to be aware of his gaze, for she straightened slightly, tossed her hair back from her face and, at the last moment, stole another glance at him, a smile playing on her lips for a second before she took another mouthful of wine.

'Maybe,' Tony said, absently.

'Did they hold you long, that night?' Duggan asked.

It took a second for Tony to refocus on the conversation and realise to which night Duggan was referring.

'Nah. I was out at dawn. You?'

'A bit later than that,' Duggan said. 'They held me the guts of the three days.'

'Jesus, why?'

'They must have thought they'd get something on me eventually. Fuckers think they can wear you down.'

Karen finished the last of her wine and, a little unsteadily, stood and began picking her way towards the kitchen. Tony drained his pint and stood. 'I'm going to grab a drink. Do you fancy something?'

'Not as much as you, obviously,' Duggan said, glancing past him to where Karen squeezed her way through the mass of partygoers. 'I'd keep it in your pants, big man. She's a cold one.'

Tony nodded in acknowledgment of the advice even as he dismissed it. He pushed his way through the group near him and made his way into the kitchen. Karen was standing at the sink, examining the boxes of wine set up there.

He could see her better now. She was lithe, medium height, her brown hair loose and curling around her shoulders. She stood with her head cocked to one side, studying the choices in front of her. When Tony spoke, she turned to him, a smile already ghosting her lips, her eyebrows raised suggestively.

'What kind of wine do they have?' Tony asked.

'It's a Chilean Chardonnay,' she said. '1986.'

'I meant was it red or white,' Tony asked, deliberately thickening his Derry accent.

'You're on the beer anyway,' she said, laughing. 'You shouldn't mix the grain and the grape.'

'I'd offer to buy you one, but it's free. Can I pour you a drink?'

She nodded. 'I'm Karen,' she said.

'I know. I heard your friend calling you.'

'I noticed,' Karen said. 'That was a subtle way of asking you *your* name.'

'I'm a Derry man,' Tony said. 'Subtlety is wasted on us. Tony Canning.'

'I'll bear that in mind, Tony Canning.'

Later, someone produced a guitar in the living room and, as the conversations died, they started singing rebel songs. Tony and Karen stood together at the entrance to the kitchen and listened. At one point, as she shifted to allow someone to pass her, she pressed against him, their arms touching, the heat of the skin of her arm electric against his, her hand hanging loose, her fingers brushing against his fingers. He looked at her and she smiled, though the contact did not go any further and, after a moment, she shifted wine glass from one hand to the other as she joined in the chorus of 'The Ould Triangle', her voice soft and light.

After one, she told him that she had to go home.

'Are you far?'

'A mile or so,' she said. 'I'll get the night bus.'

'I'll walk you,' Tony offered.

'The bus is quicker. And safer.'

'I'll come with, if you like. I'm out that way myself.'

She raised a disbelieving eyebrow, then laughed lightly and nodded. 'If you like.'

The streets were busy, the bars spilling out their customers on to the streets, taxi queues stretching off the pavements, the air rich with the scent of spices from the kebab shop they passed. Police officers milled about in pairs, high-visibility jackets and soft caps. It still took Tony by surprise to see them unarmed, without bullet-proof vests and an army escort. This, he thought with a stab of resentment, must be what it's like living somewhere normal.

Karen walked beside him, her arms wrapped round herself for heat, the light jacket she wore no respite from the deepening chill of the early spring night. Tony walked close beside her, hoping to recreate the physical proximity of the party, but she hugged herself tighter. Finally, he took off his coat and draped it round her shoulders. She smiled, gratefully, staggered a little, whether with the wine, or her heels, or by design, and he found his arm around her, her body, still shivering lightly, close beside his.

They waited for the bus together, sitting side by side on the plastic seat in the shelter. Once, he felt he might have a chance to kiss her. He'd told some story about a party at university, one that even he realised lacked any real punchline or relevance to anyone who had not been in attendance at the time. Yet she had held his gaze, her head tilted a little to one side, her brown hair falling across her eyes so that she had to try to blow it away with a puff of her breath. He leaned towards her, saw an almost imperceptible change in her expression, then saw a more obvious shift as she stood. 'The bus is here,' she said.

On the bus, she sat across two seats, her back against the window, her legs outstretched, her feet just over the edge of the seat. Tony swung into the seat behind her and, leaning on the handrail, continued their conversation. But the opportunity to kiss had passed. He'd paid for the bus for them both and now handed her one of the tickets. She took it, then returned it to him. 'You can keep it,' she said. 'My gift to you.'

'You're all heart,' Tony laughed, taking the ticket back, putting it in his pocket, his own balled up and lying on the floor.

In the brighter light of the bus, he could see her better now and realised that her eyes were two different colours, one green, one a light hazel.

'I'm a chimera,' she laughed when he told her this.

'I'm a Gemini,' he said. 'What's a chimera?'

'I've two sets of DNA. I think it means that I was to be twins in my mother's womb but we merged or something. Or I ate my twin.'

'That's gross,' Tony said, pantomiming disgust as he sat back in his seat, away from her.

'My daddy used to say to me, to tell any boys I met when I grew up that I ate my own twin. That I was not to type of girl to mess with.'

'Why? What'll you do?' Tony asked.

'Put up your dukes,' she said, a little sleepily, 'and I'll show you.'

She raised her own fists and swung a light punch that glanced against his cheek, mimicking the sound of the impact with her tongue clicking against the roof of her mouth as she did so.

'I won't mess with you so,' Tony joked, folding his arms.

'Good,' Karen said, smiling mildly as she closed her eyes and leaned her head back against the window.

They alighted at her stop and he walked her the hundred yards to her flat.

'I'll head on so,' Tony said, half hoping she might disagree and invite him inside, but she didn't. Instead she took off his jacket, shivering at the renewed chill.

'Thanks for the jacket,' she said. 'You're a Derry gentleman.'

She opened the door. 'Goodnight then,' she said, pausing on the threshold.

Tony berated himself his slowness. 'Can I see you again?'

'Maybe,' she said, then went in and closed the door. He heard the slide of the security chain inside being slipped into place.

He stood for a moment, wondering whether he should knock on the door and ask for the number, but just as he moved forward to do so, he saw the hall light go out and, a few seconds later, the small upper window light briefly illuminated. Then Karen appeared at the window and, without looking down, pulled the curtains, dimming the light.

Tony cursed himself for missing the chance at the bus stop. But then, he'd seen something in her expression, just as she thought he was going to kiss her; not fear exactly, but certainly not longing either. Maybe she'd just wanted someone to walk her home safely, he thought. But her eyes, her smile, the jolt of excitement that had caught him sideways as they stood together and her fingers touched his. He was sure he'd sensed something.

He started walking the three miles back to his uncle's, pulling up the collar of his coat, pressing his face against the material, and breathing deep the scent of her perfume, which still lingered on the cloth. He jammed his hands in his pockets for heat, felt the bus ticket she'd handed back to him and which he'd kept. He repeated her name over to himself, trying it in his mouth, a mantra that kept him going through his journey home. 'Karen Logue. Karen Logue. Karen Logue.'

CHAPTER EIGHT

'Karen Maguire,' she said, offering her hand to Barr who'd arrived simultaneous to her, three glasses of whiskey in his hand.

'I've spilled some,' he said, sucking the excess alcohol off the back of his hand before wiping it dry on his trouser leg and taking hers. 'Richard Barr. We spoke on the phone.'

Karen nodded. 'Hugh,' she said, shifting the newspaper she'd held in one hand and clamping it between her arm and her side. A beat. 'Tony,' she said, her glance just missing his.

'Do you want a drink?' Barr asked. 'What are you having?'

'I'll get a Coke,' she said. 'Sit where you are. Bit early in the day for me and whiskey.'

Tony watched her as she walked away. She wore jeans and a white top. Her hips had widened a little, but that aside, it was as if the past three decades had not touched her frame; her waist still pinched, her legs fine. Unbidden, he saw her as he had seen her that first night as she walked to her front door, as if time had set itself in abeyance just for her.

'She's aged well,' Duggan said, whistling softly to himself. 'Not like us two old codgers.'

'Speak for yourself,' Tony said, half-jokingly. But he considered how he must look to her; his face rounder and fuller, his body saggy, his pot belly a permanent feature, his hair thinned and greying. He took off his glasses, as if that defect might be just one too many for her.

Maguire, she'd said, not Logue. He'd expected she'd be married, a girl like her; he was still disappointed, though, that she had moved on with her life. It was hypocritical, of course; he too had married, after all. But that seemed different, somehow. And without ever having met the man, he felt immediately a sense of bitterness towards her husband.

Had she waited for long, he wondered. He'd met Ann in his thirties. He'd been back in Derry almost ten years at that stage. She was a primary school teacher, already settled into her routines and with that habit that those who work with children have of speaking to other adults as if they are infants. Ann hadn't particularly wanted children. He remembered hearing the sobs from the bathroom the morning she took the test and found out she was pregnant.

And again, the sobs in the hospital, six months later, when she found out the child had died.

It was that which convinced her; that realisation that grief was the inevitable cost of having loved, even something which she had not held in her hands, even as she held it inside her, near her heart.

Tony had remained solid, pragmatic, dependable on the ward and when he took her home. He'd cleaned the house, bought flowers for the hall and kitchen, set up the portable TV in the bedroom for her. Once, while she slept next to him with fitful dreams, he allowed tears to slide down his face as he mourned his lost child. And, in that moment, he had remembered Martin Kelly's tears so that, in his mind, the two losses were fused into one. The loss of this life was a balancing for his role in the loss of another. Both deprived of a proper burial; his own son's remains taken by the hospital to be 'disposed of': the doctor who took him masked and shrouded as Charon.

'Safe crossing,' he'd whispered to the dark. His unborn son's journey across the river Styx made that bit less lonely by his father's voice should he somehow hear him.

'Tony?'

He realised he'd lost track of the discussion at the table. Barr stared across at him, apparently shocked at his vacancy.

'Sorry,' he managed. 'I was daydreaming. What are we talking about?'

Barr cleared his throat. 'We can stop for a bite to eat along the way, or would you rather eat now on the boat?'

'I'm easy,' Duggan said. 'Best eat here and get a move on, make the most of the daylight.'

'That's fine by me,' Tony said.

Behind Duggan's head, he saw Karen approach the table again, a glass of cola in her hands. She caught his stare and smiled briefly, a curt acknowledgement, then looked down at the glass, as if to ensure it did not spill its contents as she walked. When she reached the table, she sat at the head rather than the free seat next to Tony, with Duggan and Barr opposite him.

'We're just discussing the plans,' Barr said. 'We're going to head straight to the forest; there's a car park now on the same side I was told you went in from.'

'Has it changed much?' Karen asked. 'I've not been back.'

'They put a motorway near it about twenty years ago and the old road went out of use. Plus part of it was destroyed in a storm a few years back, apparently, and they've replanted it. But that's a section on the east side of the woods, so it shouldn't affect us too much.'

'We might never find it,' Duggan muttered. 'This is a fucking joke. A waste of time.'

'Uncle Sean says it would help a lot; give the family some closure.'

'Surely that defeats the point of burying him there to begin with,' Duggan hissed. 'That was part of the punishment.'

'For him,' Karen said, sipping at her drink. 'The family don't deserve to be punished for something he did. Not now.'

'You've gone soft, I see,' Duggan said.

Karen shrugged. 'I was never as hard as you, Hugh. But I've a different perspective now. Stopping someone burying their own child is... Well, it's barbaric.'

'War's barbaric,' Duggan muttered.

'The war's over,' Tony offered.

'For you anyway,' Duggan said. 'And it never fucking started for you, son, so you can keep your mouth shut about any of this.'

The last comment, aimed at Barr, seemed to physically hurt him. He had already been getting agitated, clearly sensing he'd lost control of the table. 'I'm here at Uncle Sean's request.'

'If Uncle Sean had any balls, he'd be here himself,' Duggan snapped. 'Instead of sending a child, wasn't even alive back then.'

'It has nothing to do with him,' Tony said, meaning Barr, though Duggan misunderstood.

'Didn't it?' He glowered at Tony who wasn't sure how to answer the question.

'Either way, the family are looking and it's the right thing to do,' Karen said. She took the folded newspaper she'd been carrying when she came in and laid it in from of them. She'd folded it to the relevant article. 'They give the paper out free in the foot-passenger lounge,' she explained. 'That's why I saw it.'

The piece took up half an inside page. Tony had no choice but to put his glasses back on again to read the report. It detailed the recent attempts by the Kelly family to find Martin's remains. The story mentioned the disappointment of the lead technician on the recovery team, that they'd once again found nothing. They'd been searching in bogland about two hours north of Glasgow, based on an anonymous tip-off. Two pictures accompanied the story. The first was a grainy colour image of a digger being loaded on to the back of a transporter, its job complete. It was the smaller second picture towards the bottom of the story that caught Tony's eye: Martin Kelly's sister.

She shared his soft features, though she was older now than he had been then. Her hair was pulled back from her face, evidently being interviewed at the site of the latest dig.

Tony scanned down through the piece. It offered scant details of Martin's disappearance, only that he had vanished while living in Scotland and his family, despite frequent appeals for information, had never even had it confirmed to them why he died. 'Martin was a good fella,' his sister was quoted as saying. 'He wasn't perfect, but he was a good lad. No one deserves to be disposed of the way he must have been. What we've been put through is just cruelty.'

CHAPTER NINE

'All cruelty springs from weakness,' Tony said. 'According to Seneca, anyway.'

His sixth-form class sat in front of him. They'd been discussing Macbeth and what might drive him to try to kill not only Banquo and his son, but also Macduff's wife and children.

'Who's he?' Shauna Laird asked. She was one of the chattier girls in the class, though her comments weren't always relevant to the work being discussed.

'He was a Roman playwright. The play, *Macbeth*, is heavily influenced by his style of tragedies. He claimed that all acts of cruelty are motivated primarily by fear. Do you think that's the case with Macbeth?'

Several of the pupils pantomimed consideration of the question, enough to show they were listening but not willing to risk answering.

'S'pose,' Shauna said.

'How?'

'He was afraid he wasn't secure in position, so he killed people to make himself feel more secure.'

'But he only ends up making things worse for himself.'

Shauna angled her head a little. 'I guess.'

'Which is his tragedy. He causes a reversal of his own fortunes through his behaviour, then finds out too late to do anything to change it. Aristotle called it *perepetia*.'

Shauna raised her hand, despite the discussion having only involved the two of them anyway.

'Do we need to know this for the exam?'

'It won't hurt,' Tony said. 'Besides, you *should* know it.'

'In case I ever reverse my own fortunes and realise I did it?' she asked, smiling.

Tony joined in the general laughter. 'Exactly.'

'And does either of them give any advice for what to do in that situation?'

'Nothing. Suffer and learn.'

'The motto of this class,' one of the fellas at the back muttered good-naturedly, loud enough for Tony to hear.

Shauna's arm shot up again, but this time she did not wait for permission to speak. 'It's why his wife is able to convince him,' she said quickly, as if worried she might forget her point if she was too slow.

'What is?'

'Weakness. She's able to convince him what to do, because he's weak inside and she tells him she's stronger than he is. So he does cruel things, like killing Duncan, to try to prove to her that he's not.'

Tony nodded approvingly. 'That's pretty much it.'

'Class genius, me,' Shauna beamed.

He remembered her comment, her pride in understanding what motivated cruelty when he saw her again, six months after she'd finished school. He'd gone to Liverpool Betty's, a bar not far from his flat, to meet Hugh Duggan. Duggan had contacted him at school and invited him for a drink. Tony had suggested the place. Liverpool Betty herself was in her thirties, dark hair styled to one side, her fringe shadowing her eyes, her head declined slightly so that she looked up at you through her bangs as she spoke. But she ran the bar with an iron grip, her broad Liverpudlian accent cutting through the Celtic lilt of the vast bulk of her clientele.

'Two Jameson's, Betty,' Duggan called. 'And two stouts.'

He was significantly more affable than the previous time they had met, a few months earlier, at the party.

'They've set up a thing in Derry,' he said, 'for your Danny. For people who want to do something about it.'

Tony knew enough to understand what this 'thing' was, and what it signified. 'Danny wasn't involved,' he said.

'He died at the hands of the enemy,' Duggan said. 'The bastard that did it claimed traumatic stress and got out on disability, apparently.'

Tony stared at him, considering how Duggan knew this, considering too whether his father knew and, if so, why he hadn't shared this information with him.

'Fucker,' Tony said.

Duggan nodded. 'Lots of your neighbours and that wanted to honour Danny's memory. It's already done.'

'Does my dad know?'

Duggan shrugged, his gaze flitting towards Betty where she appeared at the bar with their drinks. 'Two stout and chasers, gents,' she said, her hands on her hips, waiting for payment.

Duggan pulled out a twenty from his wallet. 'And one for yourself, Betty,' he said. He waited until she'd moved to the till, out of earshot, and continued. 'You don't have to join. I just thought you should know, that you'd *want* to know.'

Tony nodded, sipping his pint. 'Fair enough. Thanks for telling me.'

'You'll have a free pass because you're family,' Duggan continued. 'You'd not have to sign up to anything if you didn't want to. Sean Mullan wanted me to let you know that.'

'And what do I have to do?' Tony said, wiping the moustache of malty foam off his upper lip with the back of his hand, then taking a sip of his whiskey. 'If I did want to do something?'

'Very little,' Duggan said. 'Or a lot. It's up to you, really. Whatever you feel comfortable with.'

Tony glanced across the bar as the doors opened and a group of youths poured in. He recognised a number of them from the previous year's group of school leavers. Among them, he spotted Shauna Laird. She looked very different out of uniform, her eyes heavily made up and smoky, her hair styled, her lipstick bright red. She seemed to be aware she was being watched for she looked across and smiled brightly when she saw him. She said something to her friends and moved across to where he sat.

'Hi, sir,' she said. 'How're you?'

'Tony,' he said. 'You're out of school now. What's the craic?'

She laughed exaggeratedly at the idiom and he began to suspect she'd taken something. Her pupils were wide, almost filling the iris, her mouth seeming frozen in a smile, her foot tapping to a different beat from the music playing through the bar's speakers.

'Drama Society night out,' she said.

'How's college?'

'Amazing,' she smiled. 'Not as good as your class, though!'

She laughed, then stood, waiting for Tony to say something.

'It's good to see you, Shauna. Have a good night,' he said.

'And you, sir,' she said, then corrected herself. 'Tony.'

He watched her walk away, her skirt barely reaching halfway down her thighs, her legs bare.

'She's only out of school?' Duggan whistled. 'She'd get a man in trouble.'

An hour and three pints later, Duggan excused himself to go to the toilet. A television played soundlessly above the bar. The report focused on a boat, the *Eksund*, which appeared to have been boarded by the French police. The officers in question beamed at the cameras as they displayed an array of weaponry. One of them held a small, red hexagonal block, the size of an altar candle. The report cut to footage of a car exploding on Royal Avenue in Belfast, then back to a reporter standing on a docks, behind which the police could be seem carrying boxes off the boat.

'Hey, hey! Martin!'

The sound of Duggan's voice, raised in greeting, caused Tony to turn. Hugh was shaking hands with a younger man, heavy built, soft featured, his hair cut tight to his scalp, who wore a satchel across his body so the bag rested on his hip.

'Another one, love?' Betty asked.

Tony nodded. He already felt groggy, the stout heavy on his stomach. He'd struggle through school the next day. He'd a Year 8 class who were over-enthusiastic to say the least. That first thing in the morning, combined with a hangover, didn't bear thinking about.

Duggan came across, just as Betty set down the pair of single malts.

'Good man,' he said, raising the glass in a toast. '*Slainte*,' he said, then drained it. He spotted the tail end of the news report.

'Fucking awful business,' he said.

Tony glanced up at the screen again, shrugging. 'What happened?'

'An arms shipment from Libya, intercepted by the French.'

Tony tried to keep focused on the images, which had now shifted to reports from a football match.

'Bad news for the men at home,' he said. 'And here.'

Tony nodded, lifted his glass, and spilled some as he missed a little bringing it to his mouth.

'Martin's one of us, too,' Duggan confided quickly, his breath warm against Tony's cheek. 'Martin Kelly.'

'The guy with the bag?' Tony slurred.

'The Man who Walked the Earth, I call him.'

Tony shook his head, one shoulder raised in inquiry.

'Caine. Kung Fu?'

Another shake of the head.

'I'm older than you's the problem,' Duggan said. 'You're just a fucking kid yourself.'

Tony stood, his hand on the bar to steady himself. 'I need a slash,' he said.

He made his way to the toilets at the back of the bar. The group of students who'd come in earlier were seated in the booths nearest the back. He kept an eye out for Shauna, but she must have left already, he figured.

The urinal in the men's toilets had been broken, the ceramic bowl lying in two pieces on the floor. The cubicle had been stuffed with toilet paper holders to the point that it was filled to overflowing with water and piss, on which sailed the remains of a broken cigarette.

Tony decided against adding to the mess, which would only have overflowed onto the tiled floor, and instead went back out and tried the door of the accessible toilet, which was locked.

He stood waiting, leaning against the partition of the nearest booth, his body suddenly heavy, his head dropping a little as the floor seemed to slide beneath him.

The Engaged sign on the door of the toilet flicked to Vacant and the door opened. Martin Kelly walked out, ostentatiously zipping his trousers. Behind him, straightening herself up, was Shauna Laird, one hand on the sink for support, a cellophane-wrapped block of hash in the other, her knees red raw with the imprint of the pattern of the tiled floor.

In his state, swaying where he stood, Tony could not understand what he had witnessed. It was only the following day, as he remembered the expression on her face, the blush rising in her cheeks, that he guessed at what form of transaction Kelly had enacted in the toilet, and how he had wanted the patrons of the bar to witness the young girl's shame.

CHAPTER TEN

'Shame the fucker didn't show that goodness when he was alive,' Duggan snapped, pushing the paper away from him.

Karen took it and folded it, neatly, then laid it next to her glass. 'So, how has everyone been?' she asked, lifting her drink and sipping from it, as if aware of the absurdity of the question.

'Just peachy,' Duggan said. 'Are we getting something to eat or not? I'm starving.'

Barr straightened a little. 'I thought we could stop on the way from the boat,' he said.

'Good luck finding anything open this time of year,' Duggan said. 'I've already told you, we should eat here and we can stop for a smoke break along the way.'

'You still smoking?' Karen asked.

'It was a figure of speech,' he said. 'Gave them up five years back.'

Karen nodded approvingly. 'Good for you.'

'Waste of time, to be honest,' Duggan said. 'So, are we eating?'

He stared at Barr, making it clear that the younger man would be paying for their lunch.

'What do you want?' Barr asked, hands open in a gesture of magnanimity.

'I'll take one of those all-day breakfasts,' Duggan said. 'Wi' tea, not coffee.' He pushed himself up from his seat and, gathering the small leather bag he'd been carrying since he got out of the car, headed off across the lounge.

'Make that two,' Tony said, looking at Karen with a brief conspiratorial smirk.

'Three,' said Karen. 'And make mine a coffee.' She returned Tony's smile, stifling a laugh.

Barr nodded. 'Four fries,' he repeated, then headed to the food counter to place the order.

'He's very earnest,' Karen said.

'Eager to impress, I think. He called Hugh Mr Duggan.'

Karen, an expression of mock offence, pushed the folded paper on the table away from her. 'Are we not good enough for him? I didn't even get a Karen.'

Tony laughed lightly. 'How have you been, anyway? It's good to see you again.'

He studied her closely now. He could still see the girl he had known; the arch of the eyebrows, the thinness of the nose, the crinkling of her eyes when she smiled were still the same, though the crinkles had lengthened and deepened.

'And you,' she said. 'All good, thanks,' she sat back in the seat a little, crossed her legs. 'How have you been?'

'Good,' Tony said, aware of the absurdity of the word. 'What have you been doing?'

'For the past thirty years?' Karen said, shrugging. 'I started my own business; I run my own estate agents now.'

'Impressive,' Tony said. 'Where are you living?'

'Outside Belfast,' she said.

'You never went back home?'

She shook her head. 'There was nothing to go there for – nothing good. What about you? Did you end up back in Derry?'

'You can take the man out of Derry but… you know the rest,' he said.

'Still teaching?'

'No, I… ah… I gave it up a few years back. I help out in the local church now, cleaning and that. A sacristan of sorts.'

'You found religion?'

Tony nodded. 'I rediscovered it, I guess.'

Karen looked to the table, pulling the paper closer to her again, straightening it so that its edges ran parallel with the edges of the table itself.

'Did you… any kids?' he asked, his mouth dry, his tongue cloying against his palate.

'Two,' Karen said, offering him a brittle smile, not quite raising her eyes from the paper. 'Two boys.'

'Boys,' Tony said, louder than necessary. 'That's lovely. What ages are they?'

'Twelve and eight,' she said. 'What about you? Any kids? I bet you ended up with loads of them running around you. A football team.'

Tony laughed mirthlessly. 'No,' he said softly, Martin flashing momentarily in his mind. 'No kids.'

'I'm sorry,' Karen offered, motioning towards him, her hand outstretched a moment as if to touch his arm. But the movement faltered and she brought the hand back safely to nestle with her other on top of the paper again.

He felt a strange disloyalty to Ann, in not mentioning her. Karen had two children; whether she'd married or not, she'd moved on with her life, he reasoned. It seemed only right that he should acknowledge Ann's place in his.

'We lost one,' he said, the words catching in his throat.

'Oh, Tony, I'm so sorry,' Karen said. 'That's terrible.'

'We didn't try again after that. And then my wife died last year and so, that's that. That's my life; thirty years in thirty seconds.'

His comment hung in the silence between them as both tried to determine how best to move on past it, past the tone of disappointment that lay implicit in his words.

'I'm sorry,' Karen repeated simply.

Tony feigned nonchalance. 'I've killed the mood,' he said, then immediately regretted the choice of words. 'Excuse me. I'm going to the toilet.'

As he made his way through the lounge, the ferry, which till now had been creeping up Belfast Lough, began to accelerate, the engines roaring into life, the surge of motion causing him to stumble as he walked. To his left, a collection of amusements clattered and jingled brightly. Two lorry drivers sat, backs turned on each other, feeding coins into their respective machines.

He pushed out through the side door, on to the deck, a thick buffeting wind catching the door and slamming it shut behind him. The water was slate grey, reflecting the cloud heavy sky above, and foamed with the wash from the ferry's wake. Seagulls hung low over the ridged surface of the lough. Further along the deck, a couple stood kissing. Both wore plastic raincoats over shorts, pinched at the waist by bum-bags. The mahogany of both sets of legs suggested they were tourists, swapping the bright heat of home for the perpetual gloam of Ireland.

Whether they were aware of his presence or not, they did not stop. She stood on tiptoe while he was leaning down to her, cupping her face in his hands. Tony watched their ease a moment. He remembered that with Karen, that final night. He'd felt at ease with her, not self-conscious in his nakedness as he had with Ann, and she with him, even after twenty years of marriage. Sex in a darkened room, always the same position, always the same responses. Even their kisses had become mechanical, perfunctory. That didn't mean that he didn't love her, of course; just that they hadn't fulfilled each other's needs so much as kept them at bay.

Tony realized that the two tourists were watching him now, eyes bright and alive with amusement under the dripping fringe of their hoods, damp with sea spray. He muttered a silent apology for intruding on their intimacy and tugging open the door, moved back inside.

He cut across into the toilet to pass a few moments before returning to the lounge, so as to ensure he would not be left alone at the table with Karen again. As he went inside, the ship rose suddenly on one side and then dropped again, having hit a swell, the jolt making itself felt in his bladder. The movement caused the doors of the cubicles to swing open. In one, Hugh Duggan sat on the toilet, the lid down, his leather bag on his clothed lap. He held a blister pack of tablets in his hands and was pressing out a tablet into his mouth.

For a fleeting moment, Tony saw Martin Kelly, coming out of the toilet in Liverpool Betty's, his stash in his bag, while Shauna Laird gathered herself off the floor.

Duggan held his stare a second, then lifted another blister pack and repeated the process over again.

'Sorry,' Tony muttered, aware as he said it that he'd done nothing wrong.

Duggan did not acknowledge his comment, merely saying, 'I have to take them before I eat.'

CHAPTER ELEVEN

'I have to take it before I eat,' the young girl said. She was a Year 8 student, eleven or twelve, he guessed, though only because of the year badge she wore on her uniform; looking at her, he would not have put her even at that age. She was slim, slight, with dirty fair hair pulled back from her face in a harsh ponytail. Her blouse looked a size too big for her, the collar encircling her neck too loosely. The sleeves of her blazer hung past her hands, her fingers curled around their edges in an almost defensive grip.

Tony had walked into his classroom to find the girl standing, her shirt pulled out from the waistband of her skirt, part of her stomach exposed as she injected herself. He'd excused himself instantly and waited outside until she'd tucked herself in and come to the door, knocking to let him know she was finished.

'I had to take my insulin,' she explained. 'Before lunch. But the toilet is locked and I couldn't find anywhere else to do it. Your room was free and it only takes a second.'

Tony nodded, trying to place her accent which melded together a Scottish lilt with something closer to home.

'I have to take it before I eat,' she said. 'Or I get sick.'

'Don't worry about it,' he said. 'You might be best to go to the school nurse the next time, though. You don't want anyone else walking in on you.'

The girl smiled, her features brightening. 'You're from home, sir,' she said, her accent more discernibly Northern Irish now.

'You're Irish?' Tony asked.

'Coleraine,' the girl said.

'Derry,' Tony said.

He could see her momentary reaction, perhaps attempting to reconcile Derry and Londonderry as the same place, the name politicised to the point that the choice of nomenclature signalled the religion of the speaker.

'What's your name?'

'Alice, sir,' she said.

'How long have you been over here, Alice?' Tony asked. 'You've a bit of a Scottish twang about you.'

The girl's face reddened a little. 'The other girls laugh at how I talk,' she said.

'They shouldn't,' Tony said. 'That's not nice.'

The bell above them rang, the girl's expression changing. 'I'm going to be at the back of the canteen line, sir.'

'Go, then,' Tony said, clapping his hands. 'Get down there and beat the queues.'

Alice laughed, then turned and ran up the corridor, her thin legs kicking out to the side as she did so.

He mentioned the girl over lunch in the staff room. One of the other teachers, an art teacher whose face Tony knew but whose name he'd never learned, knew the girl.

'She's a bit strange,' she said. 'Alice Hamilton. They moved here about eighteen months ago. She was at the primary school down the road for her last year or so. One of my friends taught her.'

Tony nodded, angling his head to catch the contents of his ham and cheese sandwich, sliding out before it made it to his mouth.

'She came over in May of Primary 6. Took her a while to settle. The wee pet was still wetting herself. Annie said she had to keep spare pants in the class in case the wee'un had an accident.'

'In Primary 6?' someone else chipped in. 'She needs a scalping across the arse if she's at that at that age.'

'She lost her mammy,' the Art teacher said. 'Cancer,' she added, mouthing the word as if to say it too loudly might upset some of those in the room. 'It's just her and her daddy. You want to see the state of her some mornings. He's doing his best, I know, but you'd think he'd never seen a comb.'

As she warmed to her gossip, Tony found himself losing focus, thinking again of the girl, injecting her own insulin, settling into a new school, a new country where they laughed at her accent so far from home. Or was this now home for her?

That evening, he met Duggan again in Liverpool Betty's. They'd chatted about home and how events there were unfolding. Tony had spoken with his mother on the phone earlier. His initial reluctance to come to Scotland had been slowly replaced with a sense of freedom that he knew living in Derry would not have afforded him. The phone call had been perfunctory, his mother's voice without colour or energy. He suspected Danny's absence from the house weighed more heavily on both his parents than his; after all, he'd been away from home at university. They would have already grown used to his bed being empty each night as they went in to check that all the sockets were off and the blinds pulled. Danny's bed being empty was a more palpable absence for them, he suspected, and more raw.

He felt guilty that Danny's death had not upset him more. In quieter moments he certainly felt mournful at his passing, but the permanence of his absence had not yet registered with him. And while he was a little ashamed to admit it to himself, he also felt some relief that, in having come to Scotland, he had escaped the chronic grief of his family home.

'I was chatting to a friend of yours the other day,' Duggan said. 'Karen Logue.'

Tony feigned ignorance. 'Who's she?'

'The wee girl you pretended you lived on the wrong side of the city to so you could sit on the bus with her a while back.'

Tony blushed lightly; if Duggan knew that, he assumed that Karen had, too, which made him all the more annoyed that his journey had been in vain in the end.

'She was asking about you,' Duggan said.

Tony wanted to ask what she had said, but that it would sound infantile, begging to know what a girl thought of him. Instead he lifted his pint, supped a mouthful.

'I'm going to a party at the weekend that she'll be at, if you fancy coming along.'

Tony shrugged. 'I might,' he said.

'You might like fuck,' Duggan laughed. 'You'll be there like a rat up a drain pipe.'

Tony shared in his laughter, not disagreeing with him.

'In return for that, I need to ask you a favour,' Duggan said.

Tony straightened a little. Ever since the discussion about Danny, he'd been waiting to see what price Duggan hoped to extract from him for establishing a memorial to his brother. 'I need you to get something for me from your school.'

Tony sipped his pint again, smaller sips this time, in a non-committal response to the request.

'It's nothing illegal,' Duggan said quickly. 'Nothing you'll get into trouble for. I need a few thermometers.'

Tony put down his pint, wiped the stout from his lips. 'Thermometers. Can you not just buy them?'

'Easier if they come for free,' Duggan said. 'No one will notice a few going missing in a school; they must get broken all the time in the science labs.'

'I don't teach science,' Tony said.

'I'm not a match-maker either,' Duggan said, 'but I've set you up rightly this weekend.'

Tony sighed. The request was not what he'd been expecting. In fact, it seemed fairly simple.

'I need four or five, if you can,' Duggan said. 'But they have to be mercury thermometers now; the alcohol ones are no good to me.'

'What do you need them for?'

'To take the fucking temperature,' Duggan laughed. 'What do you think I need them for?'

Tony joined half-heartedly in the joke. 'No worries,' he said, wondering not just how he was to manage to steal thermometers from his school, but for what purpose Duggan really needed them.

'Don't worry,' the older man said. 'No one will know you'd anything to do with it.'

Tony shook his head, as if the thought had not occurred to him, but he noticed Duggan's expression darken, as if he had somehow failed a private test the man had set for him. And strangely, he found himself keen to prove himself to the older man.

'Five thermometers,' he said. 'No problem.'

'That's it,' Duggan said, slapping him on the upper arm. 'Good man yourself.'

CHAPTER TWELVE

'Good man yourself,' Duggan said, as Barr laid two plates of breakfasts onto the table in front of them before heading back up to the service area for the rest. Tony, just arrived back from the toilet, felt a pang of guilt at the manner in which the young man was being treated, and the eagerness with which he accepted such treatment.

'I'll give him a hand,' he said to no one in particular, and followed Barr to the food counter.

He was standing, his wallet in hand, pulling out two twenty-pound notes, his legs apart in order to accommodate the increased swaying of the boat as they made their way out into the Irish Sea.

'I'll just get your tea. Do you need a receipt, love?' the cashier asked.

'No thanks,' Barr said, pushing the crinkled tenner change she'd handed him back into his wallet.

'Yes, he will,' Tony said. The younger man looked at him. 'You shouldn't be paying for our dinners,' Tony explained. 'Claim that off your uncle. Or whoever is paying for this.'

'I don't mind,' Barr said. 'It's a real honour, meeting you all. Mr Duggan's a legend. I mean, you're all legends, but–'

'I'm no legend, son,' Tony said. 'I clean the church twice a week to fill my days.'

Barr didn't disagree. 'Uncle Sean said to make sure you were all well looked after. We appreciate what you're doing here. It's not easy.'

We, Tony thought. He was learning the political lingo already, despite his youth.

'It's the right thing to do,' Tony said. 'Even if it is dragging up some memories I'd rather have forgotten.'

They waited until the cashier came back with three small pots of tea that she placed on a second tray, which Tony lifted and followed Barr. The younger man stopped near an empty table, the swell of the sea shifting the boat. He leaned his arm on the back of the seat to steady himself. Tony drew alongside and waited for the swell to subside a little.

'I don't think Mr Duggan likes me,' Barr asked, as if finally feeling he could articulate his deepest concern to someone.

'Do you care?' Tony asked, a little needlessly for it was clear that the youth did. 'Hugh can be prickly. Give it time. And for God's sake stop calling him Mr Duggan.'

Barr smiled, nodding curtly, then continued on with the tray to where the others sat.

Hugh had already eaten half his breakfast fry while Karen had cut the rind off her bacon but had clearly waited for Tony and Barr before starting to eat.

'So, we know how each of us got involved in all this,' Karen said when they'd all sat down and started their meal. 'How did you get involved?' The question was directed at Barr, emphasised with a jab of her fork in his direction.

'I studied political sciences at college,' Barr said. 'I specialized in the Northern Irish conflict as part of my final year. After Dad died, we moved down to Galway. I'd always wanted to move back to the North again.'

Duggan glanced at Karen and Tony, shook his head lightly, then turned his attention to his plate again.

'When I was old enough, my mum sent me back to live with Uncle Sean.'

'My mother sent me to Scotland to keep me away from men like your uncle Sean,' Tony offered with a rueful laugh.

'I got into a bit of trouble at home,' Barr admitted, smiling bashfully. 'I broke into the local Garda station and stole a uniform.'

'What?' Karen spluttered as she chewed. 'Why?'

'To see if I could. They nearly went mad looking for it.'

Duggan chuckled. 'Time was, I'd have done something similar myself,' he said. 'I remember stealing my teacher's car when I was at school to run myself and some of the lads down for a riot. We drove back up afterwards and left it back in the staff car park and the dozy bastard never even knew it was gone.'

Barr smiled warmly, happy to be part of the sharing of tales of past glory.

'But why did you get involved in all this?' Karen asked. 'How did you get politicised?'

Barr frowned. 'I don't know what you mean?'

'She means why did you want to be part of something the rest of us have tried to forget,' Tony explained.

'Speak for yourself,' Duggan muttered, spearing a piece of sausage on his fork then chewing it.

'The war's not over,' Barr said. 'Not as far as I'm concerned. There's unfinished business.'

Karen looked at Tony and rolled her eyes, though whether at the earnestness of the young man's comments or his actual views, Tony could not say.

'The problem with that,' Duggan said, as if stirring himself to speak, 'is that the fuckers who sent us out to fight, they were playing a game all along, except we didn't know. Some of them taking the King's shilling while they did it,' he said, then added, darkly, 'That's not changed.'

'It wasn't a game,' Karen said, her voice soft, but with a steeliness Tony recalled even from three decades earlier. 'Whatever you call it, it wasn't remotely a game.'

'Not to us,' Duggan said. 'But those fuckers that sent us out to kill or die, sitting in the pockets of our enemies the whole time. Or once they got into their pockets, sitting in power joking and laughing with the very fuckers they sent us out to fight in the first place.'

'People change,' Tony offered.

'Bollocks,' Duggan snapped. 'People don't change. They just become older and more extreme versions of themselves. Look at us. We're no different now from what we were back then. Just more extreme versions of what we were.'

'I've changed,' Tony said.

'No, you haven't,' Duggan said. 'I remember asking you to get me a few thermometers, to see if you were right for what we needed. I could tell you were shitting yourself about doing it.'

'That's not true,' Tony said. 'I just was uneasy with stealing things from a school.'

'See what I mean? A conscience.'

'You say that like it's a bad thing.'

'I've done rightly without one.'

'You don't regret anything?'

'Me?' Duggan laughed, without humour. 'I'm that French bird, Piaf. *Je ne regrette rien.*'

'Not even Martin Kelly?' Tony asked.

Duggan stared at him, his eyes vacillating between anger and pain, then clouding and becoming unreadable once more.

It was Karen who spoke. 'There's times I get the smell of burning cloth in my nose and I'm back in that forest again. Those moments aren't happy ones.'

'And how do you deal with all that shit in your head?' Duggan asked. 'What do you do with all your pity and guilt?'

'I try to forget it,' Karen said. 'I go about my day, go to work, make dinners, pack lunches, live a normal life. I've spent the past thirty years trying to forget.'

'See,' Duggan said, using his fork to point in Karen's direction, though he spoke to Tony. 'No change. She's as pragmatic now as she was thirty years ago. Just more so now.'

'I didn't say I always succeeded in doing it. But I was doing OK until I got dragged back into this,' Karen added. 'You can't forget when people are forcing you to remember.'

'You had your reasons for doing what you did, back then,' Duggan said. 'For why you got involved. That never changes. Your reasons for joining.'

'We all had reasons,' Karen countered. 'Mine was no better or worse than anyone else's.'

'Why did you get involved? Barr asked.

'Various things,' Karen said, her gaze drifting towards Tony momentarily. 'That's all.'

'What about you, Hugh?' he asked, the assonance of the words causing him to stumble on the final one, despite his best efforts to say it as casually as possible.

'It was my duty.'

CHAPTER THIRTEEN

Tony's duty on a Tuesday involved him patrolling the corridors for a period before lunch, in case a colleague needed support. Tony used the period as a chance to read ahead of his senior class on their novel. He'd deliberately circled round past the science labs four times, waiting for the classes to finish for lunch and for the staff to go to the staff room or canteen. He knew that only the science technician remained behind in the department and they always took their lunch in their own prep room. If he waited until the lunch bell rang, he could get in and out of one of the labs without being seen. He'd been on cover the day before and had, by chance, spotted a drawer of thermometers in the teacher's desk. He hoped that this was standard. There were two labs, so he reckoned the best thing to do would be to take the thermometers from the two different rooms so as not to draw too much suspicion

On his final circuit of the corridors, the last teacher to leave, an English man called Peter, with the air of one who had studied for and left the priesthood, was just leaving his room. He looked up at Tony coming towards him, his open book in his hand. 'At your breviary?' Peter said.

Tony laughed, a little louder than necessary and felt absurdly guilty in doing so. It was cut short when he saw Peter stoop and lock the classroom door.

'Do you not trust the wee blighters?' he asked.

Peter shrugged. 'You always lock the lab,' he said. 'Last thing we need is some little thug turning on all the gas when we're out of the room.'

Tony nodded. 'Very wise,' he said, slowing his pace to allow Peter to get well ahead of him. He knew there was little point in checking Peter's class. The next door down belonged to the prep room, then a second lab on the far side of that. Both labs could be accessed through the interconnecting doors of the prep room, but it was there, he suspected, that the technician would be having lunch.

He passed the prep room, confirming his assumption with a quick glance through the glass pane in the door. The technician was moving around inside, gathering up apparatus, as far as he could tell.

He moved past the prep room to the second lab and tried the handle. It too was locked. He knew that the doors could be unlocked from the inside; if he could make his way into the lab through the prep room, he'd be able to get back out again through this door.

He lingered a moment at the end of the corridor, then turned and came back again, passing the labs and glancing once more into the prep room. The technician had a grey apparatus tray in his hands and was heading towards the rear of the room, to where the connecting doors into the two labs where positioned. Tony saw him turn into the right and pulling open the door, go into lab 1.

Almost without thought, he opened the prep room door and, as quietly as he could, made his way up to the back of the area. He glanced quickly right to where the technician stood, his back to the open door, unloading equipment at the fume cupboard. Just as quickly, Tony opened the door of the lab to the left and went inside, pulling the door softly closed behind him.

Only when he reached the desk and put his hand on the handle of the drawer did he realise he was shaking, his legs jittery with adrenaline. He puffed a breath, glanced about him, then quickly checked the corners of the ceiling for a security camera. The burglar alarm monitor winked red at his movement and, for a second, gave him reason to pause.

He steeled himself, then slid open the drawer. The thermometers were still there, where he had last seen them. There were seven in total; he took two, putting them carefully into his inside pocket. He slid the drawer shut.

'Are you OK?'

He jolted around, swearing audibly with shock at the voice. The lab technician stood, the same grey tray in hand.

'I was covering here yesterday and forgot my book,' he said, holding aloft the novel which he had been carrying. His initial pride at the speed of his lie was immediately countered by a realisation that, having now seemingly found the book, he had no reason to go into the other lab. 'I think I left work in here, too,' he added, rolling his eyes. 'Head like a sieve, you know?'

'Do you need a hand?' the technician asked, looking at the desk which was completely clear.

Tony shook his head. 'I was covering for Peter at the time. This is his room, right?'

'Next door,' the technician said, heading across to the fume cupboard.

'Thanks,' Tony said, moving back to the door into the prep room.

'Mary must have borrowed your book,' the technician offered as he unloaded the beakers of solution into the unit.

'What?'

'If you left it in Peter's room, but found it in here; Mary must have borrowed the book to read.'

Tony nodded. 'Yeah,' he offered in half-hearted agreement.

'I'd not have taken her for a reader,' the man added.

Tony managed a second murmur of amusement, then headed into the prep room and straight across into Peter's room. He made straight for the desk and slid open the drawer. Empty.

Swearing silently, and aware that the technician might come back into the room at any moment, he quickly opened the doors of the cupboards behind the desk.

The speaker in the corner crackled into life. 'Mr Canning, contact Reception, please,' a voice lilted through the static.

Tony felt himself flustered. He pulled open the next door and finally, found a small cardboard box in which rested about a dozen thermometers. He lifted three of them and stuffed them clinking into his inside pocket.

Just as he closed the cupboard door, he heard Peter's voice.

'That place is getting worse. The curry looks revolting!' He'd clearly brought his lunch back up to eat in the prep room.

Tony wondered, momentarily, whether to brazen his way back out through the prep room, but to do so would involve having to use his excuse with Peter, and something about the man suggested he would remember whether or not Tony had been covering his class over the previous week or two.

Instead, he cut across the room, clutching his jacket tight against his breast to stop the glass thermometers from clattering together or, worse, breaking in his pocket.

He reached the handle, turning the knob slowly until he heard the dead bolt click back from its place. Turning the handle, he backed out of the room, keeping an eye for either Peter or the technician, closing the door softly behind him.

He turned and swore a second time when he saw Alice staring at him. She was seated on a window bench, which had been built into the alcove opposite Peter's door.

'Hi, sir,' Alice smiled.

Tony felt his heart thud in his chest, imagined he could head the mild clink of the glass rods striking against each other with the vibration.

'What are you doing here?' Tony said, more crossly than he had intended. 'You're not meant to be up here during lunch time.'

The girl's eyes filled instantly. 'I forgot my lunch money, sir,' she said, her lip quivering.

Tony instantly regretted the tone he had taken. At that, perhaps hearing the raised voice, the prep room door opened and Peter glanced out. Evidently, seeing Tony standing out there, and knowing that he had been on corridor duty earlier, he felt no suspicion.

'Everything all right, sir?' he asked. He looked at the girl. 'What's wrong now, Miss Hamilton?'

'I forgot my lunch money, sir,' she repeated.

Peter tutted. 'Again?'

'My father forgot to give it to me, sir,' she said, her voice reedy.

Tony studied her, her hair pulled back, with frazzles of hair having escaped the loosely tied elastic that held the ponytail in place. Her eyes were dull, her skin pale. Grey as dishwater, his mother would have said.

'Have you nothing to eat?' Tony asked.

The girl shook her head, not quite meeting his gaze, her head lightly bowed. Tony realised why she was sitting here now; the alternative would be to sit in the canteen with her classmates who would find cause, no doubt, to comment on her having no lunch and no money.

He put his hand into his pocket and pulled out three one-pound notes. He offered them to the Alice.

'Buy yourself something nice. What do you fancy? Chips?'

She stood, her head bowed, her cheeks registered colour for the first time since he had seen her as she blushed with shame. She did not touch the money.

'Listen, Alice,' he said, hunkering down in front of her, the glass thermometers in his pockets jutting awkwardly through the cloth of his jacket at one end, jabbing into his knee at the other. She raised her head a little, looked him in the eye. 'Us Irish ones need to stick together. I'm famished and I'm heading to the canteen for my lunch. I'll be buying two plates of chips. If you don't help me eat them, I'm going to turn into a fat pig!'

Despite herself, the girl giggled at his comment.

'Now come on. What do you think? Chips?'

Alice nodded and, for a second, Tony felt a pang of something twist inside him. He wanted to put his hand on her shoulder, ruffle her hair, do something to let her know she was not alone.

In the end, he stood and nudged her playfully with his arm. 'Don't forget to take your insulin. Then I'll race you to see who's finished their dinner first.'

CHAPTER FOURTEEN

Duggan finished his meal first, then sat back, his arms folded across his stomach as he waited for the others. Karen was still picking at hers. Despite claiming she was famished when the food arrived, she'd cut it into pieces and rearranged it on the plate rather than eating it. Tony thought he understood now how she'd managed to stay so trim. As he wiped up the last of the egg yolk with the corner of his toast, he was aware of his own belly, the pressure of the table edge against it as he ate. Almost instinctively, he breathed in a little, aware of the futility of the gesture even as he did it.

'What are your kids called?' he asked and, for a second, imagined he saw a flicker of something darken her expression. Was she annoyed at *him* asking about them? Or that he had done so in front of the others? Despite the time they'd already spent in each other's company, none of them had offered anything too personal to the conversation, as if they were skirting around each other. Too much time had passed, he decided, for them to know where to start to catch up with the others. And of course, what had united them thirty years earlier, what had driven them to kill and bury someone together, he considered a little ruefully, had long since passed.

'Desmond and Daniel,' she said a little stiffly, annunciating each syllable.

'Daniel or Danny?' Tony asked with a smile.

'Danny to me,' she said. 'Daniel to everyone else.' Her back was erect, her posture frozen in the moment of gathering food onto her fork.

'Danny's a good name,' Tony said, thinking of his brother.

She nodded, her eyes dropping from his face to the space between them, as if for the first time she realised the connection between them that the name had created.

'So's Daniel,' Barr said. 'Daniel O'Connell.'

She managed a brittle smile at the comment. Hugh, for his part, did not engage in the conversation.

'Have you family, Hugh?'

'Two ex-wives,' he said.

'I'm sorry,' Karen said.

Hugh held up his hand. 'Don't be. I'm not. You know they say marriage is an institution. Well, I'd rather not be institutionalised.'

They all smiled lightly at the joke they'd all heard before, except Barr, who seemed to echo Hugh's words, the punchline forming silently on his lips before he laughed and clapped his hands. Tony glanced at Karen who'd turned her attention to the contents of her plate again.

'What about you, Richard?'

Barr snorted. 'I'm only twenty-one,' he said.

'You're still pretty much a kid yourself,' Karen commented.

Tony looked at the young man. His features were defined, his eyes clear, his skin supple, still marked in places with acne along his throat.

'You weren't even born then,' he said, softly. 'When Martin died.'

Barr nodded. 'I suppose.'

'Why in God's name would you want to be part of it now?'

Duggan, his arms still folded, leaned forward. 'The young fella's doing his bit for the country. Like we all did. At one stage.'

Barr nodded, emboldened by Duggan's endorsement. 'What Hugh said earlier. It's my duty.'

'Were you alive when the Agreement was signed?'

'About six months before,' Barr said, a little defiantly.

'And you don't think that what's happened after it is better than what went before?'

'For who?' Duggan asked.

'For all of us?'

Duggan shook his head. 'Maybe.'

'People died so that Agreement could be reached,' Barr said. 'It justified their sacrifices.'

'Like Martin Kelly's sacrifice?' Tony asked.

'Have you gone soft in your old age?' Duggan hissed. 'He knew what would happen to him. We all did.'

'Peace happened because of politics. In spite of violence, not because of it,' Tony said.

'Violence is politics,' Duggan snapped.

'Not my kind.'

'Then why are you here?'

Duggan's question was asked almost with a smirk, as if he knew something that Tony had not yet realised.

'To do right by Kelly's family,' Tony said carefully, aware that that was not entirely truthful. Not for him at least.

'Why are we here? Duggan asked, nudging Barr with his shoulder.

'To help recover–'

'No,' Duggan said. 'Why are we *really* here?'

Tony felt his own gaze falter under the intensity of Duggan's, but could not let himself look away now. His stomach stirred and seemed to drop as his breath caught.

'We need a goodwill gesture,' Barr said finally. 'Negotiations with the other side have stalled and this would be a sweetener. It could help move things along.'

Duggan smiled, slyly. 'That's not the only reason, is it?'

Barr looked at him blankly.

'Uncle Sean is going for the leadership of the party, too,' Duggan said. 'Some of the moderates have a problem with his past. They want a goodwill gesture.'

'Is that right?' Tony asked, looked at Barr.

The youth returned his look, guileless, then nodded.

'Can we drop this?' Karen said. She had not spoken in a few minutes so they were all surprised by her intervention now. She looked down at her plate, her voice soft and without emotion.

'What's wrong with you?'

'We were used thirty years ago,' she said. 'We're being used again now.' She put down her knife and fork and pushed her plate from her. 'I'm not hungry,' she said.

CHAPTER FIFTEEN

'I'm not hungry, thanks,' Karen said.

They were standing in a kitchen near Parkhead. Duggan had made good on his promise to engineer a second meeting between them after Tony had delivered the thermometers to him, as agreed. Tony had tried to restart the acquaintance with the offer of a drink, which she accepted, and some peanuts from a single desultory bowl sitting on the counter, which she'd refused.

'Besides, do you know how many people have put their dirty paws into the middle of that?'

Tony put the bowl back, took another draught from the can he held.

'No wine tonight?' Karen said, nodding at his drink.

'You were right,' he said. 'I felt awful the day after that last night out.'

She sipped her own wine and glanced around the room. 'I don't know anyone here,' she said. 'Apart from you. And Hugh, wherever he is.'

'He's not here,' Tony said, a little bewildered. Hugh had told him Karen was going to this party and he'd invited Tony along. Now, he suspected that wasn't entirely true.

'Did you take the bus?' Tony asked, immediately regretting the stupidity of it.

Karen nodded. 'It took for ever. There was a bomb scare in the city centre,' she said.

'Here?' Bomb scares had been a feature of daily life in the North, a vague distraction or a major inconvenience depending on where the bomb was planted. For a while, the favoured target had been the city's bridge, which meant that traffic from one half of the city could not reach the other, further splitting an already divided city in half.

The sound of cheering from the living area of the flat caused them both to turn to see Hugh Duggan come in, blue bags of beer raised in his two hands. As he made his way through the room towards the kitchen, acknowledging Karen and Tony with a wink, some of the partygoers slapped him on the back.

'He's popular,' Tony said.

'Glad one of us is,' Karen said.

'Are you OK?'

She nodded, leaning towards him, placing her hand on his arm, her little finger electrifying the skin of his wrist where it touched just past the cuff of his shirt. 'These types of places make me uneasy,' she said.

'Parties?'

She shrugged. Tony looked around the room. The only face he recognised was Martin Kelly's, sitting on the sofa between two Irish girls, breaking apart a cigarette. A ten spot of dope, its corner already charred, sat on the table next to a packet of Rizla papers.

'Do you want to get a drink somewhere else?' Tony asked, his body suddenly alive, his legs seeming to vibrate with the surge of nerves he felt at having asked.

'Yeah,' she said. 'Maybe one.'

'We're just leaving,' Tony said, as Hugh made his way into the kitchen, depositing the two bags on the counter with such force it sent the nut bowl's contents scattering across the worktop and onto the linoleum floor.

'Was it something I said?' he asked, mock offended.

'It's a bit crowded,' Tony said. 'We're going to head and get a drink somewhere.'

'I'll walk you out,' Hugh said, despite the flat not being his, as far as Tony knew. 'I want to ask you something.'

'What is it?' Tony asked. He felt Karen stiffen a little beside him.

'I need to ask the two of you a favour,' he said. 'But we'll take a walk first.'

They made their way down the stairway and out into the night before Hugh spoke again.

Now, outside, he stopped. 'Can't be too careful,' he said, his voice rising over the sound of a police car siren as it sped past on its way into the city centre.'

'Trouble in town,' Karen said.

'Car bomb,' Duggan said. 'One of the other side hiding out in Glasgow. Someone put a bomb under the engine of his car.'

'Is he dead?' Karen asked.

'If he's not, he'll not be playing football again for sure,' Hugh said.

Karen shivered lightly. 'It's cold. Can we walk?'

Tony motioned to take off his coat for her, as before, but she stopped him. 'It's grand,' she said. 'I just want to keep moving.'

Hugh walked to the outside, next to Tony, Karen to the inside. 'I need you to go for a drive this weekend.'

'What?' Tony asked.

'Where?' Karen asked, simultaneously.

'Out to Paisley,' Duggan said.

'Is this something to do with your man, Martin Kelly?' Tony asked.

'What?'

'Are you looking for us to move drugs for you?' he asked, whispering the words.

Hugh laughed. 'Jesus, no. I want you to go for a drive to Paisley. Take a walk, get some dinner. There's a nice restaurant there; Watson's. I've booked dinner for the two of you for eight o'clock on Saturday.'

Tony glanced at Karen, then back to Hugh. 'What the fuck?' he asked. Arranging to have them both at a party was one thing, but booking dinner for them was too much.

Duggan said. 'Park the car in the rear car park and leave it unlocked. When your dinner's finished, bring it back into Glasgow. Pick it up and leave it back in the car park of the old church down past Bellgrove station. It'll be unlocked, with the key under the mat on the driver's side. You can lock it when you come back. The person collecting it has the spare key.'

'Listen, Hugh,' Tony said. 'I'm not sure–'

Duggan stopped, gripped his arm. 'Do you remember the fucker who drove over your brother? Do you remember that?'

Tony nodded, compelled to agree by the vehemence of Hugh's tone.

'Then we need to help shift stuff across. We've taken a bit of a hit to the supply chain recently.'

'I don't know how to–'

'You don't have to do anything,' Duggan said. 'Go for dinner, have a drink, drive home. Leave the car. That's all.'

Tony looked across at Karen who was staring at Duggan.

'What do you think?' he asked her.

'Why not?' she said. 'Dinner would be nice.'

'Why us?'

'A young couple in love is more normal than me sitting on my own for two hours and then driving back here again. Besides, people know my face; youse two are so young and sweet no one will look twice at the pair of you.'

Tony took a breath, considered his choices. The idea of an evening with Karen appealed to him much more than the thought of them carrying whatever they would be carrying frightened him.

'That night you were lifted, you told me you wanted to see someone answer for Danny. Other people agreed, volunteered. Everyone plays their part: some are more active, risk their lives; some have dinner and drive a car back into town again.'

Tony felt Karen's hand briefly take his, giving it a squeeze of encouragement.

'It's fine,' she said. 'It'll be nice.'

He felt something stirring deep inside him at her touch and the excitement of what they were going to do together. The clandestine nature of it. The visceral nature of what he hoped it might lead to. He tightened his grip on hers a moment but, when he released it, she let his hand go.

They went to a bar in the centre of town. The place was busy, though the night air was alive with the sound of sirens. It struck Tony that, having been so used to them at home, he'd become accustomed to their absence here in Scotland.

Karen seemed more at ease now, sitting forward in her seat, both hands cradling her glass. She wore a dark green, short-sleeved dress, long and belted at the waist, and a pair of brown workman's boots. Her legs crossed, Tony was aware each time her foot touched his leg under the table; indeed, conspired for it to happen.

'Hugh says your brother died recently,' she said. 'I'm sorry. That's terrible.'

Tony shrugged. 'My dad was shattered by it. You know the way you always think you're your parents' favourite – well, maybe you don't, but I did. I realised after Danny died that *he* was. Dad just sort of crumpled when it happened. Even when the cops arrested us the night of the funeral, he didn't fight back. They had to drag me down the stairs.'

'That's when you met Hugh?'

Tony nodded.

'How's your dad now?'

'Alive,' Tony joked. 'But Danny was his favourite; it'll kill him eventually.'

Karen sat back a little, as if stung by something Tony had said.

'So, were you the favourite at home?'

Karen nodded, her eyes glinting in the light from the bar. 'I'm an only child, so I was both their favourites. My mum died when I was ten so me and Dad were so close growing up. He did everything for me.'

'I'm sorry about your mum.'

Karen smiled sadly. 'Dad tried his best to be both mother and father, but it all got a bit mad for him. The whole time of the month thing just broke him, having to go into a supermarket to buy tampons. He handed me the box, made some piss-poor explanation of why it was happening and left me to figure out the rest. I had to ask my friend's mum to explain it to me properly.

'Must have been a nightmare for any boyfriends,' Tony laughed.

'Not really. He just showed them his shotgun and they behaved themselves,' she said, laughing lightly.

'Does he miss you over here? Tony asked.

She shook her head. 'He's dead now. That's when I moved across.'

'I'm so sorry,' Tony said, rewinding the conversation in his head, wincing at every comment, which, in the light of this, seemed now crassly insensitive.

She shook her head. 'Can we go? I need a breath of fresh air.'

CHAPTER SIXTEEN

'I need a breath of air,' Karen said, standing. 'Excuse me.'

The three men watched her leave, Tony rising slightly in his seat as she stood.

'She's not changed,' Duggan said. 'She was always half-hearted about it.'

'That's not true,' Tony said, a little more defensively than he'd intended. 'She was the one convinced me to help you with that first run to Paisley.'

'What run?'

'You sent us to a restaurant in Paisley, told us leave the car open and then bring it back again. She was the one convinced me that night.'

'She'd nothing to do with it.'

'We were at a party. We were leaving when you arrived and you walked us out. You asked us to drive to Paisley. I wasn't sure, but she agreed to it, convinced me to do it.'

'I don't remember that.'

'There was a car bomb in the centre of town.'

Duggan shook his head. 'She wasn't there that night. You and I met in Liverpool Betty's and talked about it. You asked could you bring her along.'

Tony frowned with bemusement. 'That's not what happened.'

'I remember the night I asked you. You wanted to do something for your brother; you asked to be more active. I asked you to do the run for me. The cops were keeping a bit of an eye on some of us at the time and you were a new face. You said you wanted to bring her with you; you thought it would be good cover to have a couple there.'

'*You* said that,' Tony laughed.

'Does it matter?' Barr asked.

'It matters if we're hoping to remember where the hell Martin Kelly is,' Tony hissed, concerned now. 'I remember that night.'

'So do I,' Duggan said. 'But not the way you're telling it.'

'And do you remember what was in the car?'

'I remember,' Duggan said. 'I'm not stupid. I've not forgotten those days. Even if the rest of the country has.'

'No one's forgotten them.'

'Of course they have,' Duggan said. 'We were soldiers sent out to fight and when the war was over, we were the villains. People apologising for things we did, things we were told to do by them. "*That should never have happened.*" What the fuck does that mean? The things that happened, they happened exactly the way they were meant to. Like this. This bullshit, going back here.'

'It's the right thing to do,' Barr said, feeling it was the only part of the conversation to which he could make a contribution.

'That's easy for you to say, son, it's not your bullets lodged in whatever's left resting in that hole in the forest now.'

'Nothing can be done with them,' Barr said. 'They're not allowed to investigate–'

'Seriously? Since when did we trust *them*? They link Kelly to other killings, they'll know I did it.'

'But they can't do anything about that.'

'But they'll know it was me!' Duggan snapped. 'And I don't want that.'

'Why?' Tony asked. 'They knew you did other things.'

Duggan folded his arms. 'But this one was different. Martin was my friend and I had to shoot him anyway because of what he did. What others *said* he did.'

He stared at Tony, but seemed to address Barr as he added, 'And this whole time since, I've been asking myself, what if we got it wrong?'

CHAPTER SEVENTEEN

'What if this is wrong?' Tony asked.

They had parked in the car park to the rear of Watson's restaurant. Tony had picked up the car from the church grounds as instructed. The key had been lying under the mat in the footwell on the driver's side. He'd gone early, hoping to see whoever left the car, but it was already parked there and, when Tony slipped his hand on the bonnet, the engine felt cold.

He'd driven to Karen's to pick her up. She'd invited him inside briefly, while she got herself ready. Her place was a one-bedroom flat, with a kitchenette abutting the living area. It was neat and clean, as Tony had expected. An oversized sofa dominated the lounge area; it was old, the velour worn on the armrests, but Karen had covered it with a knitted throw to brighten up its drab brown.

She came out of her bedroom, pulling on a waist-length leather jacket. She wore jeans and a striped blue T-shirt. She'd put on make-up, he thought, but not so much as to be obvious. But he couldn't tell whether she saw the meal as a date or a favour to Duggan.

'You look really well,' he managed.

She smiled. 'Thanks. You don't scrub up too badly yourself.'

He considered what he was wearing: jeans and a checked shirt. He'd hardly gone to town, scrubbing himself up.

Beyond her, he could make out the edge of her bed, a cabinet next to it with a picture in a frame sitting atop. He felt a frisson of excitement, a desire to be in there, to see more of her personality; the flat reflected her neatness, but nothing else.

They passed the thirty-minute journey in affable small talk. The car over-revved a little on the clutch and Tony was aware of not drawing attention to themselves, so he drove carefully, both hands on the wheel, afraid to take his eyes off the road for too long.

They found the restaurant after a few wrong turns and having to stop to ask for directions. Tony had been reluctant, in case someone remembered them later if anyone asked, but Karen had dismissed this as being a 'typical man' and, afraid to prove her right, he'd capitulated and pulled in. The youth who directed them barely even glanced at them anyway, lifting his head long enough to indicate with a light nod the direction in which they needed to go.

When they reached the restaurant, though, they realised that the car parking extended all the way around the place. Tony circled around a few times.

'Where should we park?'

'He said the back,' Karen said. 'There's a few spaces over there.' She pointed across to three free spaces either side of a street lamp.

'Maybe we need to park it somewhere darker?' Tony said. 'If someone doesn't want to be seen.'

Karen nodded. 'It's up to you. Someone over at a car in a dark corner's going to look like a car thief. Out in the open's less likely to raise any suspicions.'

'Boot in or out the ways?'

'In might make more sense,' Karen said.

Tony nodded, reversing into the spot.

'Are you sure this is it?'

Karen glanced out at the building in front of them. 'That's Watson's.

'What if this is wrong?' Tony asked, suddenly.

Karen looked across at him, held his gaze steadily in hers. 'What? The restaurant? Or the whole thing?'

'It just feels… wrong in some way.'

'Don't over-think it. We're doing nothing wrong,' Karen said. 'We're going for some food and then driving home in a car a friend lent us for the evening.'

Tony wasn't sure, but she sounded so convinced herself, and the hand she laid briefly over his on the gear stick was so warm, so soft, that he nodded. 'You're probably right,' he said.

'First lesson learnt,' Karen smiled. 'I'm always right.'

As they walked away from the car, he felt an urge to double-check that he hadn't locked it inadvertently and went back and tried the handle, then closed the door softly. The doubt still assailed him once they were inside the restaurant.

Sitting at the table, Tony could see Karen's eyes again, was reminded that she'd claimed to have eaten her own twin.

'Is it odd?' he asked, apropos the thought, which he had not shared with her.

'Is what odd?' she frowned.

'Your twin.'

'I don't have a twin.'

'I was looking at your eyes,' he explained, a comment which caused

89

Karen to blush and glance down at her hands. 'You joked that you ate your own twin. Do you feel like you had a twin? Really. Is it odd not having one?'

'I don't know. I never had one to know the difference.'

Tony blushed now, feeling silly for having asked the question and compelled to try to explain himself more clearly.

'I mean, do you have a sense of one? An absence?'

She smiled. 'I'd never thought of it like that,' she said. 'An absence? I suppose I was aware that I was alone when I was growing up. I missed having a friend. Did you have only the one brother?'

Tony nodded.

'Do you miss him?'

'He's an absence, definitely,' Tony said. 'I was away from home at university and that, so we didn't spend as much time together recently as we used to, you know? So, we kind of drifted a bit.'

He paused. He'd not, he realised, really thought about Danny being gone. Moving to Scotland had taken him from the things that would most have reminded him of his brother; he could, on some level, imagine that Danny was still OK back at home. That in some other world, Danny had stopped for a burger, or left the game early because the scoreline was already clear and he'd wanted to beat the crowds at the gate.

'It was the randomness of it,' he said, finally. 'Like it could have been anyone walking on that path. He could have been early, or late. Or not gone to the game, or met a girl or met his friends, or stopped for a drink somewhere.'

Karen did not speak, though she held his gaze, her expression soft.

'I needed someone to blame,' he said. 'My dad didn't; he just accepted it as fate, or accident, or whatever. But I couldn't do that;

someone had to be to blame, and someone had to be held accountable for what they did. Accident didn't kill my brother; a Brit did, you know?'

Karen nodded, her eyes glistening in the light thrown from the small tea candle in the holder on their table.

'If you have someone to blame, you have something you can do,' she said. 'We need to feel active; like we're doing something about what happens to us. I understand that.'

Midway through dinner, Tony excused himself to go to the toilet. He walked back by a circuitous route that allowed him to go outside for a moment, in the hope he might spot anyone near the car but it sat exactly where he had parked it, seemingly untouched.

They chatted through dessert about a mutual friend of a friend they both knew back home and about Karen's job; she worked on the reception desk at a health centre.

'That was where I met Martin Kelly,' Karen explained. 'Before I met him through Duggan.'

It took Tony a moment to remember who Martin Kelly was. 'I don't know him,' Tony said. 'I know of him; I've seen him a few times, but we've not spoken or anything.'

'He's a creep,' Karen said, instinctively rubbing her upper arm.

'Is he a dealer?'

Karen nodded.

'Why is Duggan in with him, then? At home Duggan's crew would have kneecapped him.'

'He's useful,' Karen said. 'Besides, whose drugs do you think he's selling?'

'For Duggan?'

'Not for Duggan per se,' Karen said. 'But the money he makes, he's paying a tithe up the chain. Besides, he's everywhere, meets everyone. No one suspects him because he's already suspicious.'

'There's a logic in there somewhere,' Tony said.

'How did you know he was a dealer?'

Tony sensed from the way in which she bristled slightly when she asked the question that she was afraid they had met through a transaction.

'I met one of the kids I used to teach a while back in Liverpool Betty's. I thought she was on something. At the end of the evening, I was waiting to use the toilet and when the door opened, Kelly came out zipping himself up and she was getting off her knees with a ten spot in her hand. I'm guessing she didn't have the tenner on her to pay.'

Karen grimaced at the mental image his story had conjured.

'He's a creep,' she repeated.

They drove back to Glasgow after ten. Tony wanted to check the boot, to see if anything had been placed there, but Karen advised him not to. She'd relaxed throughout dinner, having had a few glasses of wine. At the end of the meal, Tony had paid for them both and she'd not protested or offered to go half, which made him think she saw the evening out as a date. But as he drove, he wondered if she'd allowed him to pay so that it *looked* like a date, which was, after all, the cover which Duggan had suggested when he asked them to bring the car into Paisley.

The sudden flash of red lights in front of them shook him from his thoughts and he braked as he realised the cars in front of him had stopped. Flicking on the hazard lights, he glanced in the rearview to check that the drivers behind him would see in enough time to stop.

The last thing he needed was an impact from behind that might necessitate opening the boot in front of others.

Karen craned in her seat, winding down the window to see what lay ahead.

'Shit,' she said, her face blanching. 'It's the police.'

Tony felt his stomach turn. 'What'll we do?'

Karen gathered herself. He could see she was calming herself, breathing slowly, her hands raised in front of her, as if in placation.

'If they stop us, we say we borrowed the car from a friend. We didn't even look in the boot.'

'They'll not believe us.'

'There's no fingerprints on the boot door,' she said. 'None of ours anyway. And no gloves or anything in the car. Are there?' She twisted in the seat, glancing behind her, then opened the glove box in front of Tony, which was empty.

He realised with some relief and greater gratitude, why she had told him not to check in the rear. He slowed his own breathing, wiped the sheen of sweat from his hands onto his trouser leg. He felt light headed, looked around to see if he could pull in, or turn; but they were on the motorway and he was hemmed in on all sides.

As they inched forward, he could see the blue flickering of the police lights illuminating the trees edging the roadway. He guessed there must be more than one vehicle for the flickering seemed to overlap at times, and separate at others, working to its own, free rhythm.

'It'll be fine,' Karen was saying. 'We're moving forward, which means they're not stopping anyone. Not for long anyway. Have you your licence?'

'It's Northern Irish,' Tony said. 'I'm guaranteed to be pulled in. Maybe we should get out and run.'

'How far do you think either of us would get? We know nothing. That's it. Not our car, not our whatever is in there.'

As they neared the police lights, Tony realised that the two lanes of traffic were being funnelled into one with traffic cones. A policeman stood at the point where they merged, his high-vis jacket gleaming in the approaching cars' headlights.

Tony thought he would vomit by the time they'd reached where the officer stood. He had a torch in one hand, its top covered with a red cone. As they drew abreast him, he held out the torch, indicating that they should stop.

Winding down the window, the cold night air caught him by surprise, taking the breath from him.

'Evening,' he muttered.

'Wait a minute, sir,' the policeman said, glancing down at him, then across at Karen.

He walked away from the car and watched further up the roadway, where Tony could now see more blue lights pulsing into life.

'What's wrong?'

'An accident,' the policeman said, his hand outstretched, telling them to remain where they were. 'That's you now, sir,' he said, waving him on. 'Drive safely.'

They crawled past the scene a few hundred yards later. Two ambulances had just arrived, having clearly driven the wrong way up the motorway, to get to the site of the crash. A car had been upended, its underbelly exposed to the fluorescent glare of the motorway lights. The person inside remained strapped, upside down, while the paramedics lay on the ground talking to them through the opened window.

Despite the sight of the accident, Tony felt elated at having successfully made it through the checkpoint. He glanced at Karen who shared his smile. Without thinking, he reached across and took her hand. She held his for a moment, giving it a reassuring squeeze. He felt his excitement build at his very centre, felt himself buzz with it.

'Thank fuck,' he muttered.

They parked the car back in the churchyard below Bellgrove, right where they had collected it some hours earlier. After he had locked it up, Tony felt compelled once more to check the boot, to see what exactly they had been transporting past a police cordon.

'Don't look,' Karen said. 'It won't do any good.'

Tony laughed, half pleading with her to understand, to share his curiosity. 'I have to know,' he said. He moved around the rear of the car and, pulling down his sleeve over his hand, opened the rear door. The space lay empty. He pulled up the carpeted interior of the boot to where the spare wheel was kept and there saw something wrapped in a plastic bag, beneath the jack.

For the first time since they'd seen the police lights on the motorway, he began to question the wisdom of what they had done. He wondered whether Duggan had lied, whether indeed they had been bringing drugs for Martin Kelly and his like to sell to school kids in the pubs around Glasgow.

He looked across to where Karen stood, a distance apart, her hands wedged in her jacket pockets. She watched him, but showed no interest in what was inside the car boot.

Carefully, keeping his hands covered, he lifted the jack away. Beneath it, the blue-black body visible through the clear plastic wrapping, lay a pistol. He'd seen them in Derry, when the police were patrolling, but had never been so close to one before. He wanted to touch it, wanted to feel its hardness, its coldness. He felt once more that elation he had felt on the motorway, but something else beneath that, too.

He carefully laid the jack back into place, fixed the carpeting back and shut the door, then walked across to where Karen stood.

'It's a—' he whispered, but she silenced him with a raised hand.

'Don't tell me,' she said. 'I don't need to know.'

Tony felt a little deflated that she would not share with him his excitement, not allow him to reconcile that with the other, more insidious feeling he'd had all evening, that underlying sense of dread.

'Aren't you a little curious?' he asked.

She shook her head. 'No.'

They travelled back to her flat on the bus and again he walked her to the door. This time, briefly, they kissed. Her lips were dry, the skin chapped from the night air. He moved to kiss her a second time, but she responded with a quick peck on the side of his mouth.

'We'll do this another time,' she said. 'I enjoyed the night.'

'Can I get your number?' Tony asked, hurt at her preventing a second kiss.

She nodded, and wrote it on the back of his hand with her eyeliner pencil. 'You'll need to remember that,' she said. 'It'll smudge and come off in no time.'

'Can I come up?' he asked, his body seemingly electrified by the evening's events.

'Next time,' she said. 'I'm tired. Thanks.'

She leaned up and kissed him again, quickly on the cheek, her hand on his chest, as if to promise that there would be a next time.

'Are you OK?' he asked.

She smiled, without humour. 'Fine,' she said.

'Are you angry at me looking in the boot?'

She shook her head. 'No. I just don't want to know what's there. I'd rather you hadn't.'

'Why?'

'Because if I know what's there, I might start wondering whether what we've just done was wrong.'

CHAPTER EIGHTEEN

'Wrong?' Tony repeated.

Duggan nodded. 'What if Kelly wasn't the tout?'

Tony felt his head start to spin. He put his hands to the side of his seat, as if to steady himself against the ship's movement.

'You said he was,' he said.

'I was told he was,' Duggan said. 'But what if it was a lie?'

Tony studied the man opposite him, trying to tease out the subtext in what he was saying. 'Do you think it was one of us?'

'I know it wasn't me,' Duggan said. 'But I knew Kelly. He was my friend. I trusted him. He knew things, worse things, that no one knew about and never a word said. The more I've thought on it, the less certain I am.'

'I've not thought about it at all,' Tony lied.

'That's not true,' Duggan said. 'I'd believe it if the ice maiden out there said that. But not you. Nor me. And I've thought about it a lot more since this idea was pushed, digging him back up again. You can't dig up a grave without disturbing some skeletons.'

'Who... who do you think was if not him?' Tony asked. He wondered if Duggan had noticed him stumbling on his words, whether he would read something into it.

'It doesn't matter now,' Barr said, blithely. 'What's done is done. All we're looking at is closure for the family.'

'Closure,' Duggan said, staring at him. 'What the fuck is that?'

'An ending,' Barr explained, hesitantly, unsure if Duggan's question had been rhetorical.

'An ending? There is no *ending*. Things don't end; they're abandoned, unfinished. Do you think Martin Kelly had an ending? Like his story was done?'

'He's right,' Tony said, nodding at Barr, but speaking to Duggan. 'What's done is done. We can't change it, and we don't have to investigate it. We just need to remember where he is and let the family come and find him.'

'And what then?' Duggan asked. 'Do you think that'll be enough? You don't think they'll want to know why? Don't you want to know why?'

'No,' Tony said. 'It doesn't matter.'

'It matters to me,' Duggan hissed. 'It matters to me. I never did nothing that I wasn't sure about. Every single thing, every person, I knew why and I knew I was right. When I face my maker, I'll have their names in my mouth and not an ounce of guilt in me for I know why I did them and why they deserved it. But not with Martin. And I want to know why.'

Tony held his gaze. He thought of the tablets he'd been taking in the toilet, about his thinness, the jowls of skin hanging at his throat. 'Are you sick?' he asked.

Duggan's anger flared for a second, then died away as quickly. 'None of your business,' he said.

'I don't know if Kelly was the right person or not,' Tony said, then added hastily, 'I know it wasn't me,' but his comment lacked the conviction of Duggan's comments. 'And I trust Karen. But we can't change what we did. We can only hope to make up for it, if we were wrong.'

Barr looked from one to the other of them. 'Men, no one's worried about what happened. We just need to give the moderates something to keep them happy. No one cares about Kelly.'

'His family does,' Tony said, tapping the paper.

'You know what I mean,' Barr said. 'Uncle Sean wanted to make it very clear; the family just want the body back to bury him properly. For closure,' he repeated, seemingly pleased with the word.

'I'll see how Karen is,' Tony said, standing up, the boat's rocking causing him to stumble a little and have to grip the back of the chair again for a moment to steady himself. He felt a heaviness in his chest, had felt it intensifying as he and Duggan had talked, dismissed it as indigestion, caused by the greasiness of the fry they'd just eaten.

Karen was standing on the deck, facing towards Scotland, the wind cutting along the sides of the ferry lifting the ends of her hair. As a consequence, Tony could not tell if she had been crying, though her eyes were reddened and glistening.

'Are you OK?'

She nodded, her arms gathered around her. She raised her face to the wind.

'I just thought this was all over. Thirty years ago.'

Tony nodded, stuffed his hands into his pockets and silently regretted having not lifted his coat to come outside to where she'd stood.

'Me too.'

Karen looked at him, as if testing the veracity of his comment. 'Have you thought about it? About Martin?'

He nodded. 'Quite a bit.'

She shook her head. 'That was another life to me. I came home and put it all behind me.' She paused a moment, as if realising that, in so saying, she was including her time with Tony in the comment. 'It was the only way I could deal with it. I used to wake up, thinking about him; the stench of burning so strong in my nostrils, I'd get up and turn on the light, looking for a fire.' She looked at Tony. 'It's the smell I can't forget.'

'It was the crying for me,' Tony said. 'How vulnerable he was, naked, alone. We never let him say what he wanted us to tell his mother.'

'Were we wrong?'

'Hugh thinks so.'

'Hugh does?' she asked, incredulous.

'Not wrong to do it; wrong in the person we chose. He thinks Martin wasn't the one.'

Karen turned once more to the east, to where the Scottish headland loomed on the horizon. 'Who does he think it was?' she asked.

'He's not said.'

'Was he not the right one?'

'To be a tout?'

'To die?'

Tony shrugged. 'That's not my call to make.'

'When you stood there, watching him, did you know for certain it was him? That's he'd been the one passing on information?'

'If that's what Hugh was told, we had to go with that.'

Karen nodded. 'Funny how we can rationalise things,' she said. 'I turned my back on my whole life and started over. You're pretending that Hugh's decision was binding for us all.'

'I don't pretend anything,' Tony said. 'I know what we did; what I did.' He felt a sudden anger towards her, spurred perhaps by her admission that she'd forgotten him when he had not, could not forget her. 'My brother and wife and son all died. And when my son died, I thought of Martin. I thought it was the universe or God or something balancing the books. I took someone's son, so they took mine. And when Ann died, I tried to work out why and do you know what? It was because of Martin as well. It's like Death follows me because of what we did, punishing me for it.'

'That's not true,' Karen said. 'My family, I've lost no one. You can't blame what's happened now on what happened then.'

'It's cause and effect,' Tony said.

Karen shook her head. 'I don't think the universe missed Martin Kelly that much,' she said. 'You know what he was like.'

'It's the breach in nature,' Tony said. 'That's what Shakespeare said.'

'You and your books! Is that why you became a sacristan?' Karen asked. 'For penance?'

Tony considered the question. 'I suppose so.'

'And has it worked?'

He laughed without humour, raised a shoulder. 'I don't know. But when I die and make that last crossing, I know I'll see Danny, and my parents and my wife and son standing at the far shore waiting for me. But I worry every day that Martin Kelly will be standing there, too.'

'And do you think helping find him will stop that from happening?'

Tony nodded. 'I suppose so. Maybe I'm looking to be forgiven or something.'

'Fair enough,' Karen said.

'Why did you agree to it?' Tony asked, scuffing at the deck with the toe of his shoe.

'I've kids now; I can only imagine how horrendous it would be to lose one of them and never know what happened to them. I'd never stop looking for them. His family are going through that and we have the power to spare them that pain.'

'Is that the only reason?'

'The only one,' Karen nodded. 'I never wanted to go back here again.'

Tony considered the response, and how she had moved on seemingly so easily. 'Then we all have our reasons.'

'I know yours and mine,' Karen said. 'And that young lad's being used by his uncle for politics, so I know his reasoning. Why's Hugh Duggan agreed to this if he doesn't actually agree *with* it?'

'I think he's looking for answers,' Tony said. 'I think he's not well.'

'He looks awful,' Karen said.

'He was taking medication in the toilet,' Tony explained. 'I think he's sick and looking to protect his legacy.'

'And what if the truth comes out and he doesn't like what he hears?'

'Which truth?' Tony asked. 'Whose version of it?'

'Any of them. All of them.'

Tony shrugged. 'You know him as well as I do,' he said. 'Is he the type who'd look to make amends now?'

'Hugh's a wounded dog,' Karen said, looking in through the window at where he and Barr sat. 'He's spent his life running around looking to bite someone for his pain.'

'We were no different.'

'Then,' Karen agreed. 'But we moved on. Hugh didn't. He's as angry now as the first time I met him, after my daddy was shot.'

CHAPTER NINETEEN

'My daddy was shot,' Karen said.

They lay together in her bed, both still wearing underwear for she'd insisted, as he started to unclasp her bra, that she wasn't ready to have sex. Instead they'd touched each other, become comfortable with each other's bodies, then lay curled together, legs entwined as they kissed. She had her head on his chest and was playing with his chest hair, twiddling several strands in his fingers, twisting them, teasing them gently, the pain at once sharp and sensual.

It was their third date following their bringing the car back from Paisley to Glasgow. He'd not seen Duggan since. He'd tried Liverpool Betty's a few times, but there was no sign of the man; nor Martin Kelly either. But he had seen Karen; they'd gone to the cinema on their second date. *The Living Daylights* was still playing on the multiplex in town and they'd gone to it. There'd been a handful of couples in the cinema and they'd had the whole back row to themselves. It was there that they'd kissed properly for the first time.

After that, they'd gone for dinner again, this time without having it arranged for them. The conversation had been easy; Karen had picked an Italian she'd wanted to try. They'd sat at a small table with a candle guttering in a wax-encrusted wine bottle and talked about home. Afterwards, she'd invited him in for a cup of coffee and they'd kissed again on the sofa, before she announced she had work the next day and needed to get to bed.

The third date, she'd suggested she would cook for him. She'd made lasagne with a salad. He'd brought a bottle of white wine in the off licence near her flat and they'd drunk it between them before finding themselves tumbling into her bed together.

As he'd undone the clasp of her bra, he'd felt her stiffen, felt her arms close against her side, preventing him from removing it completely. 'I'm not ready to have sex with you,' she'd said.

'That's OK,' he said. 'I understand.'

She'd looked up at him, her eyes wide and guileless. 'I'm not... I don't want to yet.'

'That's OK,' he repeated.

They'd kissed again, slower, more tenderly now, the passion spent a little by her interruption. Then she'd lain against him, running her hand down his chest, across his boxers, over the length of him. He'd held her against him. Her room smelt of potpourri to disguise the faint mouldy smell of the apartment block. Outside, the noises of the street drifted through the thin curtains she'd already pulled. He looked now at the picture on the bedside cabinet he had seen before. It was her, younger, with a man.

'Is that your dad?'

She nodded against his chest. 'He was shot,' she said, simply.

'What?' Tony raised his head a little to better see her, but she kept her head where it was. Pressed against his chest, her gaze directed away from his.

'My daddy was shot,' she said.

'By who?'

She shrugged. He could feel the growing dampness of her cheeks against his skin, could hear the catch in her voice, her tone thickening with tears.

'He was a solicitor. He represented a couple of people who were connected, so I think maybe he had a name for being one of them. Someone decided he was a legitimate target. We were watching TV. It was a Sunday evening; I remember because *That's Life* was on. Every time it was on, dad would pretend he was that dog, you know, the one that said "Sausages". "Rausages" he'd say, laughing to himself, like it was the first time he'd thought of it. He'd just done it, just said "Rausages", and there was a banging on the door. He went out to answer it; sometimes people called late at night needing his help for some of their family that had been lifted or something, so it wasn't anything odd. I followed him out to make a cup of tea. I was being nosey, to be honest, trying to see if I knew who'd been lifted this time. When he opened the door, there was a man standing wearing a motorbike helmet, with the visor down. Dad didn't have time to do anything, not even to turn. The man was holding a gun and it fired, three times, one after the other, like short, sharp cracks. Dad didn't scream, didn't cry; he just dropped to the ground. I just stood there, frozen, looking at this man who'd shot my daddy. He stepped into the hall and I thought he was going to shoot me too. He raised the gun again and tried to shoot Daddy again, but the gun must have jammed or something. He looked at me and said something, but I couldn't make out what it was, because the helmet muffled him, you know, and my ears were still ringing from the gunshots. But he said something, a word. Then he turned and ran outside to a bike with another man already on it waiting and they drove off.'

She shifted her head slightly, moving her hand to wipe away a tear, then sniffed.

'I went over to Daddy and sat with him. He was breathing funny, like he couldn't catch a breath, and there was blood bubbling from a hole, from the gunshot wound in his chest. A second shot had hit his shoulder and the third had gone through his cheek. He was trying to talk, but it was like the words weren't there, like his breath wouldn't come right to make them. I knelt down beside him and the ground was already soaked with his blood. I started shouting for help, but some of the neighbours were coming running and I could hear screams and crying from outside. I took his hand, and it was warm and he had this blister from where he'd been gardening that day and I was worried that I'd hurt his hand when I held it. I felt him squeeze my hand once, and then he gave this really deep breath and the bubbling at his chest stopped. And when I looked, the light had just slipped from his eyes.'

Tony lay still, afraid to speak, knowing that whatever he uttered would be completely inadequate. And, he sensed, the story was as much for her benefit for his, as if she'd not had a chance to tell it to anyone else and needed to talk.

'The man next door was in by then and kept saying over and over that an ambulance was coming, to hold in there. But Daddy had already gone by then. The man started saying an Act of Contrition and he held Daddy's other hand in his. I leaned over and kissed my daddy on the forehead and when I looked, I thought I'd left a lipstick mark, but it was blood. His blood.'

She raised her head and wiped her face and nose with the edge of the bed sheet. 'That's what happened to my daddy.'

'Jesus,' Tony said softly. 'I'm so sorry.'

She nestled against his chest again, her gaze still directed towards the foot of the bed. 'The police never got who did it. I tried to describe the man I saw, but it made no difference. They didn't really care; Daddy had represented so many people they'd been trying to put away. One of my uncles said afterwards that he thought the cops had probably helped his killers, but what can you do with that? Who do you go to when the people breaking the law are the law?'

She lay a moment, her fingers still playing with his chest hair, then finally lifted her head and looked up at him.

'Sorry,' she said.

'Jesus, don't be. I'm glad you told me,' he said, and realised he meant it. He tightened his hold on her, felt her press against him.

'That's how I met Hugh Duggan,' Karen said. 'He came to the funeral with a guy called Sean Mullan. Daddy had represented him at one stage. He called a few times afterwards and I told him I was moving and coming over here. Then, when he moved across here, he contacted me and asked me to help him with something. Some details about a patient of the practice. An address was all he needed. And then another week he needed me to find out what time someone collected their morning paper from the shop opposite the health centre.'

'Mullan came to Danny's funeral, too,' Tony said. 'Then I met Duggan for the first time that night. We were both lifted for a cop who was shot in retaliation for Danny's death.' He thought no more about the similarities in their stories, the manner in which Mullan and Duggan had recruited both of them, raw in their grief.

She peeled off her bra now and pressed herself against him, the softness of her breasts against his side. But the gesture was not sexual and he made no effort to make it so. She held onto him and, after a few minutes, her breathing became low and even.

'Are you sleeping?' he asked, himself drifting a little, his mind wandering back to Danny, to his father, to the sight of his brother in the coffin. For the first time since the funeral, he felt tears slide down his cheeks, felt a sudden pang of grief gripping him as he grasped, fleetingly, the permanence of his brother's absence, the immensity of the breach his death had caused. He tried to stifle the sob building in his chest.

'Are you OK?' Karen murmured.

'Yeah,' he managed. 'I'm sorry for what happened to you. To your dad.'

She looked up at him sleepily, her eyes red rimmed. 'I've never told anyone, but I always thought that what he said – the man who killed Daddy, I mean – I think what he said was "I'm sorry." And I never told anyone because, if I believed that, that that's what he thought the minute he took my daddy from me, then I'd not be able to be as angry any more. And that's all I've got to keep me going. My anger.'

CHAPTER TWENTY

'Are you still angry? About your dad?' Tony asked. The breeze buffeted them as they stood, Karen's jacket flapping against her legs, cracking with wind whipping. Beyond her, the Scottish coast was clearly visible now, the houses spotted along the crags.

'No,' she said.

'Not even a little?'

She shrugged. 'I'm just sad now, when I think of Daddy. I wish he'd met my husband, my children – his grandchildren. That's what killing him deprived me of – those moments that I wanted to share with him. So I ache at his absence. But I'm not angry anymore. The guy who... shot him... he was a kid himself. I could see in his eyes, he was young. Whatever drove him to our house, whatever hatred, or bitterness, or maybe his own family tragedy, it had nothing to do with my daddy. He was a victim of something too.'

'That's very understanding of you,' Tony shivered.

Karen smiled. 'It's practical. My anger wouldn't change anything. Nor my hatred. The only person it would damage is me.'

'I got angry for a bit after my son died,' Tony said. 'I got angry at God, at Ann, at the doctors for not being able to do more. But it didn't help. Instead, sometimes, I'd imagine him alive. I'd try to imagine what he'd look like, what team he'd support, what sport he'd play, what music he'd like.'

'It's easier for me,' Karen said. 'I know those things about Daddy. When I hear a certain song, like when Frank Sinatra comes on the radio, I think of him, humming along to it in the car. Maybe in some parallel universe he's still alive, still singing along to 'These Foolish Things'. Maybe you have a son.'

'I think I wasn't meant to have a child,' Tony said. 'I don't think I'd have been a very good father.'

'You'd have been a great father.'

Tony smiled mildly at the compliment, even as he dismissed it with a shake of his head. 'No.'

'You were great with kids when we were… back when. You'd a real soft spot for them; you talked about them all the time, sure.'

'Other people's. I don't think I'd have been a good role model for my own, somehow.'

'You only think that. Before my first was born, I remember panicking one night, lying shaking in bed, thinking about how I was going to be responsible for this person and I could barely look after myself. I was shaking so hard it woke Seamy.'

Seamus Maguire, Tony thought. Karen's husband became a fraction more real with his name.

'What did you tell him about this trip?' Tony asked, suddenly.

Karen smiled bemusedly at the question, the change in topic.

'I said I was going to a meeting about buying into a franchise for the business,' Karen said. She staggered slightly as the boat slowed, having entered the lough that would lead them, eventually to their harbour.

Tony instinctively reached out to steady her and, for a second, she took his hand in hers. Her skin was slightly slick with lotion.

'He doesn't know about what happened,' she explained. 'It just wasn't something you could bring up, you know. No one asks you over dinner if you've ever killed anyone.'

Tony laughed wryly.

'It was another world,' Karen said. 'And I was a different person, then.'

'Not so different,' Tony said. 'You've changed less than I expected.'

A faint flush rose at Karen's throat and Tony realised he had inadvertently revealed that he'd been thinking of her. She didn't reciprocate, but asked instead, 'Did your wife know? About Martin?'

Tony shook his head. 'No. Sean Mullan called at our door one time electioneering and she commented on him scaring her because he was wearing loafers.'

Karen laughed exaggeratedly.

'She meant that his ordinariness scared her; the fact he was a murderer who looked just like everyone else. It was hard to tell her after that, so I didn't.'

'Did you feel guilty about not telling her?' Karen asked, holding his gaze.

'Sometimes,' Tony admitted. 'You?'

She nodded. 'I guess. It makes me wonder what he's hidden from me, too. And he's not like that, don't get me wrong, I don't think he's hidden anything,' she added quickly, as if her comment had been an act of disloyalty. 'But a bit like your wife said; that someone can look ordinary and have done something terrible.'

CHAPTER TWENTY-ONE

'Something terrible is happening to me,' Alice Hamilton said.

Tony had just come out of the staff room, having been checking for post in the staff pigeonholes when he met Alice running down the corridor. She stopped at the girl's toilet but it was locked. She gripped her skirt in her fist in front of her groin and, for a moment, Tony assumed she needed to use the toilet. But when he looked again, he realised that tears were streaming down her face.

'What's wrong, Alice?' he asked.

'Go away, sir,' she said, almost doubling up where she stood.

'Alice!' he said, a little harsher than he intended. 'What's wrong?'

She looked at him mournfully and straightened. At first he couldn't tell what concerned her until she lowered her head and, following her gaze, he saw the blood badging the insides of her legs.

'Something terrible is happening to me,' she said.

'It's OK, Alice,' he said, blushing heavily. 'It's natural.'

'I think I must have cut myself, but I don't know how.'

'It's not...' Tony began, but wasn't sure how to continue. 'It's a thing that happens to girls when they reach a certain age,' he said. 'It's completely normal. Have you a ... have you anything with you?'

'Like what?' she asked. 'I wanted some tissue paper to try to stop it but the toilet's locked.' She doubled over again.

'I'm going to get someone,' he said. 'Go into the staff toilets and I'll get someone to come in and help you.'

He led Alice across to where the two staff toilets, male and female, sat side by side and, knocking first to see if any female staff were already there, he directed Alice inside. Then he went down the corridor, glancing into each room until he found a female member of staff. The first teacher he found was Mary, in the end science lab, from whose room he had taken several of the mercury thermometers.

'Miss, can I have a moment?'

She looked up at him, safety goggles on, a strip of magnesium in a set of tongs held in front of the Bunsen flame.

'Can it wait?'

He shook his head.

Mary tutted, just loudly enough for him to hear, then shutting off the Bunsen, took of her goggles.

'Copy down the method,' she said to her class. 'We'll get back to the experiment in a moment.'

'Sorry to interrupt,' Tony explained when she came out of the room. 'Wee Alice Hamilton is in a bit of a state. She's in the staff toilet; she's taken her time of the month and it must be her first, because she has no idea what's happening. If I watch your class, would you get her sorted, with a sanitary towel or whatever it is she needs? I figured better coming from a female teacher than a male one.'

'Give me a second,' Mary said, then headed back into her room and opening one of the lower drawers in her desk, pulled out a small packet, which she put in the pocket of her lab coat. 'Mr Canning will be taking you for a few minutes, so get on with your work,' she called to the students, then came out and passed Tony.

About ten minutes later she reappeared at the door. 'Poor wee mite,' she said, her mood changed considerably. 'She was bawling and wailing in there.'

'Is she OK?'

'She's embarrassed,' Mary said. 'A wee girl at that age not knowing about her period is madness.'

'I think it's just her dad at home,' Tony said and, for a second, he thought of Karen, of how she'd told him she'd had to ask a friend's mother about her period. 'She's OK, though?'

'She's not going to die,' Mary laughed.

'I didn't want to see her upset,' Tony explained, to ameliorate his building feeling of foolishness.

'You're very sweet,' Mary said. 'She's OK and away back to class. I've told her if she's stuck again, she's to see the nurse or me. But we'll need to say to her year head, get her a little help.'

Tony told Karen that evening about Alice, and how he'd thought of her when he saw what had happened the girl.

'Maybe I shouldn't have told you that,' Karen said. 'It's not my happiest memory.'

'I'm glad you did,' he said. 'I think I dealt with it better because of that.'

'Poor girl,' Karen said. 'And her father.'

They were sitting in Liverpool Betty's again. Karen told him that Duggan had contacted her to ask for her help on something, and told her to bring Tony too. When they arrived, Duggan was standing at one of the snugs, chatting with the group sitting there. They'd got in their own drinks and sat at a table away from the bar a distance, in case he wanted to talk to them about something away from listening ears.

Duggan wandered across to them after a few minutes, his head turning as he acknowledged various different patrons of the bar as he passed, some with a nod, some with a smile, some with a shouted obscenity delivered with a laugh.

'How's the love birds?' he asked, dropping down onto the stool at their table. He held a pint of stout in his hand, his other resting on the table, already tapping out a tattoo with restless fingers.

He glanced over his shoulder as the door opened, and raised his drink in greeting to Martin Kelly who had just come into the bar. Kelly waved at him with an upraised hand, then shuffled across, pulling the sleeves of his jumper down over his hands and balling it into his fists. His bag was strung diagonally across his chest and, just before sitting, he shifted the bag from his hip to his groin.

'All right,' he said by way of greeting.

'Martin, you know Karen. This is Tony. He's a good man. Home-grown.'

'What's the craic?' Kelly said.

'How are you?' Tony managed. Karen smiled and nodded, but offered no comment.

'Listen, folks, I need a bit of a hand with something,' Duggan said, his tapping finished, now that the real business of the evening had started. 'We're looking at a man; Martin here recognised him. He's an ex-cop from the North. He'd been stationed in Derry.'

Tony felt his stomach stir, excitement and fear butterflying in his belly.

'He's a prick,' Kelly offered. 'He lifted me a few times back home. Real arsehole.'

'For what?' Karen asked, speaking for the first time since Kelly had sat down.

'You know, this and that,' Kelly said, breaking into a crooked smile. 'He wasn't slow to confiscate anything he found, and then the other side would be selling it a few days later.'

Tony shrugged, unclear as to why this would be of interest to them.

'The fucker blinded a twelve-year-old in Derry a few years back. There was a riot, the usual, and some of the school kids were out watching it. The cops were firing all over the place. This wee lassie, Paula, comes running out of the house to get her brother in for his tea and this fucker turns and shoots her in the face with it. He was about ten feet away from her.'

'I vaguely remember that,' Tony said, though he couldn't be sure if he actually did, or if it was simply because Duggan had described it in some detail.

'The family got nothing for it, the wee lassie needing to be looked after all her days and the cops did fuck all. Northern Ireland Office told them there's a backlog of claims.'

'That's desperate,' Karen offered.

'Well, at the same time, this fucker got a package; went out with stress, after shooting a child. He vanished off the radar altogether.'

Duggan glanced at Tony as he spoke and the younger man nodded. The similarity with the man who'd killed Danny and then been put out to pasture was not lost on him.

'Until now?'

Kelly nodded vigorously. 'I spotted him in the supermarket. The bloody supermarket,' he repeated.

'Wow,' Tony said, for something to fill the silence Kelly had left, waiting for them to share his incredulity at the chance encounter.

'Right?' Kelly agreed, nodding.

'I've spoken with Sean and he'd be happy for us to do whatever we can with this bastard. That's where I want you two to help me.'

Karen stiffened in her seat, shifting herself, her back erect, her expression brittle.

'Karen,' he said. 'I want you to look for him on the health centre's files to see if you can get an address for him.'

She angled her head, slowly, as if considering the implications of the actions and whether she could justify them to herself. Evidently she could, for she nodded. 'What's the name?'

Duggan handed her a sheet of Rizla paper on which something was written. She glanced at it, nodded and handed it back to him. He took out a cigarette lighter and set the paper alight. It burst into flame, then guttered out just as quickly, the fragments of ash crumbling into the ashtray on the table.

'Once we have details, I'll need you to take a drive by the house a few times, check out his routines,' he said. 'Basic things. Is he working? Where? Times he leaves the house, all that kind of thing. Does he check under his car every time he goes out in it?'

'I'm working,' Tony said. 'I can't be at someone's house in the morning; I have to be in school.'

'One of us will cover the mornings,' Duggan said. 'You'll be given your own times to do. The pair of you can go together if you like.'

'Why us?'

'He might remember me if he sees me,' Duggan said. 'And there's a chance he might remember Martin from back home. You two he'll not know from Adam. A changing procession of faces will make it less likely he'll start noticing any one of us.'

'But he uses our health centre,' Karen said.

'I wouldn't recognise someone works at the back desk in my health centre,' Duggan said. 'I think we'll be all right.'

Tony glanced at Karen, laid his hand on her knee in an attempt to show her solidarity, but she shifted her knee away, quickly, from under his touch. He looked at her, but she would not return his gaze as a blush bloomed on her cheeks.

'I'll also need another few thermometers if you can get them,' Duggan said.

Tony frowned, the thought of what he'd gone through to get the first set still fresh in his mind.

Duggan clearly misunderstood his response though for he said, 'Mercury. For the tilt switch.'

With a shock, Tony thought again of the bomb attack in the city centre the night of the party where Duggan was cheered as he arrived, the night he had asked Tony and Karen to drive to Paisley. He realised, for the first time, the role he had already played in events that evening.

'They're going to start noticing them gone.'

'Another two or three will be fine. It'll be time enough for a few days, anyway. We need to do the recon on–'

'Marty, Marty. Smelly Kelly!'

The girl's voice rang out across the bar as she entered. Almost before looking up, Tony knew who it was. Shauna Laird came in, surrounded by her friends who made a beeline for the bar. Shauna headed straight for Kelly.

'All right, girl?' he said, by way of greeting.

Shauna extended her arms, stepping light footedly from side to side as she approached, like a temple dancer. Her expression changed when she recognised Tony.

'Sir!' she said, though she glanced from Martin to Tony and back, as if attempting to reconcile in her mind why the two were seated together.

'Hi, Shauna,' Tony said, trying to ignore the wink of Duggan across to him and Karen as the older man mouthed 'Sir,' mockingly.

Her demeanour changed, though she knelt down level with Kelly and muttered something to him. Almost without Tony noticing, he'd already his hand in his bag and was pulling out a small wrap. He slipped it to her as he leaned across, as if to give her a hug. In turn, she palmed him a note, which he pocketed.

She stood up, fixing herself, and glanced across at Tony, as if waiting for him to react.

'College still going OK?'

'The best,' she said, smiling. 'Gonna catch up with my friends. See you after, sir.'

'She doesn't call me sir,' Kelly said, watching her as she walked away. 'But she'd suck the chrome off a tow bar.'

Karen winced in disgust at the comment, while Duggan chuckled before he drained his pint. 'You're a dirty bastard, Kelly,' he said, standing. 'My round.'

'I taught Shauna last year,' Tony explained, sitting up a little in his seat. 'She's a good girl. Very bright.'

'Yeah, she's a fucking genius, right enough,' Kelly said.

'She shouldn't be messing with that shit you're peddling.'

'She's an adult, trust me. She can make her own choices.'

'She's too smart.'

'Only stupid people do coke? Seriously.'

'It's not how I'd choose to make a living.'

'It's how I choose to support the cause. Rather this than stealing thermometers out of school science labs.'

'I'm not hurting anyone,' Tony said, without thinking.

Kelly laughed. 'Really? Tell that to the guy lost his two legs in Hugh's last piece of work. He might beg to differ.'

'In my job,' Tony muttered through clenched teeth, trying to keep his voice down, aware that others might overhear what they were discussing.

'You may as well go over and tell off the barmaid for selling them booze. It's a drug, kills hundreds of people every year, you've no problem with that.'

'Alcohol's legal,' Tony said.

'Yeah, you know why? The government's the dealer wi' that one. All that tax. And you judge me? Go fuck yourself.'

'I'm not judging you. I'm judging what you do.'

'What I do is none of your fucking business,' Kelly said. 'Hugh needs us to work together and that's what we'll do, but you keep your nose out of what I do. I'll keep mine out of what you do.'

'Will we go?' Karen said. Tony only briefly became aware of the fact she had not spoken for some time.

'Sure,' he said, draining his drink. 'Tell Hugh I'll owe him a pint.'

'Yeah, whatever,' Kelly said, his face flushed with anger.

'Goodbye,' Karen said, lifting her coat and walking out. Tony moved to follow but Kelly stopped him with an outstretched hand.

'Wee Shauna's not the only one knows a trick or two,' he winked with a grin, then moved away so quickly, Tony had barely time to react.

They went back to Karen's flat for a while after they left the pub but, despite Tony's evident willingness, Karen did not bring him into the bedroom. They kissed on the sofa and, when he began reach under her top to peel it off, she placed her hand on his and directed him away from doing so. Finally, a little frustrated, Tony sat back on the sofa, ignoring the confusion he could see building in her eyes.

'What's the story with Kelly?' he asked, trying to raise the issue of what Kelly had said to him as he was leaving, but reluctant to ask straight out. After all, despite a few dates, their relationship had remained chaste. He found himself seething a little at the idea she had been more sexually active with Kelly than she was being with him. And he was simultaneously aware of just how unreasonable was such a feeling.

'He's a dealer,' Karen said. 'And a scumbag. There's not much else to it.'

'You got very quiet,' Tony said. 'I thought maybe the two of you had a history.'

'What kind of history?' Karen asked, her voice steely.

'Did you go out with him?'

'Would it matter?'

Tony shrugged. 'I just want to know.'

'I think it's time you went home,' Karen said. 'I've work in the morning.'

'So that's a yes?'

'That's a go home, before this gets out of control,' Karen said, firmly.

'Fine,' Tony said. 'There's nothing happening worth staying for anyway.'

Hurt flickered momentarily in Karen's eyes, and then her expression hardened. 'Just leave then.'

For a second, Tony regretted ever starting the row, though could find no way to stand down now and save face. Then his own anger grew and he stormed out of the flat.

He fed the anger for a day or two, before he sat one evening, wondering what she was doing, wanting to call with her, privately admitting that he had behaved abominably, having been played by Kelly.

He'd called to see his uncle and aunt, having promised them when he leased a flat for himself that he'd still visit once or twice a week so they could reassure his parents that he was alive and well and looking after himself.

'You not going out with Karen tonight?' his aunt asked him as he sat on the sofa next to her where she was watching the evening soaps, once they'd cleared up the dishes from the dinner she'd made for him.

'No,' Tony said. 'We'd a bit of a row.'

'You'll get it sorted,' she said. 'You're a good person. So is she by the sounds of it.'

'She is,' Tony admitted.

His aunt nodded, already turning her attention back to the drama unfolding on the TV screen. She added absentmindedly, 'You can always spot the good people.'

CHAPTER TWENTY-TWO

'I thought we were good people,' Tony said.

Karen pulled open the door of the ferry to step back inside. 'We are good people,' she said. 'We're doing the right thing. We *did* the right thing.'

'With Martin?'

'With everything,' she said. 'You're foundered with cold; come on inside.'

Duggan and Barr were sitting where Tony had left them, Barr staring at his mobile phone, Duggan finishing his whiskey and watching a TV show playing soundlessly on one of the ferry TV screens. 'Do you watch these?' he asked, gesturing with his glass, when he saw them return.

Tony glanced up at the screen. A tall blonde woman was standing with an older couple in what appeared to be a sunny Mediterranean street. The camera cut to them walking into a kitchen and looking around. Even without the sound, he could guess at the type of show.

'Not so much,' he said.

'What about you, missus?' he asked.

Karen, her demeanour restored, shook her head. 'I'm normally working at this time of the day; with family life and that, we don't get to watch TV until ten at night sometimes.'

'I love them,' Duggan explained. 'All these people thinking they can run away from their problems, and then airing them in public instead. It cracks me up, it does.'

'We're going to be arriving soon,' Karen said. 'Should we head on down?'

Duggan glanced out through the windows to their left. 'We've another ten minutes maybe,' he said. 'We'll get one more round in before we go.'

Karen glanced at Tony. Duggan was already well oiled; another drink or two might push him past good humour and into belligerence.

'Same again, Hugh?' Barr asked. His enthusiasm had waned a little as the crossing had advanced.

'Perfect, son,' Hugh said, winking at the others as they sat, watching the youth cross to the bar once more.

'Do you remember where we're going?' Karen asked. 'Once we get here; do you know the way?'

Duggan did not respond for a moment, then feigned surprise that she had been talking to him. 'I remember the entrance. We'll work it out from there.'

'You're being a bit unfair on the young fella, Hugh,' Tony said. 'He's that keen to impress you, he'd be buying you drinks all day.'

'Fuck him,' Duggan said. 'He's a fucking ghoul. They all are, these kids hankering after the good old days. What does he know about it?'

'He is just a kid,' Karen said. 'He's not much older than we were when we first met.'

'We had our reasons,' Duggan said. 'You and your brother; you and your father; me and half my family. What reasons does he have?

125

Too many days listening to shit being spouted by his da and his uncle.'

'Tony tells me you think we were wrong with Martin?'

'It's a thought.'

'Why?'

Duggan shrugged. 'Gut feeling,' he said.

'Is that it?'

'Tell me this,' Duggan asked. 'Were you ever lifted after what happened?'

'No,' Karen said.

'Never?'

She shook her head. 'Never. Why?'

'See?' Duggan said, looking at Tony. 'None of us were questioned about it, none of us were touched.'

'And?'

'You don't think that's odd? Not one of us was lifted?'

'That proves nothing, Hugh,' Karen said. 'Maybe they knew we had nothing useful to give them, anyway.'

'I had plenty,' Hugh said. 'Besides, Martin was my friend. We'd been though a lot. I trusted him more than I trusted any of youse.'

'He'd not be the first person to abuse someone's trust,' Karen said, glancing at Tony. 'You *know* why Kelly was blamed.'

'I know,' Duggan said. 'But I had my doubts, still. And he denied it, said there'd been a mistake. It was Mullan made the final call.'

'And?'

'At the time, I didn't think anything of it. He was the quartermaster, we did what we were told.'

'But?'

'But the more I think of it, and the more I hear, the more I think Mullan wasn't being completely straight.'

'You think he was covering for someone?'

'I think he was covering for himself,' Duggan said. 'I think he was the one that passed on word of what we were doing.'

'Why?'

'Do you think it's an accident that he is where he is now? He's being controlled.'

Karen frowned as she looked at Tony.

'Are you sure, Hugh?'

Duggan nodded. 'I'm certain of it. If you drank in the bars I drink in, you'd hear plenty of stories about him. I asked him to come with us for this and sure didn't he send the boy in his place.'

'Maybe he can't be seen to be getting his hands dirty.'

'His hands are dirty!' Duggan snapped. 'If he wants the boy to take his place, so be it. The boy will take his place,' he added, darkly.

'What does that mean?'

'We've all got our reasons for being here. Youse two might be looking to find Martin's grave, but me, I'm looking to find answers to what happened back then. And when I do, someone will pay. The last time I set foot in that forest, it was to punish a tout. If I got it wrong then, I won't be getting it wrong now.'

'What are you talking about?' Tony said.

'Someone pays,' Duggan said. 'That's how it is.'

'You're not thinking of hurting the boy? He's nothing to do with this.'

'Mullan sent him in his place. That was his choice. Whatever happens to the boy will be on him.'

'You can't–' Tony was cut short by Barr himself returning from the bar with Duggan's drink.

'Everything all right?' he asked, looking from one face to the next.

'Great,' Duggan said. 'Take a pew.'

The tannoy buzzed into life as the announcer instructed car passengers to begin returning to their vehicles.

'That's us,' Barr said, as Duggan drained his whiskey, slamming the glass down on the table when he was done.

'Let's go,' Duggan said, lifting the bag he'd brought on board. 'We've a bit of a trek ahead of us. Better get started.'

He looked at Tony and Karen who remained seated, unsure how to react. 'Come on. No time to waste. We've a job to do.'

CHAPTER TWENTY-THREE

'We've a job to do,' Karen said. 'Let's leave it at that.'

It was two weeks after the row. Tony had resisted calling her, reasoning that she might not want to hear from him. So the first time they met again was in Liverpool Betty's at the behest of Duggan. Karen had arrived almost half an hour late; Tony assumed she did so to ensure she wasn't left alone with him before Duggan's arrival. As a result, he'd had to sit with Martin Kelly for twenty minutes while they waited.

Kelly was less belligerent than on their previous meeting. He bought a round and, when Tony went to get one in his turn, asked only for a 7UP. He had the bag over his shoulder as always.

'How'd you end up in this?' Tony asked, the conversation having run dry.

'This the bar? This Scotland or this my living?'

Tony shrugged. 'All three, I guess.'

'The bar because Hugh called. My living was something I got into at home. I was shifting weed and stuff in the student blocks around Derry. Shrooms, shroom tea, whatever. The school I went to over there had this big field next to the playing fields, that magic mushrooms grew in. I'd forget my PE gear every week and when the rest of them were getting stuck into a game, our PE teacher just ignored anyone not playing; I'd sneak over into the other field and pick a batch when everyone else was playing football. I mind this one time, I made tea and then we froze it in lolly moulds with the sticks and all, and me and my mates went into school after lunch eating magic lollies right in front of everyone. It was the fucking trippiest Biology class I've ever spent.'

Tony smiled, nodded his head, quietly wondering if any of his own students had done such a thing in his class, to help them survive his lessons. After all, 'Suffer and learn,' was his motto, they'd said.

'Anyway, someone inside heard what I was at and I got a call to present myself at the local community centre. There was a couple of them sitting. One of them wanted to shoot me on the spot. Hugh was there and he stood up for me, argued I could help them out. So, I was told I could either keep selling for myself and get kneecapped, or I could start selling for them and be protected. They took eighty per cent, I kept twenty. So that's what I done.'

'How did that leave you in Scotland?'

'The cops started leaning on me. They must have realised who I was selling for, considering the areas where I'd managed to get a patch. They picked me up one night and offered me five hundred quid to be a tout. If I didn't, they said they'd lock me up. They'd nothing on me, though. I had a few blocks, end of the night stuff, and I claimed it was for my own use. But Mullan reckoned I was no use if the cops were going to be lifting me and leaning on me every whip-round, so he set me up over here. Same arrangement, different country. Then Hugh arrived over a few months after anyway, so it was just like home!'

He'd just finished his story when Karen had come in. She stood in the doorway, surveying the bar, looking for them. She saw Tony, her glance avoiding his, settling in the middle distance as she came across to them.

'All right, girl,' Kelly said, his tone, his very stance, changing at her arrival.

'How are you?' Tony asked, aware that he was starting to blush.

She offered them a brittle smile and sat down on a chair at the head of the table.

'What's your poison?' Kelly asked, before Tony had a chance.

'Tonic water and lime,' Karen said. 'Please.'

'Coming right up,' Kelly said.

'I was going to call you,' Tony said, when Kelly was out of earshot.

'We've a job to do,' Karen said. 'Let's keep it at that.'

'I wanted to say sorry,' he added. 'I was an arsehole that night. I'm sorry. I was in the wrong.'

'You were,' Karen said, allowing a brief glance in his direction.

'I'm sorry,' he repeated. 'Are we OK?'

'There is no "we",' Karen said. 'An apology in a bar two weeks late doesn't change how things went that evening.'

'I know,' Tony said. 'I just hoped—'

'You hoped I'd been pining for you for the past fortnight, waiting for you to call?'

'I hoped you'd give me a chance to make it up to you.'

They had no further chance to discuss it, for Duggan arrived and, a moment later, Kelly returned with the drink. Duggan waited until Kelly sat, then began.

'Karen has got us an address for our friend,' he said. 'We need to keep an eye on him for a while, work out his patterns, his hours, the whole thing. I've taken a drive by a few times, just to get used to the place and his hours. He leaves at 8.10 every morning but comes back at different times each day, with no real pattern. He does, though, go to church on a Sunday, same time each week, and he does his grocery shop on a Friday night, usually after 7pm.'

'What do you need us to do?' Kelly asked.

'Can you keep an eye on the supermarket on a Friday night, see if that's somewhere that might be viable, see where he parks and that. Likewise with the church. And help me out with the morning watch every other day?'

Kelly nodded.

'What about us?' Karen asked.

'You've played a blinder getting us the address in the first place. Any luck with the thermometers, Tony?'

Tony shook his head. 'Not yet.'

'We'll need them fairly shortly,' Duggan said. 'In the meantime, I'll need the pair of you to do surveillance on the target's home every other evening. Keep an eye on his patterns, his behaviour. Does he check under the car? Start changing his routine? Anything that might suggest he's getting suspicious, more cautious, you flag it up to me.'

'And then?' Tony asked, his voice trembling a little. He could not tell if the adrenaline rushing through his system was as a result of excitement or dread.

'We kill him,' Duggan said, simply.

CROSS COUNTRY

CHAPTER TWENTY-FOUR

'You're going to kill us,' Duggan said, gripping the moulded dash in front of him as Barr wove once more out into the opposite lane of traffic. 'There's no way past them, son; you may just calm yourself until you get to an overtaking lane somewhere.'

The disembarkation had been straightforward. As they'd driven out of the bowels of the ferry, they'd joined a queue of lorries, all heading in the same direction. Barr had tried drifting in and out behind the lorry ahead, hoping that the driver might see him so doing and let him pass, but with a dozen lorries ahead of that one, it was a futile exercise.

'Enjoy the scenery, eh?' Duggan added, twisting in his seat and winking lightly at Karen and Tony, as if sharing a private joke.

Tony managed a brief smile, though it died on his lips even before he'd turned his head to look out at the road, which rose up to their left and along which traffic was already moving. Karen sat in the back seat with him, though had left a gap between them, her bag placed on the middle seat. As she looked out of the window towards the road, he studied her profile, the curve of her jaw, the sweep of her neck and felt again the irony that their intimacy had created almost a greater rift between them than there appeared to be between her and Duggan.

'It's brighter here,' he said, simply. The mist of rain, which had shrouded their departure, had broken into watery sunshine now.

Karen turned briefly to him and smiled. 'For now.'

'So, what's Uncle Sean at these days?' Duggan asked.

'He's over here actually,' Barr said, easing his way around the roundabout and up towards the junction leading out of the docks.

'Is he now?'

'He was speaking at some EU peace conference in Glasgow.'

'Is he indeed?' Duggan said. 'He could meet us after all.'

'He's a busy man,' Barr offered, laughing.

'We're all busy men. And women. He could take a fucking moment. Do what he said he would. Make himself available. It would be in everyone's best interests if he did. Even yours.'

The atmosphere in the car darkened with the comments. Tony could see, with some pity, Barr glancing furtively in the rear-view mirror at Duggan to judge whether he'd spoken even slightly in jest.

'Did you hear about this bridge idea?' Tony said, by way of distraction.

He could see Barr's shoulders sag a little with relief as he gratefully seized on the change in the topic of conversation. 'What bridge?' he asked over his shoulder as he started building speed on the incline. 'The one on the news?'

'Yeah. This idea of a bridge between Ireland and Scotland, to cut out the ferries. It's only about twenty-five miles across.'

'It's madness,' Duggan said. 'Between that lunatic in America building walls, and the lunatics here looking to build bridges. Fifteen billion it would cost, something like that. Better investing that money in the community.'

'Or the health service,' Karen added. 'I think some communities have been riding the investment gravy train long enough. Spending it on health would spread it more fairly.'

'Spoken like someone who doesn't live in such a community anymore. Where are you now? Bangor?'

He exaggerated the final syllable, parodying the middle-class pronunciation of the place.

They lapsed into silence once more. It was as if Duggan's mood had festered since the ferry, as if he had realised that, if Kelly had not been the tout, then it was likely that one of them must have been.

'The problem is Beaufort's Dyke,' Tony said, scrambling to again lift the tension, which was almost palpable in the car.

'I knew a few dykes in my time, but not that one,' Duggan said, though neither he, nor any of the others, laughed at the comment.

'It's a marine trench that the Ministry of Defence have been dumping old munitions into for years, apparently. We passed over it on the crossing. They reckon there's over a million tonnes of weaponry down there.'

'If we ever need to rearm for the struggle, that's where we should start,' Barr laughed.

'So Sean's over talking about peace, and you're chatting about rearming,' Duggan said. 'Which is it?'

"I didn't mean nothing by it,' Barr said, with some bewilderment.

'Give the kid a break,' Karen said. 'He was obviously joking.'

'Sure, so am I. He knows that,' Duggan said. 'Don't you?'

'The joke's gone a bit far, Hugh,' she continued.

'No, I'm genuinely interested,' Duggan said. 'Tell us, then. Why are you so keen on things starting up again?'

'I'm not keen,' Barr said.

'But part of you is sorry you missed those days, aren't you?' Duggan asked slyly.

Barr shrugged. 'I'm prepared to do what needs to be done.'

'Would you kill for it?'

'I'd rather not, but if I had to.'

'Would you die for it?'

Tony glanced at Karen, shaking his head lightly. He felt complicit in leading this youth to the slaughter but powerless to do anything to stop it.

'Again. I'd rather not, but if I had to.'

'Do you think your uncle Sean would die for the cause?'

'I'm sure he would,' Barr said. 'You know him better. He'd not go out of his way looking for it but–'

'You're right there, son,' Duggan said. 'He'd go a long way to avoid it, the same boyo.'

'Uncle Sean did his bit, like everyone else.'

'Worked out better for him than for the rest of us, though,' Duggan said.

'He risked the most–' Barr began, but Duggan cut his short.

'Risked? He risked nothing. He sat and gave orders to the likes of me – and them,' he added after a short pause, nodding towards where Karen and Tony sat.

'He said you didn't like him,' Barr said.

'Don't like him? I fucking despise him.'

'He brought peace–'

'He was a tin-pot general. He still is.'

'He's my family,' Barr said. 'That's all the matters to me.'

Duggan stared at the side of the youth's face as Barr concentrated on the road. 'Right you are, son. Martin Kelly was my friend, but I still shot him like an old dog, because your uncle gave the order.'

'That's what soldiers do,' Barr said. 'When they start questioning orders, the war's already lost.'

'Do you hear that?' Duggan asked, leaning back towards Karen and Tony. 'That's what soldiers do.'

Barr's driving had become increasingly aggressive, in keeping with the mood in the car. He swerved past one lorry, pulled in, then attempted to overtake a second, making the manoeuvre with such speed and suddenness that Karen was shunted across against Tony momentarily. He felt her pressure against him, the brief lilt of her perfume and, for a second, he was lying with her again in his student digs.

'Sorry,' she said, straightening herself.

He gave a light rise of his hand. 'We'll be lucky if we survive the drive there,' he said.

'Right enough. Take it easy, son,' Duggan said to Barr, one hand gripping the plastic handle above the passenger door. 'Kelly's not going anywhere. He'll still be there if we're a bit late.'

Barr slowed the car a little, seemingly embarrassed at having been riled by Duggan.

'Have you anything to drink?' Tony asked. The bacon from his fry had left him parched, his stomach heaving a little too at being a backseat passenger with the erratic nature of Barr's driving. 'Could we maybe stop somewhere and get a drink of something?'

'That's a good idea,' Karen said. 'Maybe stretch our legs.'

'OK,' Barr nodded. 'I did bring some stuff, but no drinks. I've crisps and energy bars in the back there somewhere,' he said. 'Provisions.'

CHAPTER TWENTY-FIVE

'I brought provisions,' Tony said, pulling out a bottle of Coke and two Mars bars from a holdall. 'I've never been on a stake-out before.'

He and Karen were sitting in her car in a layby around the corner from where the policeman lived. Duggan had suggested to them that they take a quick drive to where the cop lived, both to orientate themselves and to pick out the best spots from which they could keep an eye on his house. Tony had asked twice what the man was called, but to no avail. 'Best you don't know,' Duggan had said.

'Karen knows.'

'If you know nothing, no matter what they do to you or ask you, you'll not be able to give them anything. It's for your protection. And ours.'

Tony nodded, a little frustrated at the sense of exclusion he felt. On the other hand, the less he knew, the easier it was to reconcile himself with what he was doing. And what was he doing, he asked himself? This guy had shot a child and got away with it. Just like the driver who'd killed Danny.

'I don't like caramel,' Karen said, refusing the Mars. 'I'm not hungry anyway.'

Tony nodded, then put them both back in the bag. 'How have you been since?' he asked.

'All right,' Karen shrugged. 'You?'

'Good,' Tony said, keen to keep talking to fill the awkwardness of the silence between them. 'School's busy. I'd dealings with that wee girl, Alice, again today.'

Karen nodded absentmindedly, taking out the small pocket map and opening it up. 'He's on Hollows Avenue. The house should be up there,' she added, nodding lightly towards an estate to their left.

She put away the map and started the ignition, then pulled out onto the main road.

'What happened? With the wee girl? Alice?' she asked, glancing at him.

Tony had been covering for one of his colleagues in the English department who'd phoned in sick with a migraine. The class he was covering, it transpired, was Alice's.

The child had been sitting on her own at the rear of the room, the rest of the class paired up, two sharing each desk. They'd been left work to complete, an acrostic on their favourite person. He'd wandered around the room, glancing over some of the kids' shoulders. Most were writing poems about their parents or their favourite footballer.

Alice had caught his eye as he'd been moving through the gaps between the desks, smiling timidly at him. He'd made his way down to where she sat, half expecting that she'd been composing the poem about her mother. For an absurd moment, he'd wondering if she might have written it about him, then dismissed the idea; he'd only had one or two dealings with her, after all. It didn't stop him feeling just a little disappointed when he saw it was written for her father, even as he scolded himself for the unworthiness of his feeling.

'How are you getting on?' he asked.

She sat back, allowing him an unfettered view of the page.

'*Daddy is my favourite man.*

Anything you want, he can

Dedicate himself to it and try

Despite the fact he wants to cry

Y–'

'Are you stuck on the last line?' Tony asked.

She nodded.

'What do you want to say?'

'That even when he wants to cry, he has to forget about himself and think about me.'

'Why does he want to cry?'

'Because of Mum,' she said, simply. 'I hear him sometimes, at night, but he doesn't want me to know, so I pretend I'm sleeping.'

'I'm sorry to hear that,' Tony said. 'That must be tough.'

She nodded. 'I want to start with Y but there's only You that could be used and he's not Your daddy, he's my daddy, so that doesn't make sense.'

'What about, 'You can always count on him'?' Tony offered.

Alice tried not to react, but could not hide the lack of enthusiasm she felt for his suggestion.

'Let me think about it,' Tony said, feeling just a little embarrassed at his lack of skill.

'It is a fairly shit line,' Karen said now, as Tony recounted the story. 'The wee girl's better at it than you are.'

'I felt sorry for the man,' Tony said, having taken mock offence at her comment. 'He sounds like he's struggling. I feel even more sorry for her.'

'Why? Her dad's obviously looking after her.'

'He's doing his best, maybe, but she's just not fitting in. Even in class, no one would sit with her. Kids can be really nasty to one another.'

'So can adults,' Karen said. They passed a row of houses, before turning again, up the left. As they drove up along the crescent, Karen counted off the numbers of each house silently to herself.

'That one,' she said, with a barely perceptible nod.

It was one of four terraced houses in the block, narrow, with beige pebble-dashing. The garden, small and square, was a little overgrown, as if the last cut had been missed. A small wooden gate, sun-bleached and blistering, gave way to a short pathway leading to the front door. A red Ford Cortina was parked on the street outside, one side elevated because he had parked it up half on the pavement, the other side on the road.

'Small house for a cop,' Tony said.

'Maybe he's renting,' Karen said. 'If he got out on disability, he'd have got a decent payment for it.'

Tony looked out of the passenger window and could see shops down below the estate, separated from it by the main thoroughfare. A number of cars were already parked at the front of the shops.

'We could park down there and watch up,' he said.

They stopped in front of the shop units. In addition to a small supermarket, there was a hairdresser's, a pharmacy and both Chinese and Indian takeaways. Tony offered to go and buy a bag of chips to eat in the car, giving them a pretext for staying in the parking area, he reasoned.

'Maybe later,' Karen said. 'I'm OK for now.'

'I am sorry about that thing with Kelly,' Tony said after a few moments silence. 'I was being a tube.'

'You were,' Karen agreed.

'I was totally out of order.'

'You were,' she repeated.

'Am I forgiven?'

'I've not decided yet,' she said, with a faint smile.

'Are you sure you don't want something to eat?' Tony said, his voice just the right side of plaintive.

'I'll take half your Mars.'

'I thought you didn't like caramel!'

'I've forgiven it. Besides, you don't need it all. You'll get fat.'

'Don't hold back now,' Tony laughed, glad that she was teasing him.

'You've a lot to make up for,' Karen said, her smile fully alive now.

'I could write you a poem.'

'Not based on the evidence from earlier,' she laughed.

They sat in companionable silence a moment. Suddenly, the front door of the house they were watching opened and a thin, slightly stooped man stepped down into the driveway. His movements were small and precise like a sparrow's as he picked his way to the car, opening it and getting in without any hesitation.

'He didn't check under it,' Tony noted.

They watched as his red Cortina pulled out of the driveway and headed up the street away from them.

'Job done,' Karen said, starting the car ignition and, after waiting until the cop's car had a good head start, drove off.

'Alice came back to me,' Tony said, as they headed back into Glasgow. 'At the end of the day.'

The line had clearly been annoying her. Through the rest of the cover class she sat, head lowered, her teeth worrying the skin at the side of her thumbnail as she scored out draft after draft of the poem. Finally, she sat up, staring at the far wall, then lowered her head and scribbled once more, closing the book just before the bell rang and Tony dismissed the class, standing at the doorway to collect in their work as they left the room.

'See you, sir,' Alice said as she passed him, the last to leave the room.

'Did you get it finished?'

She nodded. 'I'm going to write one for Mummy, too,' she said.

Tony nodded his encouragement as she laid her book on top of the pile he held.

Before he left the room, he flicked through her exercise book to see her finished draft. Her handwriting was small, neat, her tailed letters contained, showing no signs of ostentation or showiness.

'Daddy can be happy
And sometimes sad he'll be.
Damaged by life and the
Death of his wife
Yet I know he loves me.'

'Now, that is sad,' Karen said, after he'd recited it to her. 'You're a good man, you know that? Despite being a tube.'

They'd reached Glasgow now and Tony wondered whether Karen would drop him off somewhere or suggest going back to hers. In the end, she did neither, instead asking him if he wanted to get something to eat. They went to O'Reilly's, a traditional bar that incongruously only served pizza, and shared a pizza and a few drinks, before picking up a bottle of wine and a few cans from behind the bar and heading back to Karen's.

Around eleven, Tony suggested he would head on home. He stood in the doorway, his coat over his arm.

'Thanks for a good day,' Karen said. 'I'm glad things worked out.'

'Me too,' Tony said. 'I feel like a proper grown-up now, dealing with an argument without throwing the head and walking away.'

Karen laughed lightly and standing on tiptoe, kissed him.

'You can stay, if you like,' she murmured, as he closed the door again and moved back into the hallway and into her room. They pulled the clothes off each other, not even bothering to turn on the light.

He lay on his back on her bed, the street lights from the road beyond blinking through the thin fabric of her curtains as she straddled him, felt the warmth of her, heard the catch in her breath, her hands gripping his shoulders, a faint blush rising along her throat and for the first time since he'd arrived in the country, he felt like he was home.

CHAPTER TWENTY-SIX

'So where is home for you, Richard?' Karen asked Barr. 'Derry or Galway?'

'Derry, completely,' Barr said.

'Not Galway, with your mum?'

Barr shook his head. 'No. Galway's nice and all, but you can't beat Derry.'

'It feels like a city that's in the act of rediscovering itself, these past few years,' Tony said. 'Like it's taken a lot of the stuff that happened to it and tried to find value in it.'

'In what way?' Karen asked.

'I don't know. Things like using the river to bring the city together rather than splitting it up. I see things now that, when I was young, I hated, but they seem to have changed.

'Do you think if you'd lived through all the events it survived, you would feel the same way you do now, about the cause?' Tony asked.

'I'll never know. But I think so. We get shaped in the crucibles of fire, Uncle Sean says.'

Duggan glanced across at the youth with barely disguised disdain, while Karen smiled lightly at the absurdity of the image.

'Do you like working for him?' Tony asked.

'It's great. You feel like you're making a difference, you know. Doing things that matter.'

'He has a knack for that, does Sean,' Duggan said, clearly still seething.

'What?' Barr asked tersely.

'Making kids feel important.'

'I'm not a kid.'

'You are to me, son. And I was younger than you the first time your uncle sent me out to do a job. He was one of ours who joined the cops. Your uncle wanted me to pop him. That's how he put it, like it was nothing. Not shoot, not kill – pop, like a balloon at a party.'

'Did you?' Karen asked.

Duggan nodded. 'He was coming out of the Rialto with his girl. We'd got word he was there, at *The Shootist* of all things. Him and her comes out, with the rest of the crowd and starts walking down the Strand towards their car. I was hiding up on the walls opposite the picture house. When he started walking, I comes out and across the street, behind him. I'd a parka on, the hood zipped up around my face so I couldn't see properly, and my own breathing loud as anything inside the hood. I'd my piece in my coat pocket and a pair of gloves on. Just as I went to pull it out, he turned and looked at me. And he knew. I could see his eyes, he knew what was coming, as if he'd been waiting for it all along. He wasn't surprised or hurt. It was like he was disappointed, like he'd thought maybe he'd have been given a pass on it.'

He paused, as if he was back there, in that moment, facing the man once more. When he spoke again, his voice was wet and timbrous.

'He turned and shoved his girlfriend to the ground. I remember that; other fuckers have pulled people in front of them, used them like shields, but not him. He pushed her to the ground just as I shot. The gun bucked a bit when I fired, so the first shot caught him in the stomach and the second on the neck.'

The silence hung in the car. Tony glanced at Karen whose eyes were bright with tears and he suspected that she was spooling the shooting of her father inside her head. He reached across and took her hand in his, clasping it. He felt her open her fingers a little and splaying them, interconnect them with his.

'He was my first. Cooney, his name was. I always thought the fucker was noble, throwing the girl to the ground. He drowned in his own blood by the time the ambulance arrived.'

He turned and looked over at Barr. 'That's the work your uncle sent me out to do for him while he sat in the bar, holding court. I was sixteen at the time.'

'Do you regret it?' Karen asked.

'What? What I did?'

She nodded.

'Never. Except with Martin,' he said. 'But we'll take care of that today. Isn't that right, Richard?'

'Any sign of a shop?' Tony asked, keen to change the subject.

'Did you ever see it?' Duggan asked, as if Tony had not even spoken.

Barr, to whom the question had been addressed, glanced quizzically at him. 'See it?'

'*The Shootist*? It's a cracker of a film. John Wayne's this gunslinger or something, aw, what's this his name is? Not Cogburn, that was the other one. That'll annoy me all day now, his name. Anyway, he's got cancer and is dying and does one last job. It was Wayne's last film. He died of cancer himself a few years later. I was sorry to hear that; his films were always good. "Truly this was the son of God",' he drawled.

Karen looked at Tony in disbelief either at the mental gymnastics that Duggan had just performed in the conversation, or the fact that the only sympathy which he'd expressed had been for an actor he'd not known rather than a man he'd gunned down himself in front of his girlfriend.

'Do you mind that one? Him a Roman centurion talking with a Texas drawl. Like Connery commanding a Russian submarine with a Scottish accent. Those guys weren't actors; they were stars. Didn't matter they were always playing themselves.'

'What happened to Cooney's girlfriend?' Karen asked, leaning forward and, in so doing, releasing Tony's hand. He felt a pang of regret, could still feel the pressure of her skin on his. He'd not held Ann's hand in such a manner for years before her death and felt a strange disloyalty and simultaneous thrill at having done so now with Karen.

'Fuck knows,' Duggan said. 'The last I saw of her, she was lying on the pavement outside the Rialto.' He coughed noisily, then spat up something into a tissue he pulled from his pocket. He balled it up and pocketed it again. 'There's services in two miles,' he said, nodding out at the sign ahead for Monkton.

'We'll stop for a few minutes,' Barr said.

'Get us a Coke and a Double Decker, would you, son?' Duggan said, twisting in his seat to face his fellow travellers. 'What about youse?'

Tony reached into his pocket, pulling out a ten-pound note. 'A bottle of water for me. Do you want one?' he asked Karen, who nodded, ran her little finger along the lower eyelid, fixing a faint run of her mascara.

'Put your money away,' Duggan said. 'The party'll cover it, won't they, Richard?'

Barr avoided the question and took the note from Tony with muttered thanks.

'It's the new dispensation for the old guard. Haven't you heard?'

CHAPTER TWENTY-SEVEN

'You hadn't heard,' Liverpool Betty said. 'God, I'm so sorry. I thought you'd have known.'

They'd arrived in the bar after 8pm, having arranged to meet Duggan there. They'd taken turns doing surveillance on the cop's house, for a week, sometimes together, sometimes alone. They'd alternated cars, too, so that none of them would be seen in the same car twice, nor was the same car used on two consecutive stake-outs.

Duggan wasn't there when they arrived so Karen had taken a seat in one of the booths to keep it for them as a private place to talk, while Tony had gone up to get drinks.

'You're the teacher,' Betty had said as she pulled a pint of stout and set it aside to settle.

'That's right.'

'That was sad news, wasn't it?' she said, taking his proffered note and turning to the till. 'About Shauna.'

It took Tony a moment to work out whom she meant. 'Shauna? Shauna Laird?'

Betty nodded.

He shook his head lightly. 'What news? Did something happen to her?'

'You hadn't heard,' Betty said. 'God, I'm so sorry. I thought you'd have known.'

'Known what?'

'She died last night.'

'Shauna Laird?' Tony repeated incredulously. 'The wee girl doing drama.'

Betty nodded.

'She died?'

Betty handed him his change. 'I'm sorry.'

Jesus!' Tony slumped on to the stool next to which he had been standing. 'What happened to her?'

Betty leaned a little over the bar, exaggerating her pronunciation even as she lowered her voice. 'She took a couple of E tabs apparently. Her mates were telling me. They're down the back, having a wake for her.'

Tony left the drinks back with Karen and explained that he'd be a moment. He moved down towards the grungier area at the back of the bar where he recognised a group of Shauna's friends. One of them, a girl a little shorter and broader than Shauna, stood at his approach.

'All right?' Tony said. 'You were one of Shauna's friends, isn't that right?'

The girl nodded. 'I'm Emma. Did you hear?'

'Betty told me,' Tony said. 'What happened?'

'We were out for the night. We came here first, then onto The Tunnel.'

Tony nodded. He knew of the place, though had never been, dance music not being to his taste.

'She had a couple of tabs. She took one before we went in, but after about forty minutes she thought it wasn't working, so she took a second one. It wasn't doing it either and she thought she'd been sold duds, so she took half of a third.'

Tony groaned, already knowing where the story was heading.

'They all seemed to kick in at the one time. One minute she was standing with her drink, the next she was bouncing around the place. She was totally hyper, like she couldn't stop, she was all jittering, she was downing water like it was going out of fashion. She wasn't even making sense, half of what she was saying. She said she felt sick and went to the toilet. I went in with her and she went into the cubicle to see if she could make herself throw up, get some of it out of her system. The next thing, she'd just taken this, like, fit on the floor. She was lying just shuddering, her arms and legs all over the place. I went out and got help, one of the bouncers like, but by the time we came back in, she was already still.'

Tony shook his head as he gently touched the arm of the girl, standing in front of him, tears streaming freely down her face at the rawness of the memory.

'The paramedics arrived, but she was already dead, lying on the toilet floor.'

The group with which she had been sitting sat in silence, listening once again to Emma recounting the facts of their friend's death. When she was finished, one of the fellas raised his glass. 'To Shauna,' he said.

The others joined in a chorus, then toasted one another and downed their drinks in their own bacchanalian memorial for the girl.

'When's her funeral?' Tony asked.

Emma shrugged. 'They'll have to do a post mortem first,' she said. 'It could be a few weeks yet.'

Tony was surprised. At home, funerals invariably happened within three days of the death, a wake marking the time the family spent keeping vigil with the remains during that period. This was different.

'Let me know when you hear, will you?'

Emma nodded tearfully and turned to rejoin her group.

'One other thing,' Tony asked, moving closer to her again and lowering his voice a little. 'Where did she get the tabs?'

Emma shook her head, not able to squarely meet Tony's gaze for the first time since they had started speaking. 'I don't know.'

'Look at me,' Tony said, sharper now. 'Did she buy them here?'

Emma nodded.

'From Martin Kelly?'

'I think that's his name,' she whispered. 'He calls himself the man who walked or something.'

'Shaved head, bag strapped across his chest?'

She nodded. Then suddenly, as if in a panic, added, 'But you can't say I told you. Please.'

'Don't worry,' Tony said. 'It'll be fine.'

By the time he made it back to his seat, Duggan had arrived and he and Karen were discussing what they'd gleaned from the surveillance.

'You all right, big man?' Duggan asked, when Tony approached.

'Fine,' he said, distractedly, as he scanned the bar, looking for Kelly.

'You sure?' Karen asked, shifting over in the seat to allow him to join her in the booth. She passed his pint across to him. He lifted it and drank in gulps, draining the pint three-quarters of the way down the glass.

'What are we talking about?' he asked, though he almost instantly tuned out of the conversation, his hands balled into fists, resting on his knees which pounded up and down to the rhythm of his anger. Her could feel his arms coursing with adrenaline tremors.

Just then, the bar door opened and Kelly walked in, his bag strapped across his chest as ever, already surveying the bar's corners, looking perhaps for them, perhaps for his evening's customers.

Tony was out of his seat and across to Kelly almost before the door had closed behind him. He greeted his approach with a smile initially, misunderstanding Tony's eagerness to see him, so that he did not expect the punch when it came.

The force of the swing, combined with Tony's own momentum, meant that the blow took Kelly full in the face and knocked him backwards off his feet. He careened into a table and low bar stools, which clattered in all directions as he fell among them.

Tony could hear the reactions of those around and, as he moved for a second blow over the prostrate Kelly, he felt hands gripping at him. He turned, raising his fists against those who were trying to stop him, when he saw that it was Duggan holding him back.

'Don't even think about it, pal,' Duggan growled and, as quickly as it had built, Tony felt his anger dissipate.

'Get him out of here,' Duggan snapped at Karen. 'We'll speak later.'

Tony allowed Karen to guide him out of the bar, looking back only once to where Kelly sat still on the floor, his hand pressed against his nose, blood streaming through his fingers.

'Fucker!' Kelly spat.

Tony turned, pulling himself free from Karen's grip, lifting his fist once more, but Duggan stepped between him and Kelly, his frame blocking an opportunity for Tony to strike once more.

'You've had your go,' Duggan said. 'Unless you want me to start on you, you'll leave him alone now.'

CHAPTER TWENTY-EIGHT

'You need to leave him alone,' Karen said, once Barr had got out of the car. They'd parked outside a family restaurant next to the service station into which Barr had headed. 'I'm not going to let you hurt him.'

'Who? *Dick*?' Duggan said.

'Yeah, leave him alone, Hugh,' Tony added. 'You've been sending him errands all day. He's not a skivvy.'

'Don't tell me what to do,' Duggan snapped. 'After all I done for them, for "the party", the least they can do is a can of Coke and a fucking bar.'

'He's not "the party". He's just a kid.'

'He's a fucking prick,' Duggan hissed. 'Talking to me about being inside. Calling me Hugh like we're old friends.'

'I told him to do that. It was better than Mr Duggan,' Tony said. He roused himself from his memories of Shauna Laird. 'Karen's right. We're all in this together.'

'*We're all in this together*. I love that! You were barely in it thirty years ago; you spent your time changing your mind. Are you sure you'll see it through today?'

'Worry about yourself, Hugh,' Tony said, trying not to get drawn down the path Hugh clearly wanted to take. He was spoiling for a fight, the drink he'd taken on the boat had made him as belligerent as Tony had feared.

'Why are you even here?' Hugh said, twisting to look at him.

'To find Martin Kelly.'

'No, I mean what's the real reason.'

'That is the real reason,' Tony said, though he could not hold Duggan's gaze, his eyes dropping to look at his hands. 'I want his family to get his body back.'

'Naw,' Duggan said. 'We all have our reasons for being here and none of them is for the Kelly family. If you'd cared that much you've had thirty years to call them and tell them where he is.'

'Then why are we all here, Hugh?' Karen asked. 'What's the real reason?'

'For Barr, it's because he wants to impress his uncle. For his uncle, it's because he wants a promotion. With you, I'd say it's because you're just looking to forget and this is like a cut that never quite healed. You think if you give Martin back to his family, you can close the door on the whole thing and just go on with your life like it never happened.'

Karen said nothing and Tony suspected that Duggan hadn't been far from the truth with her.

'But him,' Duggan said, pointing at Tony. 'I can't work out what he's looking for.'

'And what about you?' Karen managed. 'What's your reason?'

'I told you,' Duggan said. 'I'm looking for answers. And if I don't like the answers, then I'll be looking for revenge for Martin,' Duggan said.

'You'll not get any answers from me,' Karen said, opening the door.

'I've nothing to say. I'm having nothing to do with hurting that boy. You can find the fucking grave yourselves.'

'What's wrong with her?' Duggan said, watching her walk away from the car.

'She's right,' Tony said, undoing his own seatbelt and opening the passenger door. 'Martin Kelly was just a kid when we took him into those woods. I'm not doing the same again with Barr. You're on your own, Hugh.'

He closed the door and moved around to where Karen sat at a picnic area outside the restaurant. 'You OK?'

She nodded. 'I should never have come. I should never have agreed to this.'

'We thought you'd suggested it,' Tony said, earning a glimpse of incredulity.

'Why would I want to be here? With him?' she added, nodding at Duggan. 'I'm not getting back in that car.'

'Nor me,' Tony said. 'We can get a taxi back to the ferry if you like?'

Karen shook her head. 'I'm staying with family this evening and going back tomorrow.'

'I'll head back myself then,' Tony said, trying to hide his disappointment at not have the opportunity to share more of the journey with her, alone.

The door of the car opened and Duggan struggled out. He walked, stiff jointed, over to where they stood.

'We're not discussing it further,' Karen said as he approached.

'I know,' he nodded. 'You're right. I'll speak to the young fella.'

'What about?'

'Getting Mullan to meet us at the woods. He's in Scotland for this conference. If he wants Kelly's grave, he'll have to come and find it with us.'

'And if he doesn't?'

'If you two are not on board, we go no further.'

CHAPTER TWENTY-NINE

'Unless you're on board, we go no further,' Duggan said.

It was the following evening, in Betty's. They'd taken the same booth as the night before except now Karen and Tony sat on one side, Kelly and Duggan on the other.

Tony, to whom the statement had been addressed, raised his shoulder lightly in a half shrug.

'Are you in or not? All this other shit you have to ignore.'

'Ignore? A kid died taking drugs *he* sold.'

'I liked Shauna,' Kelly protested. His nose was swollen, both his eyes ringed in purple, his left eye bloodshot. Tony had resisted smiling when first he saw him, though felt silent satisfaction at the state in which he had left him. He sat erect in his seat, his own bruised fist in front of him on the table, a trophy.

'You liked her? Is that why you let the whole bar see she'd blown you in the toilets to get a ten spot?'

Kelly shrugged. 'I didn't force her to do it. Same way I didn't force her to buy anything, or take anything. She didn't need leading to anything.'

'You should have warned her.'

'Aye, right. Warned her not to take three E tabs? Who the fuck would need to warn someone not to OD?'

'Her death is on you.'

'Seriously?' Kelly asked. 'Her death is *on* me? What the fuck do you think we're doing here? The guy with no legs? He's on you and your thermometers. And this fucker–'

Duggan raised his hand and Kelly responded, lowering his own voice, leaning across the table. 'This fucker goes the same way, are you going to wash your hands of that? She has more balls than you do,' he added, nodding at Karen.

'Martin's right,' Duggan said. 'You were angry, youse had a barney and now it's done. That's it. Martin's ready to see this through, so the question is, are you?'

Tony straightened a little, glanced at Karen who stared at the table top, her fingers worried the edges of a beer mat, peeling back the layers of card beneath.

'I didn't think we'd be dealing with drugs.'

'You're not,' Duggan said. 'Everyone does what they're comfortable with. But we need money to buy supplies, to buy information. Where do you think that's going to come from?'

'Drugs is too much for me. That wee girl was bright. She was a good kid.'

Tony could feel his eyes flushing, and reddened at that realisation.

'She was an adult, who did adult things. Like we all are. I'm not debating morality anymore with you, son. None of us can judge anyone else at this table. But we have to trust each other. I trust Martin with my life. You all need to feel the same. Are you in or out? If you're out, the whole thing is off.'

Tony sat silent, wishing that Karen might get involved, might express a view. If she backed out, he'd gladly have followed her. But if she was set on going ahead, he didn't want to be the one she'd blame for it stalling.

Truth be told, he thought, he'd never really considered the reality of what they were doing. Sitting in the car, watching the house, talking with Karen, spending time in her company, going back to the flat afterwards, the sex, it all seemed like some game, a diversion from his life. He'd never considered really what would happen the man they watched, his sparrow movements, his precise nature. The truth was, he didn't particularly hate the man; in fact, he felt nothing but indifference.

Unbidden, he saw Danny in his mind's eye – crushed, broken, his limbs at angles from his body. He thought of Karen, cradling her dead father, a blood-stained kiss on his forehead. He couldn't make this choice for her, deprive her of this, if this was what she wanted. Would she resent him if he backed out now?

'I'm in,' he said.

Karen sat back, letting the pieces of broken card fall from her fingers.

'Good man,' Duggan said. 'We've things in place. Sunday will finish it. I'll take care of everything else. For now, just keep an eye that there's no sudden change in movements, change in habits. Anything that would suggest someone is talking.'

'What are you going to do?' Tony asked, and knew instantly it was the wrong thing to say.

Duggan looked at him askance. 'Better you don't know. You'll find out soon enough.'

'Be innocent of the knowledge till thou applaud the deed,' he muttered.

Duggan looked at Kelly, who shrugged. 'Whatever the fuck that means.'

'It's Shakespeare,' Tony said, a little petulantly.

'Fancy,' Duggan said. 'You're raising the IQ in this booth by about two hundred per cent son.'

Tony knew Duggan well enough now to recognise the insincerity of the comment. For the first time, he felt totally out of place.

'And youse need to split up, now,' Duggan said. 'No more paired surveillance. He'll have had a chance to see you both together enough. Split up.'

Karen nodded, but did not speak, nor did she look at Tony. Across the table, Kelly extended his hand. 'We good?'

Tony regarded him with disdain, and would have refused to shake had it not been for Duggan glaring at him.

'Man up a bit, son, Shake his hand. What's done is done.'

Tony wondered whether the quote was deliberate, decided it wasn't. He took Kelly's hand, briefly. His grip was light, his skin soft, yet Tony could not but feel an urge to wash his hands after touching him.

Duggan nodded with satisfaction. 'Good man.'

CHAPTER THIRTY

'Good man yourself,' Duggan said, taking a bottle of Coke from Barr who had returned from the shop. They had all taken up seats at the picnic table next to where the car was parked. The sky was grey, leaden, though the sun had broken through in places, gilding the edges of the lower hanging clouds. The rush of traffic barrelling along the road nearby was overlaid with the shouting of children playing in a small outdoor play area the restaurant had provided.

'Everything OK? Barr asked.

'We think your uncle should be there,' Duggan said. 'We've chatted between ourselves and we're not going any further unless he meets us at the woods.'

Tony saw Karen bristle a little at the use of 'we', though she said nothing. Instead taking a series of small sips from her bottle of water, she focused on the grain of the wooden table at which they sat, tracing its swirls with her finger.

'He won't; he's busy,' Barr said. 'That's why I'm here.'

'You're here to drive us, son, no offence,' Duggan said. 'Your uncle was the one ordered it. It's only right that he should be there.'

'He's not here, though,' Barr said, looking around as if to evidence his uncle's absence.

'But he's here in Scotland. He's in Glasgow, giving a talk. There's nothing stopping him. He could be at the woods before us, the way we're travelling.'

'Uncle Sean doesn't know where Kelly is,' Barr said. 'Not exactly. If that's what this is about, there's no need for him to be there.'

'He may not know where he is, but he knows better than anyone *why* he's there. He was the one gave the final order for Kelly to be—'

An infant, perhaps no more than three years old, had toddled over to where they sat, a doll held up in her small fist. Duggan smiled at her, pantomimed surprise. 'Isn't that a lovely doll,' he said to the child, who gurgled her delight at his attention.

Tony turned to see where her parents were and saw a harried couple standing at the entrance to the play area. The father was in his twenties, the mother in her late teens. Their other child, a twin of this girl, Tony guessed, had wandered into the park and was attempting to lift his leg high enough to climb onto a rocking horse on a thick spring coil.

'Fuck's sake,' Barr said, moving away from them and taking out his phone. He moved out of earshot, perhaps for his own dignity.

'What's her name?' Duggan asked, glancing at where Barr went, taking the arm of the doll in his own huge paw as he did so.

The girl said something which Tony could not catch, just as the mother realised where her daughter had gone and came rushing up towards them.

'That's a beautiful name,' Duggan said, though he couldn't possibly have understood the child's response. He smiled at her, earning another giggle, just before her mother grabbed her roughly by the arm and pulled her away.

'Sorry,' she said, her voice nasal, her hair hanging in straggles in front of her face. 'Emma, don't be annoying folk.'

'She's grand,' Duggan offered in placation, but too late to prevent both the forcible removal of the child and her screaming in protest.

'I never took you for the type to play with kids,' Karen said.

'Sure, I've five of me own across two marriages,' he said. 'A grandkiddie on the way, too.'

'Congratulations,' Tony managed, the word dry in his mouth, bittered by the barren nature of his own retirement.

'They're in America. I never see them.'

'Are you going across when it's born?' Karen asked.

'Can't,' Duggan said simply. 'They won't let me in the country.' He did not attempt to explain the reason for this. 'What was I saying?'

Tony sensed Karen slumping a little in her seat, as if the flicker of humanity she had recognised in Duggan had been extinguished.

'He was the one gave the order on Kelly,' Tony said, for Karen had taken out her phone and was checking the screen for messages.

'Are you recording this?' Duggan asked.

'Jesus,' she said, holding the phone up. 'I'm checking the kids haven't called.'

Duggan raised his chin a little, mollified, then continued. 'He was the one gave me the go-ahead on Martin. He was the one said without doubt he was convinced that it was Martin that had done it.'

'Uncle Sean can't make it,' Barr cut into the conversation, causing Tony to start, having not heard his approach.

'What?'

'Like I said, he's too busy,' Barr said, attempting confidence but just missing.

'Give me the phone,' Duggan demanded, his hand outstretched imperiously.

'He's busy.'

'Call him back and give me the phone.'

'No,' Barr said, surprising even himself with the comment.

'Call him back and give me the phone, son,' Duggan repeated. 'This isn't your fight.'

Barr hesitated a moment too long, before trying to argue again, but it was clear his resolve was crumbling. After two more such exchanges, he redialled and handed the phone across to Duggan. Then he stood uneasily next to the picnic bench, waiting for Duggan to finish.

'Seanie,' Duggan said lightly, once the call had connected. 'We've been chatting here. We're not going any further unless we know you're going to be there.'

He listened for a second, nodding his head. 'You're not even an hour away: we're probably the same... I don't give a shit, pal. You don't turn up, we're not turning up.'

Tony could hear Barr muttering 'Fuck' repeatedly under his breath, as if he realised his first big job was going awry even as he watched, helplessly, sidelined from his own assignment.

'We're all in agreement. The three of us are sitting here enjoying the sun and we're not going any further. We'll all be back on that last crossing tonight, if you take too long, and we'll not make it to the woods at all.'

He listened a second longer, raising his hand, indicating an unseeable wish to interrupt.

'You need Kelly back. That's not happened until you put yourself out the same way we have. That's it. End of discussion.'

He ended the call and threw the phone back to Barr, then struggled to his feet. 'I'm going for a piss,' he said. 'You can let me know when he calls back.'

Duggan had barely made it to the end of the pavement when the phone started buzzing again. Barr answered it and listened, his attempts to respond clearly being cut off by the caller. 'OK,' he said eventually and ended the call.

Duggan stood at the fence of the playground, watching up at them, waiting.

'He'll be there in an hour,' Barr called.

Duggan raised his thumb in acknowledgment, then turned towards the restaurant once more. The child in the park had approached the fence now, delighted to see her new friend again.

'Hello, love,' Duggan said. 'You're a wee dote, aren't you?'

The child laughed her approval, holding out her doll for Duggan to take. For a moment, Tony remembered again Ann comments on Sean Mullan's loafers, on the seeming normalcy of those among us who had murdered others. Tony saw it now more clearly than ever as Duggan waggled his fingers at the child through the gaps in the fence.

'A wee doll,' Duggan's voice carried to where they sat. 'That's what you are; a wee doll.'

CHAPTER THIRTY-ONE

Later, he would tell himself it was the doll that made him first doubt what they were doing, but, in reality, the conversation in Betty's with Duggan and Kelly was the first time he'd really thought about what they were planning.

He was on surveillance on his own, Friday evening. Karen had mentioned a party they'd all been invited to and he'd arranged to meet her there later.

He watched up at the house. The car had been gone when Tony arrived and he'd assumed that the cop had gone to do a grocery shop in Paisley, just as Duggan had said was his habit on a Friday evening. Tony glanced at his watch, noted the time. He'd said he would stay until eight and it was already getting dark. He was bored, being here without Karen to talk to. He put on the radio, flicked through channels, trying to find something he could listen to, his attention focused on the dial.

As a result, the tap at his car window shocked him. He jumped, his stomach twisting. Turning in panic, he saw two teenaged boys standing outside the car, one with an unlit cigarette in his hand.

Tony wound down the window.

'A'right, mister. Have ye a light?' The youth held a cigarette aloft.

'I don't smoke.'

'Yer car has a ciggie lighter, don't it?' the other one asked.

Tony nodded, his thoughts tumbling. 'Of course. I forgot. I don't smoke,' he repeated. He pressed in the lighter, willing it to heat up quickly.

'You said already,' the first one commented. 'Are you from Belfast?'

'No.'

'Where then?'

'Derry,' Tony said, then cursed himself for having done so.

'Never heard of it. You'd know your accent a mile off. My da's from Belfast.'

Tony nodded.

'He plays the fife in the bands. Do you play?'

Tony shook his head. The lighter popped out and he drew it out, his face briefly illuminated by the orange glow from the element.

'I don't.'

The young fell lit his cigarette. By the flaring of his smoke, Tony could see pockmarks from acne scarring his cheeks and a line shaved through one eyebrow. He glanced up quickly, to recover the lighter, then looked away again, trying to remain in profile so the youth wouldn't have clear sight of his face.

'Are you Rangers or Celtic?' the second youth asked, taking the lighter and trying to light his smoke from it, but the lighter had already cooled too much to be of use.

'Gone do that again,' he said, handing it back to Tony who pressed it into its slot a second time, his heart thudding so strongly now, he could feel the seat vibrating beneath him with each pulse.

'Blues or Hoops?' he asked again.

Tony cared nothing for football, but knew the significance of the question. He took a guess, based on the comment about the father of one of the boys playing the fife.

'Rangers.'

'Billy Boys all the way!' the second lad laughed.

'What are ye doing sitting here?' the first one asked now, puffing at his smoke, the cigarette held between thumb and first two fingers so that his hand cupped it as he took a drag.

'I'm waiting for someone.'

'Yer girl?'

'Aye.'

'Is she the one normally sits wi' ye?'

Tony looked up at the speaker more closely now. Had they been watching him and Karen all this time? Would they know their car? Remember the registration number?

'We seen ye, sitting here one night. Ye were sitting an hour. We saw her giving you a wank.'

'Is that what you're waiting for? A wank?' the second boy said, laughing.

The lighter popped and Tony handed it to the youth. 'I need to go,' he said, hurrying the boy along.

'Are you not waiting for her?'

'She must be held up.'

'He's getting hee haw the night,' the first boy sniggered.

The second boy handed him back the lighter, his cigarette lit now. 'Do you see Rosie over there?' he said, pointing down towards the chippie. Tony glanced in the rearview and saw a group of youths standing watching over.

'Rosie's the one in the white,' the youth explained. 'She'll suck you off, if you buy us two bottles of Mad Dog from the offie down the road.'

'I have to go, lads. Take her handy,' Tony said, starting the engine and winding up the window.

'One bottle then,' the youth called in negotiation.

They stepped back as Tony made to drive off. 'Wanker,' he heard them shout in his wake.

He rounded the corner of the estate, cursing as he saw that the cop's car was sitting in the driveway; he'd been so preoccupied with the two boys, he'd missed his return. As he drew near the house, he fleetingly saw a figure go the front door, the floral-patterned wallpaper visible as a light switched on. The man must already have gone inside, leaving the door open, perhaps so as to come back out for the rest of the groceries, Tony reasoned.

He was surprised then when he saw the driver's side of the car open and the sparrow-like man step out and open the rear passenger side. Someone else must have been in the car with him, he thought. Someone had opened the front door.

As he drew level, he saw the man straighten as he lifted bags of shopping from the rear seats along with something else. An old rag doll.

He was passed before it really registered, but had the presence of mind to glance into the open doorway where he saw the retreating figure of a child, small and thin, turn and enter one of the rooms off the hall.

He made it as far as the lay-by on the main road before he had to stop. His heart was thudding in his chest, his breaths short and quick, his head dizzy.

A doll. A child. There was a child in the house. And if Duggan followed through with his plan, planted a bomb in the man's car, there was no guarantee that the child would not be as likely a victim as the man.

Added to that, he'd been seen by the two boys: they'd recognised him as a Northerner; he'd told them he lived in Derry; they'd seen his face; they'd seen his car, albeit with the plates changed, as Duggan had insisted.

'I don't think I can do this,' he admitted to himself.

CHAPTER THIRTY-TWO

'I don't think I can do this,' Tony said.

'We're nearly there,' Karen said.

'We've not even reached the woods yet,' Tony protested. 'And he's working to God knows what agenda of his own,' he added, pointing over to the retreating figure of Duggan. Barr had returned to the car, humiliated at having been forced into calling his uncle.

'We know why he's doing it; he's been very clear about it.' She waited a beat, then added, 'Regardless, it's the right thing to do. We'll find whereabouts it was, tell Mullan, and go home. You'll never see any of us again.'

Tony looked up at her, a little mournfully, and she must have recognised his sadness, for she laid her hand on his arm. 'You know what I mean.'

'I often wondered where you'd ended up,' Tony said, prompted by the tenderness of her touch.

She smiled lightly, briefly. 'I'm sure you'd plenty of other things to keep you busy.'

'I still thought of you. After all that had happened. I hoped you were happy.'

'I was,' she said, gently. 'I am.'

'I should have just walked away, thirty years ago,' Tony said. 'When I saw him with the doll, I wanted to. I went to Duggan, but it was too far gone.'

'I wish you had. That night after you and Kelly fought.'

'We didn't fight. I hit him,' Tony said, with mock offence.

'I recall it a little differently,' Karen laughed. 'You weren't a scrapper, even then. But when Duggan called the meeting for you two to make up and he gave you a choice, I wanted you to walk away.'

'You should have said.'

'I did.'

'You didn't. You were playing with a beer mat. I looked to you, hoping you'd tell me to leave it, but you didn't.'

'I asked you to walk away. You said no.'

I don't…' Tony started, then stopped. In his head, the scene played out again, differently now. Duggan had put the question to him. He'd straightened up, glanced at Karen. She was looking at him, nodding lightly. 'Please,' formed on her lips.

'I'm not out,' he said, finally.

Karen sat up, tearing the final strips of card from the beer mat and dropping them to the table in frustration.

'I'm sorry,' he said, now. 'I thought you hadn't.' He was still confused, unsure which version of the past was the right one. If either of them were.

'We saw it through then,' Karen said. 'For good or bad. We have to do so now.'

'I don't want to see Mullan again,' Tony said.

'He's hardly going to do anything,' Karen said, misunderstanding his comment.

'He sickens me,' Tony said, realising in that moment that he had become his own father. He understood now the man's revulsion when Mullan had laid his hand on his by Danny's grave. Understood too why his father had sent him away, to this place, thirty years ago. And yet, through Tony's own fault, he had blindly walked into an event that had blighted his life since. And knowing that brought him no comfort, no profit gained from his wisdom. Shauna Laird came to his mind, sitting in class, hand held high. And again, in Betty's, getting off her knees while Martin Kelly exposed her shame. And again, the last time he saw her, on the morning of her funeral, before the lid was screwed down on the coffin.

For a moment, he felt that the past had overlaid on the present, as if the girl's death had only just happened. Perhaps it was being back here again, perhaps it was being with Karen again, the touch of her hand, the calmness in her voice, the light in her eyes as she smiled at him.

'Are you OK?'

'She was just a child,' he said.

CHAPTER THIRTY-THREE

'He has a child,' Tony said.

He was standing in Duggan's flat, his first visit. He'd called the man from a phone box once he'd made it back. Duggan had not wanted to talk on the phone, had cut him short and told him to come directly to him instead.

'A child,' Tony repeated, a little incredulous that Duggan showed so little reaction to the news. Then it dawned on him.

'Did you already know?'

Duggan nodded. 'Of course. We've been keeping an eye on him, sure. He goes out with her every morning.'

'And you're still going ahead with it?'

Duggan nodded again. He'd not invited Tony to sit, had met him at the door and allowed him no further than the entrance to his living room. Behind Duggan's head, Tony could see a single shelf, mounted on the wall, with a scattering of political books. On the wall above, a family coat of arms, a blue shield embossed with nine golden stars, and at the centre of which curved what looked like a crescent moon, sickle-shaped. A TV set jabbered somewhere out of sight.

'We can't.'

'You need to hold it together,' Duggan said, his jaw clenched. 'This pussying about, one minute you're in the next you're not; you need to suck it up and settle your head.'

'I can't agree with killing a child.'

'Who said we were going to kill her?'

Her again. Tony winced each time he said it, as if assigning the child a gender made her more real, their plan more violent.

'Bombs aren't an exact fucking science, Hugh!'

'Keep your voice down and pull yourself together. It'll happen when the kid's not there, if we can manage it.'

'I think we should stop.'

'Do you? You think we should all be held hostage to the whims of your conscience.'

'This is wrong.'

'So was blinding a kid. Shot her in the face with a plastic bullet. Why is his child more important than that one?'

'That's not what I'm saying?'

'What are you saying?'

'I can't… It's not right. She's just a kid.'

Tony realised how weak his argument sounded, but could not articulate his thoughts and feelings. He realised that it was his fault that only now was the extent of what they were planning really registering with him. But he could not admit that he'd been involved so far without giving any thought to what the final consequences might be.

Duggan seemed to sense he was struggling to explain himself. 'Look,' he said, his tone reasoned. 'I understand your concerns. I do. And we'll try to make sure she's not anywhere near it.'

It. Tony felt his breath catch, his chest tighten, the room seemingly growing smaller around he where he stood. He felt trapped.

'We'll try,' Duggan repeated. 'But if she gets caught up in it by accident, that's just collateral damage. It's an unfortunate side effect of war. Just like your Danny didn't ask to be run over like a dog on his way home from the game.'

Tony slumped against the wall. 'You need to count me out.'

'You're out, everyone's out,' Duggan said. 'You know that. And you'll have to answer for it.'

'I don't want to be involved any more, Hugh.'

'You're already involved. You gave me the mercury for that attack a while back. That was you as much as me.'

'But that was different.'

'How?'

'He deserved it, did he not?'

'Why? You don't know whether he deserved it. You'd not seen him, didn't know him. Maybe he had kids.'

'Did he?'

'Would it matter?'

'Did he?' Tony repeated.

'You're already involved,' Duggan said. 'You need to hold your nerve and see this through. It'll be over by the weekend. Then, you can go on your merry way. But we've trusted you up until now. That's how this works. You walk, we all have to walk. And a lot of people are going to be very unhappy about that.'

Tony felt he was going to be sick. He stood, shaking the jittering from his legs.

'Promise you'll not hurt the kid.'

'I'll do my best,' Duggan agreed. 'That's all I can promise.'

Tony nodded, his mouth dry, his guts writhing.

As Duggan motioned to open the door he added, 'Of course, don't be having any stupid ideas. Your folks have lost one son already; they'll not want to lose a second.'

Tony looked at him, shocked by the baldness of the threat.

'You know what happens to people who talk. That's not a threat; just a reminder.'

'I won't talk,' Tony said, sullenly.

'I know you won't. Good man. I thought you were meant to meet your lassie somewhere.'

Tony tried to order his thoughts a little. He looked at his watch and realised he was already over two hours late.

'I, ah… yeah, I have to meet her.'

'She doesn't strike me as the type will take kindly to being stood up. You don't want to keep that one waiting too long.'

The party was being held in a student house in Thornwood, near the primary school where Tony had subbed for a few weeks when he'd first come across. It was already 11.15pm by the time he arrived, and he wondered whether Karen would indeed have waited for him or not. He'd no intention of staying, but desperately needed to talk to her. He felt sure she would understand how he felt, would agree with him in his suggestion that they call the whole thing off. If both of them pulled out, Duggan would have to respect their wishes, he reasoned. He couldn't punish them both.

The place was thrumming, alive with music and movement and heat. The living room was filled with sound, people crammed together, moving as one to the beat from the small sound system set up in one corner. He knew instinctively that Karen wouldn't be there and moved on down the hallway. A smaller room, to the rear of the house, was in semi-darkness, a lava lamp providing the only illumination, the colours on the faces of those assembled in the room, gathered around a small coffee table on which lay a collection of torn-up cigarettes and Rizla papers changing through the haze of hash smoke as the waxy blob in the lamp lazily rose and fell and rose once more. He scanned the faces, though again was fairly sure that Karen wouldn't be sitting with the druggies.

Finally, he moved through to the kitchen. Someone was playing a guitar on the back step and a handful of older guests had gathered here, where the beer was kept in cooler boxes, resting on a half inch of watery ice. Just as he turned to leave, assuming Karen had done so herself, Martin Kelly wandered into the kitchen, clearly having come from the small rear room.

'All right?' he asked, flashing Tony a smile. 'You made it.'

'Is Karen still about?' he asked, a little wary at the warmth of Kelly's greeting. Kelly's sense of their rapprochement seemingly more genuine than Tony's own.

'She's up the stairs. She wasn't feeling great—'

'Thanks,' Tony said, turning to leave.

'Wait! I'd leave her, mate.'

Tony looked askance at him. 'I'll go on up, thanks,' he said. 'She's expecting me.'

'Just looking out for you,' Kelly said, his hands raised in surrender.

Tony squeezed his way up the stairs, past several assembled couples that had taken position there, though they barely noticed his passing.

There were four doors at the top of the stairs, three closed, one slightly ajar to reveal what Tony assumed to be a small toilet, judging by the noise of someone urinating in there. He knocked and opened the first door where a couple, partially clothed for the moment, lay in an embrace on the bed. The couple in the second room had progressed further, her bent over the bed, him standing, trousers at his ankles, behind her. He turned and grinned at Tony without stopping.

'Fuck off!' she shouted as she saw the cause of her partner's distraction.

Tony muttered his apologies as he closed the door, moving to the third, knocking and pushing it open.

The third bedroom was empty. For a second, Tony assumed that Kelly had been mistaken, or that perhaps Karen had given up waiting and left. Just then, the door of the first bedroom opened and the drunken couple emerged. He had his trousers still half unbuttoned while he tried to tuck in his shirt, she, head lowered, was rebuttoned her own shirt the wrong way, so that it gaped in the middle, showing her bra beneath.

'Karen?' Tony asked.

She looked up at him, her face a blear of make-up, her eyes unfocused as she squinted slightly at him.

'Tony?' she said.

CHAPTER THIRTY-FOUR

'Tony?' she repeated.

He raised his head. They were back in the car now and on their way again. He was almost surprised to see she was older, her features hardened a little with age. Yet he still felt the pain of her betrayal as something visceral, as if it had happened a moment earlier.

'Are you OK?'

Absurdly, he wondered if she'd just shared in his reverie of that night, if she felt any guilt, remorse at what had happened.

'I'm fine,' he said, more petulantly than he'd intended, earning a brief frown from Karen before she motioned towards where Barr sat.

'I was asking you, are you OK to stay over and go back tomorrow?'

'I have my bag,' Tony said. When the idea had been first discussed, they'd planned to go over and back in one day, returning on the last crossing of the evening. However, Barr had called back a few days later to suggest that they each bring an overnight bag, in case they found relocating Kelly's resting place more difficult than they thought; the woodland was likely to have changed significantly since they'd last been there. As a result, Tony had packed for a night away. Now, though, he just wanted to go home.

He realised, too, that the fluttering in his stomach was intensifying as they got closer to the wood. His anticipation of the trip had centred almost exclusively on seeing Karen again, how she might have changed, whether she remembered him. And, in his more private moments, whether they might rekindle that which they'd once shared. As he'd packed the overnight bag – Ann's bag – he'd felt guilty when he realised he was packing his most slimming nightclothes: black T-shirt and shorts. Now, he felt more embarrassment at his vanity than disloyalty to his dead wife.

'I've a funeral in the morning,' he said.

'A funeral? Whose?' Duggan asked.

'I don't know,' Tony admitted.

'You're going to a funeral of someone you don't know?'

'It's not like that; I'm a sacristan in the local church.'

'You found God,' Duggan said, as if this confirmed a suspicion he'd long harboured.

'Not quite,' Tony said, blushing at his feeling that he needed to deny the comment, as if it had been something accusatory. He wasn't ashamed of his faith, even as he was aware that, increasingly, people saw it as something old-fashioned. Even in school, staff had scoffed at his continued attendance at Mass, had questioned how he could continue to believe in something they considered so ridiculous. He'd smiled, nodded his head in acknowledgement of their derision, felt no compulsion to defend his choices. The truth was, Ann had been the religious one. Even when they'd first met, she'd been going to First Friday Masses, confessions, the whole bit. She'd even managed to convince him to go to Lough Derg with her; their first trip away together.

Lough Derg was a lake a few miles across the border in the Republic. At its centre lay Station Island, home to St Patrick's Purgatory, Europe's oldest place of pilgrimage. Tony and Ann had gone together for the three-day retreat. He'd only gone because she wanted to, but found the place, in spite of his scepticism, strangely peaceful. He trod the stations, concentric circles of rocks on which the pilgrims walked in bare feet while reciting the rosary, thinking of Martin Kelly and his final journey into the woodland. Yet, when it came time for confession, as he had done before and so many times since, Tony could not bring himself to confess what they had done. As a result, when they sat on the boat returning back to the mainland on the final day, he felt still a sort of gnawing guilt that would not ease. And he realised now, with a mild shock, that Karen was right. What he hoped to find with Martin Kelly's grave was forgiveness.

"My wife was pretty religious,' he said, glancing at Karen to see if she was reacting, but she did not look at him, her face turned towards the scenery sliding past. 'I got involved in the church with her. Then when she got sick, we became more involved.'

'Did it help her?' Duggan asked.

Tony ignored the snide nature of the comment. 'It did,' he said. 'She found comfort in it.'

'She still died though,' Duggan said.

'Hugh!' Karen turned on him now. 'That's enough.'

Duggan chuckled. 'I'm only saying.'

'She still died,' Tony agreed. 'And what about you, Hugh?'

'I'm not religious,' Duggan laughed, shaking his head. 'Not in years.'

'I mean, are you dying?'

Duggan's expression set as he turned and glanced coldly at Tony, a humourless smirk tautening his lips. 'You're getting brave,' he said.

'I've no reason not to be,' Tony said. He'd grown tired of Duggan's presumption of authority. 'As you've said so many times before, we're all in this together. I'm guessing you're not well.'

'We're all dying,' Duggan said. 'Isn't that the idea: life is the ultimate terminal disease? What killed your missus?'

'Cancer.'

'Breast?'

'Brain.'

He'd not spoken the words so baldly before and wondered why he was doing so now. When she was first diagnosed, after weeks of headaches, forgetting keys, stumbling over words, they'd been hopeful, ready to fight it. She'd even talked about doing Lough Derg again, as if bargaining with God. But the seizures that followed prevented that.

The first had been after a concert in the Guildhall, a local musical society. Again, it had been Ann's choice; she'd loved the old musicals: *Oklahoma*, *Annie Get Your Gun*, *South Pacific*.

They'd been passing the bank when two kids had slid by them on skateboards, the rattling of the wheels on stone echoing off the city walls to their left. The noise had caused Tony to start and he assumed the sudden movement from Ann to his right-hand side was the same. But then she hit the ground.

Initially, he thought one of the youths had struck her, but there was no blood; not until she began to writhe, as if her body were surging with current, her head striking off the brickwork beneath it. Then the blood began to seep, haloing her skull, badging her hair.

Tony had knelt beside her, his hands holding hers, his jacket hastily placed beneath her head, shouting for someone to call an ambulance, his own phone useless in his jacket pocket as he tried to control the seizure.

He'd sat in the ambulance with her, her hands in his, telling her it would be OK, that they'd be home soon. She couldn't remember the event afterwards. She could recall only the first song of the concert and nothing thereafter until the ambulance ride.

'I'm going to wash that man...' she sang, sleepily, lying on the stretcher. He placed his hand to the side of her face, marked her with her own blood from his fingers in so doing.

The doctor told them, the following week, that the trip to Lough Derg was impractical. There was no guarantee that she wouldn't take more seizures (indeed, she did with increasing frequency) and walking on jagged stones was not the ideal situation for her under such circumstances.

Instead, she'd listed other plans, places she wanted to revisit. Fahan beach, Griannan fort, Inch Island. They'd done all three in one day, Tony driving from one location to the next. In Fahan they sat in the car, the winter chill outside too much for Ann to bear. She watched the tide, listened to the gentle breathing of the earth with each wave that washed the beach clear, wept for all she would miss.

'That's a tough one,' Duggan admitted, drawing Tony once more to the present.

'*She* was a tough one,' Tony said. 'She refused treatment in the end.'

Karen's look caught him off guard, a mixture of sympathy and regret, he thought.

'Why?'

'She was told she was going to die either way. Treatment might give her another month or two but with no quality of life.'

She'd slipped quietly away in the hospice, her passing ultimately a relief after the horrendous final days she'd endured.

'Brave woman,' Karen said.

'So, what about you?' Tony asked, the question directed at Duggan, but the man had turned from him and whether he hadn't heard, or pretended not to, no answer was forthcoming. Tony looked out the window, prepared to let his refusal to answer slide. If he was dying, he wasn't quite ready to deal with it yet. That was OK.

'How much longer?' Karen asked.

Barr's shoulders dropped as he answered, and Tony realised the youth had been holding himself tensed since they left the service station. His relief at the innocuous nature of the question was clear. 'About twenty minutes to the car park,' Barr said. 'We take the next exit, I think.'

'We approached it from the other side,' Duggan said. 'Coming from Glasgow.'

'It might have changed,' Barr said, unnecessarily.

'Some things won't have done,' Duggan said. 'I'm guessing he'll still be in the ground. Those that go in tend not to come back out.'

He glanced at Tony, who searched for the insult in the comment and struggled to find it. Did he mean himself? Ann? Tony?

Tony looked across at Karen who looked from Duggan to him and shook her head.

'Your wife,' she said softly enough that Duggan might not catch it. 'I am sorry.'

CHAPTER THIRTY-FIVE

'I'm sorry,' Karen said, the following morning. 'It wasn't my fault.'

She'd arrived at his flat at 9.30am, just as he was getting ready to go into school. Despite being a Saturday morning, the school was holding an Open Day for prospective pupils and staff were expected to be there.

'Well, it was hardly mine,' Tony said. He stood in the living area, shirt and tie on, but stripped to his underwear while he pressed his trousers.

'I don't know what happened,' Karen protested, moving towards him.

'You didn't even try phoning last night,' Tony complained, as if this was the cause of greatest offense.

'I was out of it. I don't remember anything after the first half hour or so.'

'You must have been putting the wine away something manic.'

'I'd two glasses, max,' she protested. 'You have to believe me.'

Tony looked at her, her expression pained. Her face was freshly scrubbed, free of make-up, though her eyes looked bruised with the previous night's mascara, which had not been fully removed.

'How can I believe you? I saw the two of you lying on the bed. He had his trousers undone.' After a pause, he articulated his greatest fear, one which had riven him to the core all through a sleepless night. 'Did you fuck him?'

'Fuck him?'

'Would you prefer "making love"?' Tony spat.

'Do you really need to ask?'

'Obviously I do.'

Karen looked at him a moment, searchingly. 'No. I don't think I fucked him.'

'You don't think? Who was he?'

'I don't know.'

'You what?' he turned from her, incredulous, angry.

'I don't remember anything,' she said. 'That's what I'm telling you. I had a drink, waiting for you in the kitchen. I was talking with Kelly who'd been in selling in the back room. I don't know what happened then. I vaguely remember wakening in the room and some guy on top of me, his tongue down my throat. I pushed him off and told him I was already with someone. We got up and came out of the room and that's where I met you.'

'You expect me to believe that.'

Karen straightened. 'I don't care whether you believe it or not,' she said. 'It's the truth.'

'Being drunk doesn't change your personality,' Tony said, annoyed at himself, even as he spoke, for his priggishness, yet unable to back down. 'It just brings out the worst elements of what's already there.'

'I wasn't drunk,' Karen said. 'Or if I was, they must have had really strong wine. I've the headache from hell today.'

'Is that looking for sympathy?'

She shook her head. 'I don't know what happened,' she said. 'I'm really, really sorry. But I didn't do it on purpose.'

'I hate it when I accidentally fall into bed with someone,' Tony replied, pettily. He finished pressing his trousers and pulled them on, buttoning them up in front of her. She watched him, exasperated, and finally stood.

'I thought you'd trust me,' she said. 'I didn't cheat on you. I don't know what happened last night, but it wasn't me who did that. Anyone who knows me well enough would know that to be true.'

'Maybe that person isn't me, then,' Tony said.

'I'm beginning to think that,' Karen said.

He watched her walk out the door, desperately searching for something to say that would both stop her leaving and express just how deeply he was hurt. In the end, he could only manage, 'That's fine. Walk away.'

But she was already gone.

He endured the Open Day morning, despite the foulness of his mood. He stood with three of his colleagues while one group of parents after another processed past, regarding them as one might animals in a zoo, some smiling or nodding in acknowledgement, some averting their gaze so as not to make eye contact. Or so it seemed to him. There was a hiatus between twelve and one to allow staff and those pupils who had volunteered to come along and help an opportunity to get some lunch.

Tony followed the rest of his department to the canteen, where sandwiches and tea had been provided. The teachers sat together at two tables near the top of the room, nearest the food, and watched the line of students file past to get some lunch.

'Would you send a bairn out dressed like tha'on?' one of the technology teachers commented.

Tony followed her gaze to where she had indicated with an incline of her head and saw Alice standing in the queue. She'd stretched a little across the term, and her father had made allowance for such a change by unstitching the hem of her skirt. While it sat now across her thighs, the line from the previous fold was still evident, as were the dangling of threads from the frayed edge of the hem, which had once been hidden. Her jumper, which she'd pulled down over her hands, carried marks of green paint on the elbow and red splotches further up the sleeve.

'She'd hardly a walking advertisement for coming here, is she?'

Alice, mistaking the attentions of the faces ranged against her, lifted a timid hand and waved at Tony. 'Hello, sir,' she mouthed, and smiled brightly.

'You've a fan,' the tech teacher said.

'She's a good girl,' Tony said. 'Give her a break. She gets a hard enough time from the kids.'

'You'd think her mother would dress her right,' someone commented.

'Her mother's dead,' Tony said.

The afternoon session was the quieter of the two. Tony's anger had hardened now, moving beyond his indignation from this morning to a more settled resentment for what Karen had done and her failure to admit it.

'What books do you do?' one parent in the final group asked. She'd already spent several minutes scanning the display of texts they had set up on the tables which ran the gamut of Literature, both English and Scottish.

'All of these,' he said, nodding to the display.

'Anything else?'

Tony frowned. There were, after all, almost thirty books on the table, many of which, truth be told, would not be seen again until this time the following year when the school would spruce itself up and put on its finest display for the next prospective cohort.

'*King Lear*,' he offered, speculatively.

'Is that not a bit hard for the younger ones?'

'We wouldn't do it with the younger ones.'

'Then what would you do?'

Tony regarded her more closely. She was trim, neat, with pinched features. She clasped the prospectus for the school tightly between arm and side while she clasped her hands in front of her. She bent a little at the waist. For a moment, Tony had the impression she was a nun, were it not for the two children with whom she'd arrived who were taking turns kicking one another behind her. The elder sibling offered his crotch for the younger to kick, which he did with some vigour.

'I don't know. Depends on the class, really. Some Bernard McLaverty maybe.'

She shook her head to indicate she didn't recognise the name.

'He's an Irish writer living in Scotland.'

'I can see why you'd like him,' the woman commented. 'With your accent.'

Tony offered a withered smile, tiring of the conversation and wanting to be home.

'I'd want Brian to read something challenging,' the woman decided. 'He's very bright.'

Tony remained sceptical, as he watched Brian receive another kick in the balls from his younger brother.

'I'm sure he'll fit right in,' he said.

Once the woman left, they started packing up the books and Tony took the chance to get away early. He went down through the school and out the side door, to avoid meeting any of the senior teachers at the entrance who might comment on his leaving so quickly. It was there that he met Alice again, standing at the bus shelter.

'Hey you,' he said. 'How did you get on today?'

'It was great,' she beamed. 'We got to cut up a rat in Science. I got to take out the guts.' She laughed with joy at the memory.

'Are you getting the bus home? I can run you if you like.'

'No thanks, sir,' she said. 'Dad's coming to get me.'

'How's the year gone? Are people still giving you a hard time?'

She nodded. 'It's all right. Dad said I have to ignore them. They'll get tired of it eventually.'

Tony nodded. How many times had he given the same advice, knowing it was rarely true? Bullies were born of weakness, turned to cruelty, just as Seneca had claimed.

Once more, Shauna Laird came to his mind, herself a victim of cruelty. Did she realise, he wondered, in her final moments, that she had been the cause of her own fate, as she had joked in class? Whether she did or not, the thought angered him. She wasn't entirely to blame; Kelly had been responsible, too.

'Might be better to lift your foot and hit one of them a boot some day,' he said. 'That'll put an end to it for sure!'

'I might,' she laughed, conspiratorially.

They heard a short blast of a car horn and she turned to see from where it had come. 'There's Dad. Bye, sir,' she said, offering him a brief wave, despite being only a foot or two away from him, then turned and ran across to where a red Cortina had pulled into the bus bay at the end of the car park.

Tony recognised the car the instant he saw it, even before Alice's father stepped out to meet her. His movements were small and precise, his attitude like that of a sparrow.

Alice hugged into him and he returned the gesture, one arm around her shoulder, the other cupping her head momentarily as he kissed the top of her head then directed her round to the passenger side of the car.

Tony felt like the ground had dropped from beneath him. He'd forgotten all about what they had planned, so fixated was he on what Karen had done. Now the reality of it broke on him more forcibly than ever.

The man looked across at Tony as moment, as if aware of his gaze, then climbed into the car himself.

Tony stood, watching, his heart hammering against his chest, as the car pulled out and drove off, Alice's face spectral through the tinted glass of the passenger window as they passed.

CHAPTER THIRTY-SIX

They passed through the village below the woods, the car shuddering from the unevenness of the road surface, pockmarked with potholes and dips. To their left was a pharmacy and shop, beyond that a small, whitewashed pub, the red illuminated T sign affixed to the front the only flash of colour on the building.

'Stop here would you, son?' Duggan asked. 'I want to pick up a few tins before we head in.'

Tony could see Barr playing with the idea of ignoring him, showing no visible acknowledgment of having heard the request. Perhaps he was reluctant to stop again, so near to their final destination. Or perhaps he had tired of Duggan's demands. In the end, though, whichever it had been, he obviously thought better of it and pulled in.

'We need to be at the woodland soon if we're going to have any chance of finding it today,' Barr said.

'That's grand. Will you pop the boot for me; I need to get my wallet from my bag.'

Barr reached down and clicked the button. They heard the catch release behind them as the trunk unlocked.

'I'll not be a minute,' Duggan said, getting out and stretching, stiff from sitting so long in one position. He stood a moment, as if deliberately taking his time, his face turned towards the sun. Then he moved around to the back of the car. They could hear him unzip his bag, could hear his movements, then the sharp thud of the door closing, the car dipping lightly with the slam of the trunk.

They watched as he rounded the vehicle and disappeared into the darkness of the pub.

'I'm going to see where Uncle Sean is,' Barr said, excusing himself as he climbed out of the car. 'Encourage Hugh to get a move on, too.'

'You've been in a different world,' Karen said, when Barr had closed the door.

'What?'

'You've been somewhere else since we stopped at Monkton.'

Tony nodded. 'I've been remembered things.'

'I've been trying to do the complete opposite,' Karen said. 'No good comes of it.'

Tony smiled. 'Duggan said the past is another country. He's wrong. The past feels like it was just a split second ago, like it's just a shadow, or an echo of what's happening now.'

Karen nodded, but did not comment.

'I was thinking about Alice,' he said.

A shake of the head this time and Karen frowned to signify her failure to recognise the name.

'She was the wee girl I knew in school. The one who lost her mum before she came to us.'

'She took her period and you...'

'Thought of you,' Tony said, then immediately apologised as Karen blushed.

'I remember her now. What of her?'

'I wonder where she is.'

'She'd be grown up with kids of her own, now,' Karen said. 'She was what? Eleven then? She'd be in her forties now then.'

'I want to imagine her happy.'

'I don't… I'm not sure what you mean.'

'Camus said we have to imagine Sisyphus happy, pushing his boulder up a slope the top of which he can never reach. Even though his situation could never leave him happy, we must imagine that he found some way to deal with it, to reconcile himself with his lot. Like Prometheus did.'

'You were always too literary for me,' Karen said.

'That's not true,' Tony smiled. 'I learned so much from you. Do you remember you made me a mixtape for my birthday?'

Karen smiled. 'That sounds like something I'd have done. Cheap and nasty.'

'That was the first time I heard of Tom Waits. "Martha" was on there.'

'It's a great song.'

'It's a sad song.'

Karen, as if uncomfortable with the melancholic tone of the conversation, turned and looked out at Barr on the phone. 'Then we must imagine the singer happy,' she said.

'Even if he is still in love with Martha?'

'Even so. I think of you every time I hear "Wonderful Life".'

Tony laughed. 'Now that's another great song.'

'We saw him a while back, touring. Black. Before he died, obviously.'

We saw him. She had shared that song, a new memory of that song, with someone else, and in so doing had changed it.

'We saw Tom Waits the last time he was in Ireland,' Tony said.

It wasn't entirely true. Ann hadn't wanted to go, couldn't stand his voice. Tony had gone himself and stood at the front, alone, lost in the music.

He'd listened to 'Martha' in the car on the way down, on repeat, and was again in Karen's bed, his head on her breast, the scent of her in his hair and skin, the taste of her in his mouth. He thought of her every time he heard the song, though did not tell her that now; 'Martha' had been playing that last night they had been together. Nor did he tell her that he still had the mixtape, saved in a box in his bedroom, even though he no longer had a tape recorder on which to play it. That she had been there, a presence in his room, all the time he'd been married.

'That must have been special.'

Tony nodded. Waits had not played 'Martha' at the gig, though he had played 'Time' at the end and, for a moment, listening to it, Tony had felt truly invisible, like he had disappeared into the music, half hoping not to return from it.

He'd thought about the song one day, while he was teaching Shauna Laird's class 'Birches' by Robert Frost. They'd talked about Frost's comment that sometimes he'd like to get away for a while, climbing away from the earth but knowing he could return. Shauna had nodded when he'd explained what Frost was saying.

'Like when your ma's doing your head in, and you want to get away frae her but you don't either 'cause you'd miss her if she wasn't there. Everyone must feel like that,' she'd said.

'That's what makes it such a good poem. It's saying something you always thought but never realised you were thinking and never expressed.'

'Do you think if he was alive now, he'd be on drugs?' she asked. to a chorus of laughter from her classmates.

'He'd not be the first poet to take drugs if he was,' Tony had joked.

He'd thought of the conversation the morning of her funeral, as he'd seen her for the last time in her coffin. Should he have said something that day in class, something about the dangers of drugs? Or should he have said something when he first saw her in Liverpool Betty's? Or when he saw her getting up off the toilet floor? When should he have intervened? And would she even have wanted him to? In the end, as he said goodbye to her that morning, he decided that he should have tried.

'And you're away again,' Karen said. He felt a little sick as he was brought once more to the car, to Karen, to Barr standing outside at the door of the pub.

'I'm sorry.' He felt himself unbalanced, as the past and present merged, overlapped and separated once more, as if he was compelled to follow memory after memory, down the rabbit hole of his own making.

'Am I that poor company?'

'I didn't sleep last night,' Tony said. "I must be tired. You're not poor company at all. I'm so glad to see you again.'

He noticed a flush spreading along Karen's neck and jawline, before Barr tapped on her side window and, somewhat gratefully, she opened the door.

'Can some of you speak to him?' Barr said.

'What's wrong?'

'Take a look,' Barr said. 'I give up.'

Tony got out and followed Karen to the door of the bar. They looked inside, the room unnaturally dark after the daylight, an effect intensified by the wood panelling of the walls and the chequerboard pattern of the tiled floor. The pub was fairly quiet; a few customers sat at the bar, two women with a baby sat near the entrance and, in the far corner, beneath a gilt-edged mirror, Duggan sat, hunched over a tumbler of whiskey, four cans of Special Brew sitting on the seat next to him.

Tony went in, nodding to the barmaid's greeting, Karen following behind as they moved down to where Duggan sat.

'You nearly ready, Hugh? We're on a tight enough schedule.'

'Just a last one,' Duggan said. 'A wee Scotch for the road.'

He took a small mouthful, held it, as if to savour every aspect of its flavour, then swallowed audibly.

'I always thought wine tasters and that were talking shit, but you can taste it off a good whiskey. Turf smoke. Oak.'

'Is that you?' Tony asked.

'What's the hurry?' he snapped. 'I'm in no rush to see that place again.'

Tony sighed and looked at Karen. She surprised him by moving across and sitting on the red faux-leather seat beside Duggan, placing her hand on his arm.

'Are you ready?' she asked, gently. 'Or do you want to sit a moment.'

He looked at her, as if only really seeing her for the first time. His eyes glittered.

'Now we're here, I'm not sure I am ready.'

'We can take a minute if you like.'

He considered it for a moment, then lifted the glass and drained it, wincing a little at the burning in his throat as he swallowed.

'Do you think he's waiting for us?'

Karen frowned lightly. 'Martin?'

Duggan nodded. 'Do you think he knows we're coming?'

'I guess it depends on whether you think there's anything after death,' Karen said.

'Do you think your missus knows you're there? When you visit her grave?' Duggan asked, looking up at Tony.

'I think she does. Somehow.'

Duggan nodded, as if this was what he'd been expecting.

'Let's get this over with, then,' he said.

CHAPTER THIRTY-SEVEN

'Just get it over with,' Tony muttered to himself, sitting in the car at the row of shops opposite the estate where he now knew Alice Hamilton and her father lived.

It was Saturday night. He'd come back from school after 4pm and had wanted to call Karen, to tell her what he had learned. But things had ended so badly that morning, so damagingly to their relationship, that he felt he couldn't.

He'd felt sick since then, pacing his flat, unable to settle himself for longer than a few minutes, before the thrumming of his body compelled him to his feet and he set off once more, round and round the flat. He'd made beans and toast, convinced himself he was hungry and then thought he'd vomit with the first mouthful.

Alice would be alone. That was the heart of it for him, the thought he could not get beyond. He'd managed from to dissociate himself from the reality of a man's death by not thinking about the man as a person, by creating some sense that his death would be the corollary for Danny's. Seeing the doll, the child, had made the man a father, a figure incrementally more real than the faceless officer he'd been up until that point. But now he had a name, Hamilton, and a child, Alice, and a connection to Tony that could not easily be dismissed.

Alice would be left on her own.

Tony could not help but see Karen in the girl: bereft of a father through the violence of someone she did not know, would never meet again; set on a path that led inexorably to this, to targeting others, to becoming a killer herself. Death begetting death, spiralling from one to the next, an unending chain of cause and effect.

His father had been right, he reflected. What good would revenge do? What would the child do without even her father? OK, he wasn't great at the day-to-day stuff, but Tony guessed he was doing his best, widowed, suffering himself from all he had witnessed in the North, trying to raise a young girl in a strange country. He was empathising with the man, sympathising with his position, all the time making him more real, more concrete in Tony's consciousness. And, ultimately, what right had he to deprive Alice of a father, fate having already taken her mother from her.

He allowed himself to fixate on that thought, allowed it to ruminate through the evening, for the other line of thought was too much for him to bear – that Alice would get in the car with her father the following morning to go to church. Yet, once he allowed himself to even consider that, and the inevitable outcome of it, he could not stop the thought from imposing itself over and over.

He could not dismiss the mental image of the explosion, ripping through the car, tearing Alice asunder. He imagined her sitting in the car, her sleeves balled in her fists, her eyes bright and wild with terror as the first wave rippled the metal work, shredded the plastic moulding of the dash, tore her clothes, her skin, ripped the muscle from bone, splintered and shattered her. The thought made him sick. He thought he would pass out, found his pace doubling as he padded around his flat, his face slick with a cold sheen of sweat.

He drove back out to Foxbar and parked up a distance from the shops, away from the glare of the street lights, in a spot that allowed him a view of the parking area while he remained in shadows. He could make out the house in the distance, in the space between two of the row, which backed on to the main road. The lights were already on in one of the upstairs rooms, even though it was only beginning to turn dark, the sky thickening in the east.

He'd a bottle of water and a Mars bar in the car, which he tried to eat now. He forced himself to swallow each cloying bite of the chocolate, aware he'd not eaten since lunch time and already feeling a little light-headed, as if his blood sugar was dipping. The thought instantly brought to mind Alice, standing in his classroom, her shirt pulled up as she injected herself with insulin. How would she manage without her father? Would her self-sufficiency thrive? Or would she be lost completely, the final thread of stability in her life torn from her?

Duggan had told him that this man's death was a response to Danny's in some way, to justify his involvement. But it wasn't, and he knew that now. Danny had died. That was separate from this. There was no reciprocity of violence that would change any aspect of what had happened to him.

He stayed in the car and waited. He knew that the changeover in watches was at 8pm. Sure enough, at 8.03pm, he saw Martin Kelly drive out from the parking area at the shops and make his way home.

He waited for another twenty minutes, just in case someone else arrived to replace Kelly, but he suspected no one would. If the attack was happening tonight as he had implied, Duggan would probably wait until it was late, until people had gone to bed, before arriving to attach whatever device he had built. They had agreed that, in the hours before, they would stay away from the area. Even so, Tony got out of the car and pulling up his hood, and zipping up his coat to cover the lower part of his chin, he cut across the road through a break in traffic and up along the backs of the rows of houses facing the shops.

Some of the kids he'd seen from the previous night were gathered under the shelter of the front canopy of the small supermarket. He could hear their raised voices, their laughter, could see the glowing tips of their cigarettes, swirling through the darkness like fireflies in flight.

He wanted it to be over, but it was still dusky, the streets still busy with people heading out for the evening. He went back to the car, avoiding crossing where the kids might see him, and drove out to the promontory where Black Cart and White Cart Waters met as the River Cart.

There he stood, the smell of the mudflats along the banking sharp in the evening air, and considered, just for a moment, what would happened if he walked down into the river, allowing the water to carry him, to weigh down his clothes and bear him away, as Ophelia had done.

His parents would be broken, he knew that. His father would never recover. What of Karen? Would she care? Would she blame herself? A self-centred part of him took some imaginary joy in her suffering. And it would free him from the searing pain boring through him, the guilt of what was to come and the impossible situation he faced.

He drove back towards Paisley, stopping at a phone box below a fish and chip place on Storie Street.

'Dad?'

'Hi, son,' his father sounded groggy, as if he'd been asleep. Tony imagined him drowsing in front of the telly, the house so quiet now there was little to disturb his slumbering. 'How are you?'

'Good,' Tony managed, his voice cracking a little.

'Do you want your mother?'

It was the normal rhythm of their calls.

'No. I'm good talking with you. How's things?'

'Good, good. I was up at Danny's grave today, cleaning it up a bit, weeding and that.'

'Did you say one for me?' Tony asked.

'Every day,' his dad said. 'You know that. How's things there? How's school?'

'Ok. We'd an Open Day today.'

'What's that?'

'For the kids for next year.' He felt sick at the comment, the thought of a future. The presumption of it.

'Very good. How's you and Karen?'

'Yeah, OK,' Tony said, not wanting to have to explain. What could he say? Strangely, he still didn't want his parents thinking badly of her. 'Listen, I just wanted to say thanks.'

'What for?'

'Sending me away over here. I know why you did it.'

'Given the choice, I'd rather have you here. You know that.'

'I do,' Tony said. 'And I'd be there, too. I miss you.'

'I miss you too, son.' His father hesitated a moment. 'Is everything OK?'

Tony nodded, aware the gesture was futile. He wanted to tell his father that he had been right, the night of the funeral, when he'd spoken to Tony about the futility of revenge. And he wanted to tell him that he loved him, wanted Alice to say the same to her father.

But the words struggled in his throat; he'd not done it before and knew his father would think it strange now. Would worry. So instead he contented himself with his usual. 'I'll head on so. Talk to you later.'

'All right, son. You're sure you're OK?'

'I'm all right, Da.'

'All right, then. Speak soon. I love you.'

The comment threw him. By the time he'd responded, the line was already dead, his words lost.

He drove back to Foxbar one final time and parked at the shops, now closed up for the evening, the kids all gone. He watched across at Alice's house, saw the bedroom light go dark.

'Just get it over with,' he muttered.

He got out of the car and sprinted across the road, pulling up his hood again as he did so. He climbed over the low fence of one of the houses along whose backs he was moving and cut through their garden and out onto the street. He was on the opposite side of the street from Alice's house, about a dozen houses up from it.

He walked down towards the house, scanning the cars parked along the street, lest Duggan was already there. But each vehicle was empty.

He paused, once at the bottom of Alice's driveway, building up the courage to take the final steps. He shoved his hands in his pockets, took a few slow breaths, trying to steady his nerve.

Just then a pool of light spilled onto the drive as the front door opened and Alice's father stepped out, two empty milk bottles in hand. He wore a pyjama top over brown cords. He stopped when he saw Tony, frozen mid stoop. One bottle slipped from his fingers and clattered hollowly onto the step, rolling onto the one below where it shattered.

The noise forced Tony to act. He moved up the driveway, even as the man stood and rushed back inside, his face drawn in terror, misunderstanding Tony's presence on his doorstep this late at night.

'Mr Hamilton,' Tony said. 'I'm a teacher in Alice's school. I need to talk to you.'

'I'm calling the police,' the man said, already closing the door, but Tony managed to to wedge his foot in the gap and prevent him shutting it completely.

'Please. You need to let me in.'

The door opened a crack further, the man still holding his weight behind it.

'You need to let me in,' Tony said. 'Please. You have to trust me.'

'Mr Canning?'

He heard Alice's voice, as if from somewhere deeper in the house. She'd recognised his accent. He felt the weight behind the door shift and her father's face appeared at the widening gap.

'Let me see your hands.'

Tony held up both in surrender. 'I'm not going to harm you. Or Alice. But we need to be quick.'

Slowly, the door opened and Tony stepped inside. He heard it slam behind him, with a finality he could not easily dismiss, as if the life he had lived was over and a new reality lay ahead.

CHAPTER THIRTY-EIGHT

The entrance to the woods lay ahead of them as they trundled down an increasingly uneven roadway that led to a small empty parking area.

'No sign of Uncle Sean,' Duggan said, pulling one of the cans free from the plastic rings that held the four together. He tapped on the top twice, a trick Tony remembered him doing years back to stop the contents from spraying when the can was opened. Tony didn't know if it worked, or it was a tic Duggan had not shed.

The can opened with a wet hiss and he gulped down three or four mouthfuls before belching softly. 'We're staying put so, until he comes.'

'I'm going to stretch my legs,' Tony said, feeling he had to explain his exiting from the car to Duggan.

'I'll join you,' Karen said.

They stood together, in front of the car, their backs to the occupants, and scanned the woodland. A five-bar gate blocked the pathway leading up into the trees, a dull metal chain and padlock wrapped around one side.

'Do you remember this?' Karen asked.

'I'm not sure,' Tony admitted. 'I don't remember climbing over a gate. How could we have?'

'Did we even come in through here? Maybe the gate wasn't here back then.'

Tony looked around, trying to find some distinguishable landmark that might trigger a memory from that night, but recognised nothing in particular. It could have been the entrance to any woodland, anywhere.

'It has been thirty years,' he said, finally.

'We're never going to find him,' Karen said.

Just then, the air filled with a low rumbling which grew in intensity and pitch. They both glanced up instinctively as the sound sharpened, rising above them. They could just make out the underbelly of the jet as it emerged through low lying cloud and continued it ascent, breaking through the higher layers and disappearing from sight, its roar gradually dying with its passing.

Karen looked at Tony. 'This is the place. I remember that.'

'We don't need to be exact about the spot,' Tony said. 'They have all this technology now where they can scan the ground to see if soil was disturbed. We just need a general part of the woods. I remember there was a big oak near to where we buried him. And spruce trees. And there was a fallen tree trunk over a stream along the way.'

'I don't remember that,' Karen frowned. 'Are you sure?'

Tony nodded. 'I took your hand to help you across. We'd barely spoken since the row, the party.'

'It wasn't quite a row,' Karen said. 'That diminishes it a little.'

Tony mumbled an apology, keen to drop the subject.

'We've all kept our secrets,' she said, clearly still annoyed by his comment.

Before he had a chance to tease out the implications of her comment, a black car swept down the road, skittering loose gravel as it did so. It ground to a halt next to Barr's car and Sean Mullan stepped out.

'Folks,' he said, by way of greeting, then moved across to his nephew's side of the car and waited for the boy to get out, business-like. Impatient.

Tony studied him. The man had aged more than any of them, he reckoned. The weight of power, perhaps: uneasy lies the head that wears the crown. His moustache was narrower now, more grey-blond than the brown of his youth. His hair had thinned and, though still brushed to one side, revealed more of the scalp below. His weight had settled at his gut, his belly hanging over the top of his belt. Only his clothes were better quality, his trousers a heavy canvas, his brown walking boots supple and well-polished. Either he'd been planning on a walking holiday when he was in Scotland, or he'd had to buy them new on the way here. Or, of course, he'd half expected that Duggan would demand his presence at the wood and had come across prepared for that eventuality.

'Let's get a move on,' Mullan said, tersely. 'Hugh,' he added, acknowledging the man who had now made his way out of the car and was draining the can. 'You've started early.'

'I started on the boat,' Duggan laughed.

'So I heard,' Mullan said, deliberately not looking at his nephew who had clearly been reporting back to his uncle.

'Good to see you, Seanie,' Hugh said, raising the tin.

The informality of the nickname seemed a little forced, a little desperate, as if he were letting everyone know that his relationship with Mullan was different from theirs. But the fact that he felt he needed to do so at all suggested it was not as close as perhaps he believed.

Mullan came across to Karen and Tony and shook hands, a little stiffly, with both of them. 'Thanks for doing this,' he said.

'Happy to,' Karen commented. 'It's the right thing to do.'

Mullan nodded, though seemed a little distracted, always keeping Duggan in his peripheral vision.

'Those days are long past,' he said. 'The new future demands that we make up for some of the cruelty of previous generations.'

It was an absurd soundbite, clearly prepared for the conference he was speaking at and cribbed to use now. They *were* the generation who had carried out this act and for all his attempts to dissociate himself, Mullan's hands were as bloody as anyone's. Bloodier, in fact.

'I don't think Hugh's too happy about it,' Tony said, nodding towards the man who had moved around to the boot of the car and was recovering a bag from the boot.

'Hugh?' Mullan said, sceptically. 'Sure, it was him suggested doing this in the first place. We'd never have asked you if he hadn't already agreed.'

'Hugh suggested it?'

Mullan nodded. 'He suggested it and he suggested this date for coming across.'

'What's that I did?' Duggan asked, having approached them, his small bag in one hand.

'I'm saying you suggested this trip, to find Kelly.'

Duggan nodded in agreement. 'That's right.'

Tony frowned. 'I thought you said you thought he should stay in the ground where he was.'

'This isn't about finding Martin,' Duggan said. 'Not for me. I told you that on the boat.'

'What is it about then, Hugh?' Mullan said, making no effort to disguise the exasperation in his voice.

'We put the wrong person in the ground thirty years ago. I want to know the truth.'

'Not this again, Hugh,' Mullan began, moving towards him, making for his car. 'I've no time for your bullshit.' He stopped suddenly, half raising his hands. 'What the fuck, Hugh?'

The woodland seemed to quieten, the bird song silenced as they all turned to where Hugh stood.

In his hand, he held a pistol.

The image took Tony back thirty years in an instant, to this same place, with Hugh again standing with a gun, moving into the woods to kill someone. It appeared to him to be the same gun that had been used that night.

'We're all going back into the woods,' Duggan said. 'And we're going to finish what we started thirty years ago.'

Karen moved a step closer to Tony and, instinctively, he found himself stepping forward a little, partially blocking her from Duggan's line of sight.

'Anyone who tries to leave will be joining Martin in the ground. Let's get started.'

THE WOODS

CHAPTER THIRTY-NINE

'Let's get started,' Mullan said.

They were sitting in the backroom of Betty's. Tony had got the call to school, telling him to present himself in the bar at 10.30 that morning to discuss what had happened at the weekend. No further elucidation had been provided

It was five days since he'd visited Alice Hamilton's house and spoken with her father. The man's initial reaction had been to call the police, but Tony had begged him not to, for so doing would surely result in Tony being killed.

'How's that my problem?' the man had said, receiver in hand.

'I'm risking my own life being here,' Tony said. 'If they know I warned you, I'm dead.'

'Who is they?'

'I can't tell you.'

Hamilton dialled the first number on the phone, allowed the dial to circle back, a rapid unspooling.

'I can't tell you,' Tony said again. 'I don't want anyone's blood on my hands. Yours or theirs.'

'They know what they're getting into when they target policemen.'

A second number dialled.

'They said the same about you when you targeted a child,' Tony said, glancing past Hamilton to where Alice sat on the step at the turn of the stairs, listening.

He saw something shift, almost imperceptibly, in Hamilton's expression: a wounding, his Adam's apple bobbing as he swallowed.

'I know Alice,' Tony said. 'I don't want anything to happen to her.'

'So you're the teacher from the North who bought her lunch and that?'

Tony nodded.

Hamilton considered for a moment, not taking his eyes off Tony, then replaced the receiver on the handset. 'You've two minutes. Get up the stairs, Alice.'

They waited until the heard the child's footfalls pad across the floor above them and the creak of her bedsprings. Hamilton nodded for Tony to speak. When he did so, he still spoke in hushed tones in case the girl was listening from her room.

'Someone will plant a device under your car this evening. It might already be there. They know who you are, what you did, what your routines are. Church on Sunday, your runs to the supermarket on a Friday, when you go out, when you come back.' He could see the man's expression grow a little wilder as he recognised the details of his own weekly routine.

'How do you know all this?'

Tony held his gaze, but fear prevented him from speaking. Irrespective, the man clearly guessed at the truth for he straightened a little, his mouth curled in disdain.

'It doesn't matter how I know,' Tony said, almost pleading now. 'You need to leave here. Go and don't come back. You find the device today, there'll be another one sometime down the line. For Alice's sake, you need to leave, go somewhere else, away from Glasgow altogether.'

'We can't just leave,' he scoffed. 'What about Alice herself?'

'What about her?'

'I can't just uproot her from her school, her friends.'

'She hates school,' Tony said. 'And I don't think leaving behind friends is going to be an issue for her.'

'Balls!' Hamilton spat.

'Trust me,' Tony said, trying to keep his voice low and calm, lest she was eavesdropping. 'Alice won't miss anyone in that school.'

'She said she was happy,' Hamilton said, as if pained both by the realisation of his daughter's experiences in school and the knowledge that she had taken this stranger into her confidences before him.

'She didn't want to worry you, I'd guess,' Tony said.

Hamilton nodded. 'They'll know someone talked,' he said. 'If I clear out completely. They'll know.'

'Not if there's no come back on any of us. That's why I need you to not tell the police here. If you just go, without incident, they might think it was just a coincidence.'

'People aren't stupid. They'll guess.'

'I know,' Tony said. 'But I couldn't live with myself if something happened to your daughter. And that includes her being left orphaned if something happened to you.'

Hamilton nodded again, as if he'd been privately considering something while Tony spoke and had reached his decision. He looked around, as if trying to decide where he might begin, what were the essentials that he and his daughter might need in the days ahead.

'Alice!' he called.

The rapidity of the steps from above suggested the girl knew what was coming. She appeared at the top of the stairs, already wearing jeans and a T-shirt. It was clear that she'd been listening. The ease with which she'd accepting the move made Tony wonder how many times before she'd been forced to leave her home in the middle of the night, how many other schools she'd joined and left.

'We need to leave,' her father said. 'Pack anything important. Don't forget Rosie.'

Tony assumed this was a toy of some sort, a suspicion confirmed when Hamilton turned and said, 'It's a ragdoll. She's too old for it, but her mother bought it for her before she passed.'

Tony nodded, did not speak, did not tell him he had seen the man carry the doll days earlier.

'I know you've taken a risk. For Alice,' Hamilton said. He extended his hand, a curt, sharp gesture. 'Thank you.'

Tony took it and shook. In so doing, he felt a moment of reconciliation with what had happened to Danny, the first seed of acceptance. He nodded. 'I'm sorry it came to this.'

Hamilton shrugged resignedly. 'I hope nothing happens to you for doing this.'

'It'll be fine,' Tony said, with no hint of conviction. 'Just keep Alice safe.'

As her father nodded, Alice herself came running down the stairs and across to Tony. She embraced him around the waist, her face pressed tight against his side.

'Thank you, sir,' she said.

Tony did not trust himself to speak, merely hugging her tightly and then letting her go. 'Maybe I'll see you again some time, eh?' he said finally.

She smiled, then ran back up the stairs to pack her things.

When he motioned to go towards the front door, Hamilton stopped him.

'Go out the back and across the yards, in case anyone is watching.'

He lay in his bed that night, waiting for the knock on his own door, expecting that when Duggan reached the house and realised Hamilton had gone, he would immediately suspect that someone had talked, someone had alerted the cop to the threat. And, based on the past few days, Tony was the only logical person that might be. He'd at least expected a knee-jerk reaction of some sort, hushed calls between them telling him what had happened, or more correctly, what had not. Instead, there had been silence. No calls, no messages, no word from anyone else.

Had Duggan called that night, Tony was ready to confess, defiant almost in the certainty of his righteousness. By 4am he had convinced himself of the nobility of his sacrifice. By 6am, he was shuddering in the bed as he waited for the knock that did not come, his fear a palpable force, twisting his hands in the bedsheets, popping sweat on his skin despite the relative cold of the morning. He would confess, he still believed, but he feared the form Duggan's retribution would take nevertheless.

He'd seen the pictures; bodies lying along the back alleys of Derry, stripped naked, their hands bound behind their backs, black plastic bags tied over their heads, the skin livid with bruising, the final shot, from behind the head, designed to destroy the face so that a wake with an open coffin would be impossible.

Or failing that, a body never returned, family members never really sure what had happened to their loved one, denied the final chapter of a burial, their story abandoned, unfinished.

Tony wondered whether he should call Karen, tell her what had happened, what he had done, but his anger both at what he had witnessed at the party and the paucity of her excuse for it was still raw. More importantly, he knew that in so doing, he would be putting her at risk, making her an accessory to his actions. Regardless of what had happened at the party, she did not deserve to suffer because of something he had done.

Then he began to panic. Maybe Duggan had gone ahead with setting the device and the police had been waiting for him. Maybe he'd been shot, lying in a puddle of blood in the driveway. Or worse, Tony thought, with some shame at his blatant self-interest, maybe he'd been captured, alive. Maybe he was being questioned, right now, giving up all their names and addresses, implicating them all. He sat up at the edge of the bed, scrolling through the channels on his radio alarm until he found a news report, waiting to hear of someone being arrested. But there was no such report.

All day, he listened to news reports, bought the local papers, watched seven different TV news programmes, all the time waiting to hear something about events in Foxbar.

But nothing was reported.

By late evening, when there was still no news, no one had called, and apparently Duggan had not been arrested, Tony began to convince himself that perhaps Duggan had assumed the cop had got lucky, had gone somewhere coincidentally the night before the planned attack. It couldn't be the first time that such a thing had happened. In fact, perhaps Duggan was waiting for his return, not yet realising that the man, and (more importantly for Tony) his daughter, had managed to avoid their fate.

That being the case, he decided, his only option was to brazen it out. No one could prove that he'd had anything to do with the cop's disappearance. He would deny everything. Yes, he'd had qualms in the days before the planned attack, but surely some of the others must have had, too.

He couldn't believe that Karen hadn't once considered the morality of what they were doing, hadn't once had second thoughts, expressed doubts. Even on the drive from Paisley, that night they'd brought the car back with the gun in the boot, she'd wondered whether they were wrong in what they were doing. Surely her scruples could only have deepened when they targeted a real person. And Kelly knew the man, had a shared history with him. Perhaps he'd harboured some secret doubts himself. Only Duggan, Tony was convinced, would not have thought twice about the ethical consequences of what they were doing.

By the following day, he'd convinced himself that his best approach was to say nothing, admit nothing. To act as if nothing had happened. Feign both ignorance and innocence.

That confidence was shaken a little when, the day after, he got a phone call to school, supposedly from a parent. A voice he did not recognise, though with an accent he could place as close to home, informed him that he was required to present himself at Betty's at 10.30am to discuss recent events. That was all. The caller hung up.

Tony felt his legs weaken, felt his bowels loosen as he replaced the receiver. It wasn't Duggan, of that he was sure. Did that mean they'd brought someone in to investigate? Did that mean they suspected Duggan himself as well? If that was the case, there was no doubt Duggan would implicate him, tell them all about his change of heart when he learned about the cop's child.

That day he'd contemplated pretending he was sick. He'd phone the bar, leave a message for whomever, say that he'd food poisoning, say he'd come the next day. But he realised it would make no difference. They'd suspect him straight away, would come to his flat and forcibly remove him. If he was going to claim innocence, he had to look innocent.

Shauna Laird briefly came to his mind, and with her, *Macbeth*: 'to beguile the time, look like the time...' He'd not heard about her funeral arrangements yet, and he realized, with a sudden stab of fear, that his funeral might well come before hers. Unless he denied everything. What could they do to him then?

In fact, if the bar was busy with people about who would see him coming in, meeting this man who had called, there would be witnesses. What, indeed, could they do to him?

But he knew what they could do, which is why, by the time he reached Betty's that morning, having had to phone in sick to school, he'd already had to stop twice to vomit through sheer terror, his pulse drumming in his ears and his limbs humming with the constant drip feed of adrenaline running through his system.

He paused outside Betty's, taking a breath, wondering whether he should turn and walk away, but the door opened and Duggan stood inside, holding it ajar for him, Hades at the entrance to his kingdom.

'Come in, Tony,' he said grimly. 'We're through here.'

The bar was empty, the shutters pulled.

'Betty's not well,' Duggan explained. 'She's closed up for the day. A family thing.'

Tony nodded, tried to control his shivering, tightened his jaw a little. The empty bar wasn't a good sign.

Duggan led him through the bar into a back room, a lounge he'd not seen before, smaller than the main area; the type of place to be used by families looking to offer soup and sandwiches after a funeral, perhaps. That thought brought him no comfort.

Three seats sat behind a table at one end of the room, a single chair sat in the middle of the room in front of the table. The room was dimly lit, so Tony had to squint a little to see the two men sitting behind the table: he recognised one as Sean Mullan, didn't know the second. Duggan moved forward and took the third seat.

'Sit down, Tony,' Mullan said.

Tony shuffled slowly forward towards the seat that Mullan had indicated. Only in doing so did he hear the dull crinkle of the plastic sheeting as he stood on it. He looked down, dumbly, to see that a square of builder's plastic, twelve feet or side each side, had been set on the floor, the chair at its centre.

'Jesus Christ,' he muttered, backing away, the bile rising raw in his throat once more.

'Sit down!' the unknown man said. 'It's OK.'

Tony stood a moment, as if in a paralysis of fear, before Mullan spoke more gently.

'It's OK, Tony. We just want to talk. That's all. Sit down, please.'

His voice was so reasonable, so calm. He smiled at Tony, might have winked at him, were it not that the lights were so dim, his face so shadowed, Tony could not be certain.

Still, he moved forward and sat as instructed, swallowed dryly, waited.

'Good man,' Mullan said. 'Let's get started. We've some questions for you, Tony. You're not in trouble. We just want to talk. You know me and Hugh. We're joined by a comrade who will act as an impartial adviser. Is that OK?'

Absurdly, the situation felt more like a job interview than an interrogation, as if he were applying to work in the bar. Until the unknown man spoke.

'You know why we're here,' he said. 'All we need from you is the truth, son. Let's not make this any harder than it needs to be for anyone. We already know what's happened: you just need to tell us the truth.'

CHAPTER FORTY

'I just want to know the truth,' Duggan said. 'I want to know who set Martin Kelly up.'

The locked gate meant they'd had to walk the incline up towards the tree line, a path along which, Tony thought he remembered, they had been able to drive the last time they had been here.

'No one set him up,' Mullan said. 'You were there; we investigated it and he was the one we identified. *We* identified,' he repeated, indicating both himself and Duggan.

'Here's the thing, Sean. I don't believe you. The more I've thought about it, the more convinced I am that Martin was killed so someone else could cover for what they did.'

'No one else thinks that, Hugh,' Mullan said. 'Just you. We were all happy just letting him be forgotten.'

'No, you weren't,' Duggan smiled. 'You need his grave. Looking to bolster your leadership chances with an act of reconciliation, like a fucking vulture picking over his bones for your own self-interest.'

'And for the good of the country,' Mullan said curtly. 'What's your interest then, Hugh? What are you looking for? You're the one shot him and now here you are, looking to dig him up again?'

'I know what I did,' Duggan spat. 'I think about it often. He's the only one won't give me peace.'

'You're looking for peace?' Mullan laughed. 'Says the man with the gun.'

'Kettles and pots, Sean,' Duggan said. 'The great peacemaker with his armalite behind his back.'

'Those days are gone, Hugh,' Mullan said.

'But not forgotten. I want the truth of what happened.'

'The truth?' Karen snapped. 'Whose truth? You've heard us these past few hours; we can't even agree on our memories of back then, we all remember what happened so differently.'

'There's some things none of us will have forgotten,' Duggan said, stealing a glance at Mullan. 'No matter how many versions of the past we've heard since.'

'Whatever you think is going to happen in here, Hugh,' Mullan said, 'you're wrong.'

'We'll see.'

They moved their way into the edge of the woodland. Tony had wondered on the way across whether he might recognise anything in particular, but the truth was, it could have been any woodland anywhere in the country. Sycamore, beech and alder predominated. The air beneath the canopy was chilled and damp, rich with the tannic scent of last autumn's leaf fall mushed from winter snows. It hadn't rained for a week or so, yet the ground was still soft beneath their feet, the clay clinging to the grips of Tony's boots as he made his way deeper into the speckled shadows the late spring sunshine scattered over the woodland floor.

'It's the wrong season,' Tony said.

'What?'

'We came here in winter,' he explained. 'The trees were stripped. It's going to look different.'

'We'll be alright,' Hugh said. 'We headed due north for about half an hour. That's enough to get us started.'

They fell into natural groups: Karen and Mullan walked ahead, deep in discussion. Tony guessed she was quizzing him about how much he'd known about Duggan's planned mission and, perhaps more importantly, what they could do about it. Tony wondered at how stoically Mullan had taken Duggan's revelation of the gun. Perhaps a lifetime spent using them or in the company of those that did had inured him to them. Or else, he had suspected all along that this was Duggan's plan – that the events which began, for Tony at least, with an army Land Rover blindly careening down a street just as his brother walked around the corner, could only reach their natural conclusion in this woodland, in this way.

Rather than asking the man himself, Tony slowed his step a little, to walk alongside Barr, Duggan trailing them by some seven or eight feet.

'How are you holding up?' Tony asked, assuming the youth to be frightened by the turn of events.

'All good,' Barr said. 'Good to have Uncle Sean here.'

'This wasn't your fault,' Tony offered.

Barr looked at his quizzically. 'What wasn't?'

'All this. No one could have guessed what Duggan was planning. It's got a bit out of hand.'

'Hugh's had his problems,' Barr said. 'Uncle Sean will take care of all this. Don't be worrying.'

Tony was struck by how the dynamic had shifted, with the youth now attempting to console him. And yet, strangely, he realized that he was not worried. Not because of Mullan or anything he might do to salvage the situation but because of himself.

He thought of his empty house, the church, cavernous and echoing as he cleaned it, Ann's grave, narrow and silent, his rituals, designed to inure him to his own loneliness. He realized, with only the faintest note of pain, that if Duggan killed the lot of them, no one would really notice he was gone. He'd just be a footnote to the story of Mullan's death in the papers; no one would mourn his passing.

'Everyone's gone,' he said, and surprised himself to hear the words had been spoken aloud.

'What?'

'Nothing,' Tony said, unwilling to share something so personal.

'I trust my uncle,' Barr said, continuing with his own train of thought. 'He's come out of worse than this unscathed.'

'How long have you been working with him?'

'About three years,' Barr said. 'He took me under his wing; an apprenticeship, I suppose.'

'Do you enjoy it?'

Barr nodded. 'It's important work.'

Tony wondered at the nature of the work that he considered so important. Driving old killers around the country, listening to their war stories, or multiple versions of them? Was that important? Perhaps, it was all part of the healing process that people said the country needed to undertake before it could be whole again. But none of this felt like healing, none of it cathartic.

'I don't understand why someone of your generation would want any part of this,' Tony said. 'I don't get what the attraction is. I know why we all got involved; we lived through it, but your generation? You've a choice.'

'A choice?' Barr said, incredulously. 'There's no choice. The work that started a hundred years ago isn't finished yet.'

'What about the peace process?'

'Peace and the absence of fighting are two different things,' Barr said. 'The war never ended, the rules of engagement just changed. If we stopped now, what would have been the point?'

'Do you think there was a point? In the end?'

'My granda was interned,' Barr said. 'When I was young, he used to talk about what happened to him in front of me. He wouldn't tell his family, wouldn't tell Uncle Sean, but he talked about it to me.'

Tony tried to keep his expression neutral, even as he privately considered the wisdom of a grandparent discussing such a thing with a child.

'He was kept for weeks,' Barr said. 'Before he went in, he was a big man, delivered coal in the city. Afterwards, he was afraid of his shadow, didn't have any strength left. I remember he couldn't lift us as grandkids, like we were too heavy for him. Even my cousin's baby, he couldn't hold, said his arms were shaking and he didn't want to drop it. We'd an allotment that he worked in, was the only thing he wanted to do after he got out, and I used to help him pot the flowers. He'd give them out to all the neighbours. Didn't keep any for himself; I think he just liked the idea of putting something into the earth and watching it grow, making the streets around where he lived brighter, better, knowing no one could stop him from doing it. He used to chat while he worked, almost like he didn't realize I was there, like he was talking to himself. He had this old radio; a wireless he called it.'

He glanced at Tony to check that he was listening.

'He used to tune it to between radio stations, so it would just play, what do you call it, white noise?

Tony nodded.

'The first time I tried to change it to a proper channel, he went ballistic. He tuned it back, turned it up, listening to this fuzz of noise. 'Listen carefully,' he said, smiling, 'and you can start to hear things. I thought it was rain at first; I thought they were playing the sound of rain, but it's not rain. But if you listen you can hear a pattern to it. That's how you survive it,' he said. 'You let it wash over you and look for the meaning in it. You can give it whatever you want, because it's just for you."

He kicked a rock from the path they were treading between the trees. It skittered off through the ground cover.

'I thought he was mental. But every day he listened to that noise, as if he was looking to find something in it he'd not been able to the whole time they'd played it into his cell, stopping him sleeping, him with a bag over his head the whole time so he couldn't tell if it was day or night.'

'What happened to him?'

Tony felt his own breath shorten, wiped a sheen of sweat from his face as he tried not to register what the youth was saying, tried not to imagine it too deeply lest it brought back his own memories, ones he'd tried hard to forget. But it was too late.

'They made him confess to all kinds of things.'

'Everyone confesses in the end,' Tony remembered.

CHAPTER FORTY-ONE

'Everyone confesses in the end,' the unnamed man said, sitting behind the table in Betty's back lounge. 'But if you've done nothing wrong, you've nothing to worry about. All we're going to be doing is asking a few questions.'

Tony swallowed dryly and nodded. 'What do I call you?'

'Nothing, son,' the man said. 'My name doesn't matter. Let's talk about your Danny, shall we?'

The topic threw Tony a little. He'd expected them to talk about Hamilton, about Alice. He'd been ready for that.

'How did you feel about what happened him?'

'Sad,' Tony said, aware of the inadequacy of the word.

'Sad?' the man asked, skeptically.

'Angry. Hurt. Sad for my loss,' he said, keen to appear forthcoming. 'A little jealous, I guess,' he added.

'Jealous?'

Tony didn't know why he'd said it, why he'd felt compelled to admit something that still shamed him. He had felt a little jealous, not of Danny's death, but of the outpouring of love for his brother which had followed, for the effect Danny's passing had on his parents, the void which was left, the displaying of pictures long consigned to drawers and boxes, now revisited, reappraised, as if their value had changed irrevocably. It was not a part of him he wished to acknowledge. 'Jealous of those who could do something about it,' he lied.

The man nodded, more in acknowledgment that Tony had answered than in acceptance of his explanation, but did not speak. As a result, Tony felt he needed to keep talking, to fill the silence, to distract the three faces staring at him across the desk, as if his words might stop their unflinching gaze.

'I wanted someone to pay for it,' he said.

'Your father didn't,' the man said. Tony glanced at Mullan, clearly the source of this information, but his expression was implacable.

'My father didn't want anyone else to suffer.'

'Why? Does he not support the cause?'

Tony shrugged. 'He believes in civil rights. He's a pacifist.'

'Are you?'

'A little,' Tony said.

'Yet you still got involved?'

'I was angry. Like I said.'

'*Was* angry?'

'Am?'

'You sure?'

Tony nodded.

'So you don't share your father's views?'

'A little,' Tony said, frustrated at the circular nature of the conversation. 'But I wanted someone to pay for Danny.'

'You spoke to Hugh last week about your concerns with the recent mission.'

This was Mullan speaking now, his first time having done so since the questioning had started.

Tony nodded, glanced at Duggan, expecting to see some response, but, like the others, he remained impassive, staring at Tony.

'What was the content of that conversation?'

'Hugh's obviously already told you. Ask him,' Tony said, beginning to feel a little riled at the manner in which they were treating him. 'He's sitting right there.'

'We'd like to get your version of events.'

'I realized that the officer we were watching had a child,' Tony said, being extra careful not to use names, either for the man or Alice, which might suggest more intimate knowledge of them than would have been expected from him.

'And?'

'I was worried that, in the event of an attack, the child might be killed, too.'

'What difference would that have made?' the unnamed man asked.

'I didn't think it fair that a child should be killed,' Tony said, tamping down the tone of sarcasm in his voice that he should have to explain such a thing. Clearly he'd not tamped it down enough, for the man bridled a little and straightened in his seat.

'Don't get smart with me, son,' he said. 'What did the child of a cop matter to you?'

'She didn't matter,' Tony said. 'Beyond I didn't want to be part of something which resulted in a child's death. My own brother was just a child, really. I saw what that did to my family. I didn't want to be part of that.'

'Badly enough to sabotage the whole mission?'

'Of course not,' Tony said, then realized that he'd yet to ask why they were questioning him. His mind raced as he tried to assimilate all that had been said. Would they suspect him because he hadn't asked why they were there? Would he be expected to know that it hadn't gone ahead as planned? 'Why, did the mission not go as planned?'

'No. The target left his home in the early hours of the morning, before we could plant the device,' Duggan said. 'He's not been back since. Our sources tell us he's left the area completely.'

'Maybe something spooked him,' Tony offered.

'Some*one* is much more likely.'

'And do you think... it was one of us?'

Mullan nodded. 'Only a certain number of people knew what was planned,' he said. 'That means there are only a certain number of people who could have been responsible. We intend to find out which of them it was.'

'What's more interesting,' the unnamed man said, 'is that you've only just asked what all this is about.'

'I just assumed it was...' Tony began, but he could find no suitable excuse. 'I've nothing to hide,' he added, feeling that a protestation of innocence would be expected in the situation.

'Everyone has something to hide,' the man said. 'And like I said, everyone confesses in the end.'

CHAPTER FORTY-TWO

'In the end, they tried to blame him for a bomb attack in Belfast. He confessed to it, even though he'd been on holidays when it happened,' Barr said. 'I mind standing in the shed with him at the allotment, the radio buzzing in the background, and him holding this pot in his hands. He just stood there, the pot in his hands, his arms outstretched, just standing like this.'

He mimicked the position, standing still, arms stretched out in front of them, then began to shudder.

'He just started going like that, his arms shaking like he'd Parkinson's or something. "Can I put it down?" he asked. "Can I put it down, sir?" I tried talking to him, but he wasn't there; he was somewhere inside his head, a different place, talking to different people. I went over to him and shook him, called him "Granda, Granda," but he just looked at me like I was a stranger. The tears streaming down his face. "I can't do it no more, sir," he said. "I can't hold it no more." Then he started whimpering, like a baby, his spit bubbling on his lips. "Don't hit me, sir," he said. "Please don't hit me." Then this smell I can't forget, the piss running down his leg where he stood. I told my da that evening and he stopped me going to the allotment with him on my own. They sent him to the doctor,

I think, and he was put inside for a while. The family didn't talk about it, like it was a dirty secret, something to be ashamed of.'

'We were never ashamed of him,' Sean Mullan said, glancing over his shoulder at them, having been listening to the conversation about his father. 'He had soldier's wounds. He died a soldier.'

'What happened to him in the end?'

'He took a heart attack,' Barr said. 'I went down to the shed one day, about two years later, to leave down lunch for him. My granny had made sandwiches and a flask of tea. He was lying on the floor when I went in.'

'I'm sorry,' Tony said, quietly.

'He was a good man,' Mullan said. 'He didn't deserve what was done to him.'

'I remember for weeks after the incident with the pot, I couldn't sleep. I still dream about it, about what I should have done, should have said. I thought I should have offered to hold the pot for him, take over his torture for a while, give him a break. Instead I stood there looking at him, not knowing what to do.'

'You were a kid,' Mullan said. 'No one knew what to do. Nowadays they'd be calling it PTSD but, in those days, it was just nerves. He went to the doctor, got a bottle of valium, the tablets rattling round in his pocket everywhere he went afterwards.'

Tony thought of Hamilton and the Land Rover driver who had killed Danny, too. Both of them would have been diagnosed with the same, if then was now, he reflected. Then and now.

'I still dream of what happened to him,' Barr said. 'Since I was a kid, I dream I'm standing there, holding on to whatever they made him hold, whatever stress position they put him into. I wake and my muscles are numb with it.'

Tony nodded. He didn't admit that he sometimes dreamt of Danny, dreamt that he'd gone down to meet him and had stopped him at the corner, before he'd stepped out into the path of the car. Or that he dreamt more often of Alice. In those dreams she was still a child, standing in an empty building. Tony released that the building was crumbling around her and he needed to find his way inside, to reach her, to save her. Sometimes he did and woke with a sense of warmth, as if his sleep had refreshed him. Other times, just as he reached her, the building would collapse around them and he'd wake, frequently with a migraine aura flickering around the edges of his field of vision, and find it impossible to easily dispel his grief at her imagined passing.

'So, yeah, I think there is a point. I think on some level what happened to him was passed to me, like it hadn't been resolved, hadn't been dealt with. I don't think he'll ever be a rest until the job's done. It's like that O'Donovan Rossa line; he'll never be at peace.'

Tony walked alongside the youth, but did not speak. If he was honest, Barr's conviction frightened him. He'd assumed that most people had moved on with the relative peace, had acclimatized to the changed circumstances. He knew some communities still relied on the paramilitaries as a police force, often used them to help discipline their own children, but he'd always thought such people were the exception.

He'd taught one such child, a year or two before Ann's illness drove him to early retirement. The boy's name was Brandon. He'd been involved in anti-social behaviour, breaking windows, a little joyriding. When he'd progressed onto dealing drugs in school, the principal had called in his mother. She'd sat in the office and decried her powerlessness to deal with the boy. When the principal had suggested getting the police involved, she'd launched into a diatribe about traitors and instead promised that she would deal with it once and for all. That evening, the boy got a message to present himself the following day at 3pm to an alleyway in the city, to be shot. If he came peacefully, they'd only do one leg; if they had to come looking for him, he'd be shot in both.

At the appointed time the next day, his mother drove him up to the entrance to the alley and sat waiting in the car while he made his way along to where the man stood, masked, gun in hand. The boy's mother had made him wear shorts, to keep both the bullet wound and his clothes clean and save the expense of buying a new pair of tracksuit bottoms. She'd sat in the car, waiting for the punishment to be done, fingering a pair of rosary beads as she convinced herself that she'd done the right thing. When she heard the crack of the shot, she got out. The masked man passed her, pulling off his balaclava. 'Tell him it'll be in the head the next time, if he doesn't clean up his act,' she'd been told.

She went up to where he lay writhing on the ground. They'd shot him through the calf muscle, the bullet exiting the other side so that the wound was clean. She helped him to his feet and drove him to the hospital. A month later, he was back in school, hobbling along the corridors, on his way to the toilets at breaktime, business as usual.

Tony had reflected on the discussion in the staffroom after the events, the scornful manner in which his colleagues had spoken about the mother, about her choices. In doing so, he'd assumed that everyone felt the same way, that everyone considered this abnormal, could see that such behaviour was aberrant, and was destined to dwindle and die. Recent events had forced him to reconsider, though. The rise in populism in the community had strengthened feelings in favour of such rough justice. As such groups tightened their hold on the local estates, their rejection of the uneasy peace inculcated itself among the generations growing up. It was children such as those whom Tony had assumed would want to see a return to violence, not those like Barr whose family had suffered through it.

'I'm sorry to hear that, about your grandfather,' he managed, finally.

They'd moved deeper into the forest now. Across to their left, a huge elm had fallen, its broken bough resting against the limbs of an oak next to it, supporting its weight. For a moment, he wondered if it was the trunk they had used as a makeshift bridge, but this tree fall was too recent, the leaves still fresh on the branches. Besides, there was no stream nearby that he could hear.

At the sound of their arrival, a squirrel scampered up the bough, bounding up through the branches of the oak, frightened by their appearance. Tony stopped, gazing up. The woods were still, the road far enough away that the sounds of traffic had silenced, the soundtrack to their journey the whistling of birds, the raucousness of crows. After a moment, he heard again the familiar building of a jet engine's roar as a plane took off from the nearby airport.

'Do you recognize any of it?' Duggan asked, drawing alongside him. His breath wheezed in his throat, a sheen of sweat shining on his forehead.

'Nothing,' Tony admitted. 'Apart from the sounds of the planes. It could be anywhere.'

'I suppose you were far enough gone the last time we were here,' Duggan admitted, with a brief nod. 'After our chat and everything.'

'Our chat?' Tony repeated incredulous at the euphemism.

'Our questions,' Duggan said.

CHAPTER FORTY-THREE

'We've a few more questions,' the unnamed man said.

Tony had asked if he could use the bathroom, to which the three men opposite him had laughed.

'What's the situation with you and Karen?' Mullan asked.

'What do you mean?'

'Are you an item?'

Tony glanced again at Duggan, once again clearly the course of this information. He wondered just how much the man had been feeding back to Mullan in Derry.

'No,' Tony said, simply.

'Were you one?'

Tony scowled lightly. 'For a while.'

'How serious was it?'

'That's none of your business,' Tony said, the turn in questioning angering him.

The unnamed man stood up and walked in front of the desk. He leant against it, no more than four feet from where Tony sat.

'How serious was it?'

'That's not relevant,' Tony said, the man's size tempering his earlier bravery in challenging them.

Despite this, the man moved forward quickly, hitting Tony on the side of the head with his cupped hand, just over the ear. The blow knocked him off his chair, onto the floor.

He looked up at the man, more stunned by the blow than anything. His ear sang, a high-pitched whistling that he tried to shake away. He reached out for the chair to steady himself, in an attempt to get to his feet. The man held out a hand which he refused, scrabbling for the seat.

As he rose, the man cut in sharply near him and punched him this time, a quick, curt blow to his cheek bone, not hard enough to break it, but enough to leave his teeth hurting, his eye stinging as he hit the floor again. His head spun and it took him a moment to orientate himself enough to sit up.

He looked up at the man, reluctant to rise again lest it elicited a third blow.

'You can get up,' the man said, moving away from him. 'Don't tell us again what's our business and what isn't.'

'I don't have to take this,' he said, spitting onto the ground, the saliva thick and bloody. He prodded with his tongue, found a tooth in his upper jaw loosened a little, shifting under pressure.

'That was just to put some manners into you, son,' the man said, standing to the side of the room now. He reached down into the seats of one of the booths there and produced a length of wood tapered at one end. A baseball bat. Even in the dim light, Tony could see the glints where nails had been hammered right through the wood, their points piercing through the opposite side.

'So, you and Karen,' Mullan began. 'What's the situation?'

'We were dating.'

'Dating?

245

Tony nodded, tried to stand, righted the chair on which he had been sitting and sat once more.

'Dating, going for dinner? Dating, fucking? Which?'

'I don't–' Tony began, but the man stood, the bat in his hand.

'Answer the question.'

'Both,' Tony said.

'Dinner and fucking?'

He nodded, trying to suppress his blush.

'So why not anymore?'

'We had a fight,' Tony said.

'About what?'

'Private stuff.'

'Nothing's private. What stuff?'

'What has this got to do with the cop?' Tony said, his voice more pleading than he'd intended.

The air filled with the swish as the man swung at him. Tony tried to shift, jumping to his feet and moving back, tripping over the seat. In so doing, the bat connected with his calf, at first a dull thud which then gave way, as the numbness passed, to the piercing pain of the puncture wounds from the nails.

'Jesus,' he yelped, putting his hand to his leg, feeling the frayed edges of the holes in his jeans, already dampening with blood.

'Tony, we're trying to be civil here,' Mullan said. 'We need to find out what happened at the weekend and that means knowing what happened before that, too, with everyone involved. No one wants to hurt you, if you'll just tell us the truth.'

Tony tried not to cry, tried to stymie the tears that were burning in his eyes. 'I don't… we broke up. We're not talking.'

Mullan nodded in a manner that made Tony think that he'd already known this, that Tony was simply confirming something rather than offering them anything new.

'I was meant to meet her at a party last Friday. It was the night I spoke to Hugh about the kid. By the time I got there, she was in the bedroom with some other fella.'

'And you've not spoken since?'

'She tried to explain but I'd no interest in listening. We're not speaking anymore.'

'Do you trust her?' the man with the bat said, his tone changed slightly, less antagonistic.

'What?'

'Do you trust her?' he repeated, more slowly, his voice raised, perhaps suspecting Tony's hearing had been damaging by the blow he'd dealt him.

'In what way?'

'In any way? Trust is trust. Do – you – trust – her?'

'She didn't tell the cop about us, if that's what you mean.'

'How do you know?'

'She's not that type.'

'She's the type to fuck someone when her boyfriend's late to a party,' he said, simply.

'That's not what happened,' Tony said, beginning to get confused, unsure what the point of the discussion had been, suddenly wary that now might be just the time when he'd say something he shouldn't, inadvertently reveal her knew more than he should about the cop, about Alice.

'So what then?'

Tony felt his eyes burn, his face blaze with shame at what they had done to him, clasping his calf in one hand, the other wiping his face.

'I thought she was… she's a decent person,' he said, and realized that despite what he'd seen at the party, he believed it. 'Whatever happened that night, she's not the type that would have sold us out.'

'Now's the chance to get your own back on her,' the man said. 'You can fuck her over the same way she did you.'

Tony thought of Karen's face the morning after the party. She had seemed genuinely distressed at what had happened, genuine in her denial of her own complicity in the events of the evening. He thought of her, lying next to him, the touch of her, the vulnerability of her in the story of her father's death. None of that was fake. She was, he believed, a decent person. And she didn't deserve to suffer for what he had done.

'I *know* she didn't tell on us,' Tony said. 'I *know* it for a fact.'

He waited for a moment, to see if they would push him on how he knew it, ready to confess what he had done, to protect her.

'You know for a fact?'

The man stood, the length of wood in his hand.

Tony felt his confidence falter a little. 'Yes,' he managed, his tongue thick and dry in his mouth.

'Funny, she said the same thing about you,' Mullan said.

The atmosphere in the room seemed to almost imperceptibly shift, like a held breath released.

'Get yourself a drink,' Mullan said. There's a bottle of Jamesons on the bar over there. Take a breather. We need to talk.'

CHAPTER FORTY-FOUR

'We need to talk,' Tony said.

Duggan had stopped, seemingly getting his bearings in the woodland, affording Tony a chance to catch up with Karen and Mullan.

'What about?' Mullan said, smiling ruefully.

'What are we going to do?'

'We're going to find Martin Kelly's grave, as we'd agreed.'

'You know what I mean,' Tony snapped.

Mullan shook his head. 'Hugh's hurting. That's all.'

'He's threatening to kill one of us,' Karen said.

'Only if he discovers that the wrong person died thirty years ago. He was part of the process that identified Kelly in the first place, so he should know that that conviction was secure then and remains so now.'

Tony waited a beat before he spoke. 'And what if he discovers that Kelly shouldn't have died?'

'*Then* we have a problem,' Mullan said. 'Hugh's an attack dog. That's how he thinks. It's like you said; he's threatening. That's what dogs do, they growl. It's how they're trained.'

'I can hear you,' Duggan said.

'I assumed you could, Hugh,' Mullan said. 'You know it's true. That's what you were good at.'

'While you sat back giving orders, not wanted to get your hands dirty.'

Mullan accepted the criticism with a nod. 'Why keep a dog and bark yourself?'

Tony wondered at his calmness. Mullan continued moving through the woodland, stepping over tangles of brambles and weeds which covered the ground in areas where the sun was able to break the canopy, as if he already knew the location to which they were going, the end to which they were being drawn. Tony, for his part, knew different. They had killed the wrong person. That truth had yet to be revealed.

'I'm no dog,' Hugh snapped.

'You're a good man, Hugh,' Mullan said. 'But you're wrong in this.'

'Someone lied to us,' Duggan said. 'In Betty's that morning. Someone lied.'

'About what?'

'About Martin. Everyone confesses, Doherty said. But Martin didn't. No matter what was done to him.'

'Martin was a special case,' Mullan said. 'He'd been lifted on and off for years by the cops for dealing. Hell, even the first time we spoke to him in Derry, after we caught him red-handed, selling, he denied it to my face. He had a skill in lying. It was useful in its way, but you couldn't trust him. Not in the slightest.'

'I trusted him,' Duggan said. 'He was always straight with me.'

'Lie with dogs and you'll catch fleas,' Mullan muttered.

'What the hell is that supposed to mean?' Duggan snapped, but Mullan walked on and did not respond.

Karen stopped and surveyed around her, turning her head slowly from side to side, searching for something that might trigger recognition. 'Are you sure this is the right way?'

'Yes,' Duggan said, though without his earlier confidence.

'I don't remember any of this,' Tony said.

'I wouldn't remember it anyway,' Karen said. 'It was dark. We were almost delirious.'

'There was a tree trunk, a stream,' Tony said. 'We crossed it about half way through.'

'Maybe it's rotted,' Mullan said. 'The stream dried up.'

'The track of it will be there,' Duggan said. 'The memory of it.'

'I think we're off a little,' Tony said. 'I remember when we came in, the sun was setting already, but you could still see it burning on the horizon. My memory was that it was up to the left more, so, if we're meant to head north, that should be across to our right a little.'

Mullan looked at Duggan. 'You're the man in charge. You wanted to come here. Is he right?'

Duggan looked around him, staring straight ahead as far as he could see, then across to the right, where a path of sorts seemed to insinuate its way through the trees.

'We'll move right a bit,' he concluded. 'If the path doesn't take us anywhere, we can always come back here.'

'We'll never be back,' Tony muttered.

'What?'

Tony shrugged. '*The Road Not Taken*? He keeps one for another day but knows he'll never be back.'

He glanced at Mullan, but he seemed disinterested at best.

'I used to teach it,' Tony explained. 'How your life choices changed your later life.' He lifted eyes a little, looked at Karen, reflected that the last time they'd walked through these woods, they'd had a possible future together lying ahead. Now, they had separate pasts behind them. The problem was, Tony couldn't work out what choice he'd made which had resulted in that outcome, or indeed if the choice had been his at all.

As if sensing his gaze, or sharing his thought, Karen looked up at him, raising her eyes from the undergrowth which she was scanning to ensure she didn't trip. She smiled, a little sadly, and he wondered if it was for the graveness of the situation in which they now found themselves, or in shared recognition of the thing they had lost.

'How much longer?' Barr asked, his voice a mild shock after his long silence. The question held no tiredness, no frustration.

'We're not done yet,' Duggan muttered.

CHAPTER FORTY-FIVE

'We're not done yet,' Mullan said. 'Sit down again.'

Tony had drained a glass of Jamesons, swirling the whiskey in his mouth to help rinse away the taste of blood. He knew people used alcohol to clean wounds, so hoped that the whiskey would keep the loosened tooth clean and free from infection. His leg was another matter. The sharpness of the initial injury had passed and now his skin felt inflamed, each small wound angry.

'Can I go now?'

The question elicited a laugh from the three men.

Tony took his seat, but the three men remained standing, Mullan and Duggan leaning against the desk, the unnamed man standing to one side, nearer to Tony, the length of wood in his hand once more.

'Where were you on Saturday night?'

'In my flat.'

'Anyone with you?'

Tony shook his head. 'No one.'

'You were out during the day,' Mullan said. 'Hugh here called with you in the afternoon and you weren't there. Where were you?'

'I was working.'

The blow was sudden and sharp, the wooden bat being swung low, striking him across both shins. He almost toppled off the chair, more with the shock than the pain, though both were considerable. He looked at the unnamed man angrily, as if demanding to know what he'd done to deserve being hit.

'You're a teacher,' the man explained. 'Schools don't open on Saturdays.'

'We had an Open Day,' Tony spat. 'The school was open for next year's pupils, you fucking prick!'

The man came forward quickly, fist raised, but Tony was expecting it this time and curled himself a little in his seat, his hands up over his head and face, his stomach curved, his knees brought up, defensively. He felt a series of glancing blows on his hands and arms, waiting out the attack until he saw, through the gaps, the feet of the unnamed man retreat back to his position. He straightened himself up tentatively, wary that a second series of blows might follow if the man felt frustrated by the lack of impact of the first.

'I'll use the nailed side next time, son, you don't watch your mouth.'

Tony realized that the blow across his shins had been from the flat side of the baton, for while his shins sang in pain, he did not feel the individual piercings that his calf muscle still carried.

'Fair enough,' Mullan said. 'It was Open Day. When did that finish?'

'About four, I think,' Tony said. 'I went home afterwards.'

'And what then?'

Tony feigned ignorance. 'What? I ate my dinner.'

'And then?'

'I don't remember. I watched TV, I think.'

'What did you watch?'

Tony couldn't remember the TV schedules from the weekend, couldn't be sure that whatever programme he suggested had either been on, or that some of them wouldn't ask him what happened during it to test whether he'd actually seen it. He knew enough not to lead himself into a blind alley.

'Actually, I went to the cinema,' he said.

'Which one?'

'The Odeon on Renfield Street.'

'What was showing?'

'*The Living Daylights*.'

'What time?'

Tony tried desperately to remember what time the showing had been the night he and Karen had gone to see it. He knew the Odeon were still showing it in the smallest screen, hoped the times hadn't changed.

'It was the 8.30 showing.'

Mullan nodded, then tapped Duggan on the arm. The man rose, wordlessly and walked across to the bar. Tony followed him with his gaze, watched as he lifted a phone and a Yellow Pages from beneath the counter. He flicked through the directory, found the number and dialed, Tony's panic growing with each click as the dial revolved back into place.

The room was silent, save for Tony's breathing and the thudding of his heart which he felt sure the others must be able to hear.

'Hi, I'm looking to see if you're still showing *The Living Daylights*?'

A pause. 'You're not,' Duggan said, turning to glance at Tony.

Tony felt the room spin, placed his hand on the seat of the chair, to steady himself, swallowed dryly, the taste of whiskey in his mouth now sickening him, burning his throat and chest.

'Tell me, was it running last weekend? Saturday night?'

Another pause, a held breath.

'What time was the screening?'

Tony allowed himself a breath; at least it had been on.

'That's great, thanks.'

Duggan replaced the receiver and walked back to the desk.

'8.15pm,' he said as he passed the chair. Tony could smell stale sweat off the man and wondered whether, perhaps, he'd been put through the same form of questioning.

'I was late,' Tony explained. 'I missed the opening.'

Mullan took a moment to consider the comment, looked to the man who shrugged.

'Do you have your ticket there?'

'Not on me,' Tony said. 'I probably binned it with my drinks cup.'

'What did you think of the film?' Mullan asked, pronouncing it 'filum' as everyone at home did.

'It was all right.'

'What's the new guy like as Bond?'

Tony was wary one more, the innocuousness of the question the very thing that most frightened him. He had to assume that Mullan had seen it and was testing him.

'He was good. A bit serious.'

'The cello bit was a bit stupid,' Mullan said, his tone friendly, laddish.

'It was,' Tony agreed. 'The skiing down the mountain part.'

'Did you speak to anyone about what we were planning with the cop?' Mullan asked, the sudden shift in conversation jarring.

'No!' Tony said, mustering offence.

The man stepped forward, lifted the wooden bat and brought it down across his shoulders and neck.

Tony slumped forward onto the floor, screaming in pain.

'Quiet, son,' the man said. 'Did you tell anyone?'

'No!'

Another strike, this time across the back.

'You must have said something. Your dad? Your mother?'

'I swear!' Tony shouted, flinching in expectation of another strike. Instead, the man kicked at him, the boot connecting with his knee.

'I swear to God, son, if you're lying to me, I'll shoot your fucking da. He's a coward anyway. All it'll take is one phone call here and he'll be done. Do you understand me?'

'Yes,' Tony said, gripping his knee.

'Do you understand me?' the man repeated, this time aiming his kick higher, to the groin.

Tony arched with the pain, his stomach heaving, and he vomited all over the plastic sheeting.

'I didn't tell anyone,' he shouted, his abdomen aching. 'I swear to God, I didn't.'

Even as he said it, the words stuck in his throat, but he had no choice. If he told them now, what was to stop them killing his father anyway? They already considered him a coward, might think that Tony had involved him in some way.

'Did you go to the cops?'

'No,' Tony gasped, trying to spit the bile from his mouth.

Another blow, this time across the back with the wooden baton.

'Who did you tell?'

'No one.'

A blow to the stomach with his boot caused him to retch again, the pain in his innards searing.

'Who did you tell?'

'No one!'

Another blow, this time to the side of the head. Tony fell prostrate, his face pressed against the plastic sheeting, his head haloed in his own vomit. He lay there, looking sideways at this attacker's feet, wondering whether it wouldn't just be easier to tell the truth. They might understand, they might see why he'd wanted to protect Alice.

'Leave him,' Mullan said, and Tony saw the feet move backwards. He felt a touch on his shoulder, which stung with pain. He looked around into the face of Mullan, friendly, warm.

'We're nearly finished,' he said. 'Tell the truth now; did you tell anyone?'

Tony began to cry, the shame burning his cheeks, his words lost in his sobs. 'Leave me da alone,' he said. 'Leave him alone.'

'That's OK,' Mullan said. 'Did you tell anyone? Someone in school maybe? A colleague? Maybe a bit of chat in the staff room? You can tell us. Confess. Everyone needs to confess in the end.'

Tony lay back, tried to catch his breath. Something about Mullan's questions surprised him. They didn't know someone had spoken directly to the cop himself.

'I swear, I didn't tell anyone in school. I swear on my da's life, I didn't,' he managed, honest at least in that.

'Good fella,' Mullan said, patting him on the shoulder. 'Get yourself up and have another drink. It's all right, now.'

Tony pulled himself to his feet, using the overturned chair for support, then limped across towards the bar, holding his side gingerly with one hand, his stomach in agony, his balls cupped in his other hand. He glared at the unnamed man, spat blood and bile onto the plastic sheeting, but the man paid him no heed, moving across instead and removing something from the booth next to him.

When Tony glanced back a moment later, the man was holding a pistol.

Tony stopped, turned to look at Mullan and Duggan. 'What's going on?'

'See, the thing is, Tony,' Mullan said. 'We have a witness. Someone was spotted going into the home of the cop on Saturday night.'

Tony felt his legs seem to crumple under him.

'We already know who the tout is. We just needed to be sure.'

CHAPTER FORTY-SIX

'Are you sure? It's definitely this way?'

Tony nodded. He couldn't put his finger on what, but something felt familiar about the path they now followed, though if he were honest, it might have been simply that he was convincing himself that they were on the right track, for the trees blended one into the other. He was looking for the stream; it alone would prove that he was leading them in the right direction.

'Who was he?' Tony asked, gaining a quizzical look from Mullan. 'The third man, from back then. The one who beat us up.'

'It was hardly a beating,' Mullan laughed. 'I've got worse in the bar evenings.'

'He took a nail-studded bat to me at one stage.'

Mullan shrugged, glancing at Karen sceptically. 'I think you've misremembered that.'

'I know what happened to me,' Tony said. 'Who was he?'

'Joe Doherty,' Mullan said. 'He was one of the Nutting Squad. He helped us out.'

'He was an animal.'

'He did what needed to be done to be sure we had the right person.'

'We didn't have the right person,' Duggan muttered from behind them.

'And why were you there?' Tony asked.

Mullan looked at him askance. 'Me? I was in charge.'

Duggan spoke behind them again. '*Uncle* Sean here was the one set us all up together. He was the one sent me to the health centre to meet you, Karen. And he told me to look out for you, too, after your brother's death. We're all together now because of him. He was even the one who named the cop to us.'

'I thought it was Martin who saw him in a supermarket,' Karen said. Tony nodded, grateful at least that her memory coincided with his in that regard.

'Martin told me that Sean here sent him to that shop, week after week. Told him he'd heard a rumour that our guy was living in the area, shopping there. Martin knew him from back home.'

'Is that right?' Karen asked.

Mullan nodded, smiling a little ruefully. 'I'm surprised he told you. We knew the target was living in the area; we'd got word from someone that he'd relocated there. Kelly knew the man already; it made sense to send him out to check whether the rumours were true.'

'Martin told me everything back then. So, why didn't you come to me directly?' Duggan asked. 'Why go through Martin?'

'You always needed to feel like you came up with your own ideas, Hugh,' Mullan said. 'If I'd sent you after him, there'd have been no guarantee that you'd have followed through. Why do you think we'd sent you to Scotland? You were too awkward, too prone to heading off in your own direction.'

'That's a lie.'

'Your move over here was sanctioned at the highest levels, Hugh.

You know that. You were brought back when the ceasefire started, because there was nothing more you could do.'

'I was loyal.'

'You were,' Mullan said. 'And brutal. And effective. But you needed to feel like you were in charge. Still do.'

'What's that meant to mean?'

'Like I said, you're the man holding a gun. I told Kelly to mention to you that he'd seen the cop in the supermarket. I knew you'd come back to me, looking for permission to target him. And you did. You were predictable.'

'Not anymore,' Duggan said.

'Do you think? Why are we here? You approached me about this, first.'

'I've said; I want the truth—'

'No, why did you first think about him?' Mullan asked, smiling.

'What do you mean?'

'What first started you thinking about him, recently?'

'I'm dying. My pancreas, bowel, even moved into my lungs. I've weeks left,' he said, finally.

Despite everything, Tony felt sorry for the man, how defeated he looked despite holding a gun on them all.

'I know,' Mullan said. 'You were spotted going in and out of the cancer centre months back. News travels fast.' He offered no empathy, no concern. Business-like. 'But what made you think of Martin?'

'He was on the news. The family were looking again for him, in all the wrong places.'

Mullan nodded. 'I wonder where they got those tip-offs?'

Duggan stared at him a moment, as if piecing together what he had said. 'You?'

Mullan nodded. 'We needed to get him back; I knew you were dying, reflecting on things, according to your drinking cronies. I guessed a few high-profile stories about Martin's family and you'd be in touch. And you were. Predictable.'

'Don't push me, Sean,' Duggan growled.

'Or what?' Mullan laughed. 'What do you think is going to happen? Do you really think you're going to shoot one of us, here, with all these witnesses? Or shoot all of us? And then what? Drive yourself back home? You don't think you'll be caught?'

'I don't care if I am,' Duggan said. 'I'll be dead soon enough. But when I am, I don't want to face the dead and see Martin Kelly there, blaming me for what I did.'

'You think Kelly will be the only one waiting for you when you die?' Mullan sneered.

'Anyone else I did, got what they deserved.'

'Kelly got what he deserved, too,' Mullan said.

'I don't believe that,' Duggan said.

'But you told us there was a witness?' Tony said.

'What?'

Both Duggan and Mullan turned to look at him. He glanced at Karen. She seemed to give a shake of her head as if in warning, but it was too late.

'Someone saw him going to speak to Hamilton?' he continued.

CHAPTER FORTY-SEVEN

'Someone saw?' Tony asked. He was standing at the bar, one hand holding the brass handrail for support.

'Someone was watching the house that evening. It was a last-minute decision, apparently,' Mullan said. 'But they saw someone going into the cop's house and not coming back out again.'

Tony swallowed, glanced at the doorway. It was about six feet to his right, but limping as he was, he'd hardly be through it when the unnamed man would be on him, if he even got that far.

'Who was it?'

'You'll know soon enough,' Mullan said. 'Finish your drink and follow me.'

Tony struggled to pour himself a drink, his hand shaking so much the neck of the bottle rang on the edge of the glass several times before he managed to quarter fill the glass. He put down the bottle and, holding the glass two-handed, drained it.

His legs shook as he walked, his hands balled into fists in an attempt to control the shuddering which vibrated along his arms. As he passed the unnamed man, he tensed, refusing to look the man in the eye. All the way to the far door, he expected a bullet to strike him, flinching at the sound of Duggan's chair scraping on the floor as the man stood.

Mullan continued walking, leading him down a corridor to the door at the end which opened onto a small metal staircase. 'Down there,' Mullan said. 'Someone will be down for you in a while. Help yourself to a drink. We'll sort Betty out for it later.'

Tony picked his way down the steps, his footsteps echoing metallically off the cellar walls. Crates of empty bottles were piled to one side, while on the other wall, he could make out boxes of spirits, their labels barely readable in the penumbra of the light thrown from a single bulb in the centre of the room.

Amongst the shadows, against the far wall, sat Karen.

'Are you OK?' he said, moving over towards her.

She shifted slightly away from him and, at first, he thought she was still angry with him, but then he saw her face. A vertical line of blood had dried along one side of her face, from the cut above her eyebrow to the curve of her jaw.

'Did he fucking hit you?' Tony said. 'I swear to God, I'll…' He did not know what to say, knew how absurd such threats were in the situation and so allowed the sentence to die into silence. 'Are you OK?' he asked again, finally.

Karen sniffed, wiped at her eyes with her hand, the end of her jumper sleeve balled like a tissue in her fist. 'I'm all right. He only hit me once.'

'He hit you?' Tony spat.

She nodded. 'What about you?'

Tony blushed a little. 'Yeah, a few times. He had a bat with nails in it. I think he punctured my calf muscle with it.'

'Jesus. Are you OK?'

He shrugged. The question was offered more as a social observance than genuine inquiry, clearly, for the blood on his face was answer enough.

'What do you think they're going to do to us?' Karen asked.

Tony dropped roughly to the ground next to her. 'I don't know,' he said. 'Did they tell you who did it?'

Karen looked at him a moment, her expression unreadable. 'No. Did they tell you?'

Tony shook his head, unable to meet her eye. 'No. They said someone was seen, but that's all. Where's Kelly?'

'I've not seen him. I was told to be here at 9.30.'

'I was at 10.30. What time is it now?'

Karen glanced at her watch, angling it in the dim light. 'Almost one,' she said.

'What did they ask you?'

Karen cleared her throat. 'About you, mostly. And me.'

Tony felt his stomach churn again. They'd been asking about him. Did that mean they suspected him? But then, they had asked him mostly about her. Maybe they'd been bluffing when they said someone had seen. Maybe it had been to see if he would confess on the spot.

'What did you tell them?'

'The truth,' Karen said. 'We were going out and now, well, we're not.'

'I said the same thing,' Tony said. 'They wanted to know why we broke up.'

'What did you say?' Karen asked, suddenly apprehensive.

'I said you cheated on me at that party.'

'I didn't know what I was doing,' Karen said.

'I'm not arguing with you. They asked me if I thought we could trust you. If I trusted you.'

There was a pause for a moment, before Karen spoke. 'What did you tell them?'

'I said that we could. That I did.'

'Do you trust me? Completely?'

'Yes,' Tony said.

Karen took his hand in hers. 'We're going to be OK,' she said. 'I promise. Everything's going to be OK.'

Tony wanted to tell her the truth, wanted to unburden himself. She knew already about Alice; they'd spoken about her before. He felt certain she would understand why he'd done what he did. But then a voice niggling at the back of his mind made him wonder if this, too, was part of the interrogation. Was Karen sent to get him to confess, all along? Was she working with them? He desperately wanted to trust her, to tell her everything, but couldn't gather the nerve to do so.

In the end, their conversation was cut short by the grinding of the cellar door as it was pushed open. Duggan stood, alone at the top of the steps. He looked exhausted, his body slumped, his hands hanging uselessly by his sides.

'It's time to go,' he said. 'Come on.'

Tony struggled to his feet, put out his hand to help Karen to hers. 'Where are we going?' he asked.

'To finish this,' Duggan said.

'Where's Mullan? And the other guy?'

'They've gone,' Duggan said. 'They don't stay for this part. Mullan won't get his hands dirty.'

Tony stepped in front of Karen, his arm outstretched to stop her moving forward.

'What happens now? I'm not going anywhere until I know what's going to happen.'

'We shoot the tout,' Duggan said. 'We're taking him to Skiff Woods and we'll leave him there. All three of us need to do it. That way, no one will ever speak about it again.'

'Who was it?' Tony asked, feeling his stomach flip as he spoke as he swallowed back the rising burn of whiskey once more.

Duggan's eyes flushed and he sniffed once as he regarded something on the far wall. 'Kelly,' he said.

'Kelly?' Tony felt first a rush of relief, followed just as quickly by shame at the joy he was feeling at another man suffering for *his* crime. 'Are you sure?'

'That's Mullan's decision. We just do as we're told. Let's go. The car's outside.'

Tony looked at Karen and, for just a second, could have sworn he saw a change in her expression, from terror not to a look of relief, but of regret.

CHAPTER FORTY-EIGHT

The look of regret on Karen's face was the first thing that alerted Tony to his mistake. He rewound the sentence in his head, trying to work out the flaw. The others stood in silence, each considering the implications of his words. He'd only managed to do so himself, when Duggan himself spoke.

'How did you know his name?'

Tony feigned ignorance. 'Who? What name?'

'Hamilton,' Duggan said. 'No one told you his name. How did you know?'

'I must have overheard one of you talking about it,' Tony said.

Duggan shook his head. 'We made a point of never naming him. You shouldn't ever have known his name.' He pulled the gun free from his bag again. 'How did you know his name?'

'What difference does it make?' Tony asked, his mouth suddenly dry, his jaw tight.

'You knew his name. I want to know how.'

Tony looked from one face to the other and they were all closed against him, with the exception of Karen.

'I must have heard it somewhere?'

Duggan nodded, moved closer to him, the gun raised. 'I know that. I want to know where.'

'I don't remember,' Tony said.

Duggan progressed on him, the gun steady now. 'Where?'

Tony took a step back, felt the roughness of a tree trunk against his rump. 'I can't... I don't remember.'

'You spent that week looking to get out of it,' Duggan said. 'You hated Martin. I remember. *You* set him up.'

Tony could not move. He felt a tightness in his chest, felt the raggedy hoof beat of his heart. Duggan's gun was now less than a foot from him, the man's face set, his eyes blazing, his mouth tight with fury.

Tony shook his head, glanced at Mullan, Barr, Karen. Duggan followed his gaze to her.

'You both set him up!' he snapped. He turned now, towards Karen, pointing the gun at her, but looking at Tony. 'How do you know his name?'

Tony looked at Karen, her eyes wide, fearful. She had people to lose, people who would miss her.

'How do you know his fucking name?' Duggan shouted, the gun closer to Karen now, waving a little in his hand as he struggled to control his rage.

She looked back at him in terror. He thought again of how, when talking to Barr, he'd realized that, if he died, no one would miss him.

He thought now too of all that had happened since the death of Kelly. The passing of his son, his parents, Ann. His teaching career was over, his friendships, all with Ann's friends not his own, lost with her passing. He thought of the emptiness of his house, everything in its place, neat, the way Ann would have wanted it. And he realized, with a pang, that the life he'd been living, not just since Ann, but even before, had not been the life he'd expected, the life he'd imagined as he'd lain in bed with Karen thirty years ago, her very breaths pacing the rhythm of his heart.

And that realization brought with it resolution. He was not afraid to die; he no longer had reason to live. The thing he'd been looking for, here in the woods, he realized, had not been forgiveness at all, but confession.

'I knew his daughter,' he said. 'It was me who went to his house that night. I was the one who warned him. It was me.'

He felt strangely invigorated by the words, even as his guts tightened, his chest heaving. He glanced at Karen who groaned and wondered at her reaction.

Duggan stared at him, though remained in front of Karen, his gun still wavering before her.

'You?' Mullan asked.

'I taught his daughter, Alice,' Tony explained. 'I saw her at his house the night I went to Hugh, but I didn't recognize her until Open Day. He came to school to collect her that afternoon and I made the connection. I'd not planned it,' he added, hastily, as if in mitigation for what he'd done.

'What did you tell him?'

'Nothing important.'

'Our names?'

'No,' Tony protested. 'I told him nothing important. Just that his life was in danger and he needed to leave. I didn't give him anyone else's names, I swear.'

'It wouldn't have taken a genius to make the connection between you and us,' Duggan said. 'We drank together.'

'It was thirty years ago,' Tony said. 'He didn't care about you, or me. He just wanted to keep his kid alive. If you'd listened to me—'

'Listened to you?' he said. 'A fucking coward and a tout?'

'Better that than kill a kid,' Tony snapped, confident now in the rightness of his choice. 'That youngster had already lost her mother. She was struggling and her father was the only thing she had. She'd done nothing wrong. She didn't deserve it. She had a hard enough time as it was, just surviving. So I'm not sorry I spoke to him. I'm sorry that Martin took my place. I'm sorry that I wasn't honest thirty years ago, and sorry I didn't spare his family their grief, too. If I'm a coward, it's not because I wouldn't kill a child, it's because I didn't admit what I did back then. But I wouldn't change what I did with the cop or Alice. I was right to do it. So fuck you, Hughie. You want to shoot me, go ahead. I'm ready.'

Tony realized how quiet it had become. Even the birds above them seemed to have been silenced by his words, as if waiting to see how Duggan might respond. Tony looked to Karen, who sat on the bough of a fallen tree over to his right, her head in her hands. He wanted to apologize to her, for not telling her earlier, not telling her back then, but he didn't know what to say. For a moment, he worried that she was upset with him. He'd expected her to understand and was perturbed that she seemed not to, now.

He only realized the truth when Duggan spoke.

'You fucking bitch!' he shouted, raising the gun at her.

'Wait!' Tony shouted, rushing at him. 'It was me! Me!'

'You never named Martin,' Duggan snapped, looking at him, the gun still trained on Karen. 'That's not on you.'

She looked at Tony, tears already bright in her eyes.

'It was *her* said she seen him,' Duggan said. 'It's her fault!'

'You?' Tony asked.

Karen nodded, the tears slipping freely down her face now as Tony realized that, in confessing, he had not damned himself, but damned her; she who had lied thirty years earlier, to save him.

CHAPTER FORTY-NINE

'No one's going to save you,' Duggan said.

They'd reached the forest and stood in silence as Duggan opened the trunk of the car, in which Kelly lay, gagged and bound. His body was livid with bruises, visible because his T-shirt had become pulled up in his thrashing around the boot, as he attempted in vain to get free. 'Shout all you want,' Duggan said. 'No one's coming.'

Kelly attempted to kick out, perhaps hoping to knock some of them off balance. The kick glanced off Tony's side, though with little effect. Despite this, Duggan leaned into the trunk and punched Kelly, several times, on the side of the head, stunning him into silence.

'Grab the shovels,' Duggan said to Tony. 'He'll not hurt you.'

Tony reached in past the prone body, his head spinning. He'd not thought that, in protecting himself and denying his own guilt, they would inevitably blame someone else. They would punish someone else. And more than that, he had not considered that he would be party to meting out that punishment.

'Grab the petrol can as well and hand it to her,' Duggan instructed.

Tony did as he was told, lifting the can, the petrol sloshing about inside as he pulled it from behind Kelly's head and handed it to Karen.

'You OK?' he asked.

She nodded, not taking her eyes off Kelly where he lay and Tony knew that, in her head, she was already imagining the only possible ending of this.

Once they were ready, Duggan hauled Kelly to his feet, dragging him out of the trunk. He fell awkwardly to the ground, lay curled there, his hands grasping at the decaying leaves which cushioned his body.

'Get up,' Duggan said.

Kelly lay, groaning behind the gag. Duggan lifted his foot and kicked him hard in the balls. Kelly arched his back, sounded like he was choking against the rag that had been wadded in his mouth and taped over. 'Get up,' Duggan repeated. 'Or you'll get another one.'

Kelly struggled to his feet, but had not the energy or strength to stand. He slumped sideways, falling against the car while Duggan gripped at him to keep him upright.

'Give him a hand,' Duggan ordered, and Tony moved forward, ripe with guilt, and, putting his arm around Kelly to support him, used the shovel in his other hand to offer extra balance.

'Let's go,' Duggan said. 'The place will be empty by this time of the day.'

He carried a torch in one hand, a shovel in the other. Before he moved from the car, he put down the torch a moment and lifted a package, wrapped in blue plastic, from the boot of the car, and wedged it in his pocket.

'We head north,' he said.

The woodland was eerily still, the cries of the roosting rooks the only noise. Off to the left, the setting sun had branded the horizon in reds and gold. Tony wanted to tell Kelly to look, hoped he might see this final scene of beauty, but the man next to him kept his head bowed, watching his feet, trying not to trip, without the free use of his hands to break his fall.

Then they heard, for the first time, the sound of the jets rising from the runway of Glasgow airport, roaring overhead above them, life going on as a life here drew inexorably to its end. Tony ducked absurdly at the sound, looking up to see the plane, but he saw only the canopy of clouds.

After a while, the path veered a little to the right. It was darker now, the gloom thickened sufficiently among the trees for Duggan to switch on his torch, the circle of light bouncing between the tree trunks ahead, their upper branches lost in the ever-decreasing gradations of light. Occasionally, the lamp beam would catch a creature's eyes, shining blue-green, watching impassively their progress through the woods.

They moved in silence, save for the ragged breathing of Kelly and a low keening moan that he made every so often, a futile protest against his fate.

They crossed a small stream, only three or four feet across, using as a bridge the freshly fallen trunk of a tree, its body entwined with ivy. The watercourse lay at the bottom of an incline, which they had to jog down. Here, Kelly lost control and stumbled and fell into the water. Tony dropped his shovel and, falling to his knees, heaved him out of the water. Only when he had so done did he realize the absurdity of saving the man from drowning, like a doctor treating a condemned patient.

They walked a further twenty minutes or so, veering always to the right, making their way into the depths of the woodland. Their progress slowed as they went, the twilight darkening to night, the torch limiting the scope of their movement to all that was encompassed within the narrow beam.

Finally, they broke into a small clearing, an ancient oak at its entrance, a row of spruce at the other side, perhaps eight feet away.

'This'll do,' Duggan said.

Kelly slumped on to the ground, his body wracked with fresh sobbing.

'Should we give him a drink or something?' Karen asked.

'He doesn't deserve it.'

Kelly started to shudder of a sudden, his body seized by spasms, as if the shock of all that had happened to him and all that would had finally registered with him. The noise he made now became more guttural, as someone struggling to catch their breath.

'He can't breathe,' Karen said. 'Let him breathe.'

She ran across to him, dropping the petrol can and pulled the tape from his mouth, removing the rag it had held in place to silence him. He sucked in air greedily, gulping it down.

'Please, Karen,' he said. 'Please, let me go. It wasn't me.'

'I can't… I don't know…' She looked to Duggan who shrugged.

'He was better gagged,' he said. 'You,' to Tony, 'start digging.'

He and Tony set into a rhythmic motion as they dug, one offloading the soil while the other dug their shovel into the earth to lift a fresh load.

'I'm sorry,' Kelly whimpered.

'Strip him,' Duggan said to Karen. 'Everything off. Then burn it.'

'What?'

Karen stood, aghast.

'Take off his clothes. Everything. Even his jacks, in case he's got a wire or something on him.'

Karen looked to Tony who shrugged. She moved across and began to slowly unlace one of Kelly's shoes but he kicked out at her, striking her on the side of the head and knocking her to the ground. Duggan was up out of the shallow hollow in the earth and on him, striking Kelly's body with the shovel.

'Be a man,' he snapped. 'I'll fucking shoot you in the stomach and leave you to bleed, otherwise.'

Karen sat up, her face smeared with tears.

'He'll not do it again,' Duggan said, misunderstanding the cause of her crying. 'He'll behave himself.'

As Karen peeled off his shoes and socks, then started to work at his belt to remove his trousers, Tony tried not to look, focusing instead on the deepening grave. He knew he should confess, tell them what had happened. But he was afraid. He didn't want to die, didn't think it fair that he should end up in an unmarked grave for doing the right thing. As he reflected on it, he convinced himself that he was doing the right thing. He had saved a life, maybe two at least. Kelly had already claimed one, that he knew of, with Shauna Laird, never mind how many countless others who'd suffered taking the drugs he peddled. Kelly deserved this more than he did, Tony decided. And he almost convinced himself that that was true.

'It wasn't me,' Kelly started again, his breath back after Duggan's kick. 'I swear on my mother's life, it wasn't me, Hugh.'

'You were seen,' Duggan hissed. 'You were seen going into that cop's house.'

'That a lie,' Kelly said. 'Please, Hugh, you've got to believe me. That's a lie. You *know* me. Who said they saw me?'

Duggan did not look up, digging into the ground, the air fresh and sharp with the dampness of the earth as they deepened the hole. 'I trusted you,' he spat angrily.

'I didn't do it, Hugh,' Kelly said, looking around wildly for support, his gaze lighting on Tony. 'Was it him? He hates me, you know that, Hugh. He blames me for that girl who OD'd. You know *that*, Hugh. You *know*. Please.'

'It had nothing to do with him,' Duggan said. 'Don't embarrass yourself any more, son. You know what you did.'

Kelly was crying again now. 'Was it you?' he asked, looking at Karen, who lowered her head, tugging at his trouser leg. He kicked out at her, lightly, to get her attention. 'Was it you? Is this because of the party? It was a joke, all right? It was a joke.'

'What was a joke?' Tony said, standing, as Duggan stooped again to his task.

'The pill. It was a joke. It was a fucking joke,' Kelly said. 'I just slipped her one thing, one thing. She'd not even remember. It was a joke. It was a JOKE!'

He began thrashing now. Duggan stepped up again, his hands already curling into fists and unleashed a barrage of punches on the prone figure. Kelly curled on himself, screaming at each strike. 'I trusted you. Trusted you. I trusted you!' he shouted, each word punctuated with a blow.

Duggan leaned down, tearing at Kelly's T-shirt, ripping it up the middle and tearing it from his body. He ripped down each short sleeve, in order to remove the garment without having to undo the binds that held his arms.

'Get his trunks off him and gag him again. I don't want to hear him, anymore.'

'Please, Hugh,' Kelly cried. 'I'll not shout. I'll not shout.'

Duggan looked at Karen and nodded, then began digging again. Tony watched her removing Kelly's underwear, keeping her head averted so she did not look at his nakedness.

'He drugged you?' Tony asked.

'I said,' Karen said, her tears streaming freely now. 'I said that it wasn't my fault.'

'I'm sorry, Karen,' Tony said.

CHAPTER FIFTY

'I'm sorry, Karen,' Tony said. 'I didn't know.'

He stood next to her, his hand on her shoulder. She made no effort to remove his hand, nor did she acknowledge he was there. She stared straight ahead, her tears coursing freely.

'She was watching!' Duggan said. 'She said she saw someone going in after dark. She told us it was Kelly. Was that a lie?'

Karen nodded.

'Why?'

She looked up at him, angrily. 'Why? Why do you think? He was a scumbag. He killed that wee lassie that used to come into Betty's. He sold to kids. He drugged me. He was worse than the very people we were meant to be saving the country from and yet we were meant to work with him? Where's the morality in that?'

'Wars aren't moral!'

'Spare me the shit, Hugh,' Karen said. 'You weren't at war. You spent your days getting off on the power, on people being a little afraid of you. You mistook fear for respect. The night you maimed that guy in Glasgow, coming into the party late, bag in hand, standing with your arms up while everyone cheered you, like you were some kind of hero.'

'Don't!' Hugh cautioned her, his teeth gritted, his gun levelled at her.

'Or what? Are you going to shoot me?'

'I should have, thirty years ago.'

Tony stepped in front of Karen, blocking her from Hugh. 'It should be me. I told Hamilton about our plot, told him to leave. Karen was just trying to look out for me.'

'Don't think I haven't enough bullets for the pair of you,' Duggan said. 'And you, Sean. You took her word for it. You believed her.'

'We were all there,' Mullan said. 'You heard him; he admitted they'd broken up. There was no reason to think she was protecting anyone, least of all the ex-boyfriend she'd cheated on.'

Tony shook her head. 'Is that what those questions were about? Whether you could trust Karen?'

Mullan nodded. 'Her cheating on you saved both your lives. Ironic really. If you'd still been together, we'd have had to investigate a lot more.'

'We need to keep moving,' Barr said, surprising them, apparently, with the control he took of the situation. Tony wondered whether it was fear; what might happen to him, after all, if Duggan did turn his gun on them all?

'We'll go when I say we'll go,' Duggan said. 'Just keep your mouth shut, son.'

Barr nodded, his jaw tight. 'We need you to find Kelly's grave,' he explained. 'We can deal with all this when we've done that. Now, more than ever, his family deserve to recover his body, especially if he was innocent.'

'He was never innocent,' Karen said resignedly, standing. 'He just wasn't guilty of *this*.'

She began moving again, not looking to Duggan to see how he might react. Tony fell in alongside her, Mullan and Barr a few steps behind, Duggan to the rear.

'I am sorry,' he said. 'You should have told me.'

Karen smiled, shook her head. 'Seriously? *I* should have told *you*? Why didn't you tell me?'

'When?'

'Back then.'

'I couldn't. I didn't have a chance. I'd no time.'

'We were in a cellar for two hours, waiting for them to finish questioning Kelly.'

'Two hours?' In his memory, it had seemed perhaps twenty minutes. 'I… I wanted to. I actually was about to when Duggan came in and told us we had to go.'

'And afterwards?'

'Duggan was with us.'

'No, I mean after we came back. I risked my life for you; I'd no idea what you told them. If you'd confessed to them, I'd have been shot for lying. I trusted you to do the right thing. And afterwards, when we went back to mine, we had sex, we lay together and I waited for you to tell me. If ever there was a place or time for it, it was in those hours, lying together. I'd never have said a word, if you'd only told me, I'd have taken it to my grave for you. But you didn't. You talked about everything but and then you went to sleep and pretended everything was OK in the morning. And I knew then, we were done. You didn't trust me, which meant I could never trust you.'

'I did trust you,' Tony pleaded, turning to her, as if somehow convincing her now of this fact might change everything, might rewrite the past they didn't share. 'I told them that. I told *you* that, in the cellar. I told you I was sorry.'

'Our entire relationship seemed to be marked with milestones of your apologies,' Karen said. 'You didn't trust me enough.'

'I was ashamed,' Tony admitted. 'It's not that I didn't trust you not to tell anyone; I was ashamed. I thought if you knew what I'd done, what I allowed us to do to Martin, that you'd...'

'What?' Karen said, stopping to stare at him.

'That you'd not love me the same anymore.'

Karen nodded, even as Tony realized she was right: he hadn't trusted her to love him no matter what he had done.

'Jesus,' he said, tears springing to his eyes. 'I'm so sorry.'

'And there's another one,' Karen said, smiling sadly. 'I know you are, Tony. I knew you were then, too. But I couldn't be with someone I'd trusted with my life that didn't trust me with his.'

'We need to keep moving,' Barr said behind them.

Tony looked at Karen, wanting to hold onto this moment, painful as it was, if only because it was something they shared, something that had brought them closer together. But she moved on.

Following her, he realized they were going down an incline, into a hollow in the woods. 'This is it,' he said. 'This is the right path.'

Sure enough, a moment later, they came to the scar of where a stream had once cut through the woods, its bed now cushioned with fallen leaves.

Barr headed down to the right several hundred yards, tracing the dried stream's progress. 'Down here,' he called.

They moved down to where he stood. As they approached, Tony could make out the rotted carcass of a tree trunk, which traversed the bed of the stream.

'We're on the right track,' Barr said. 'How much further?'

'Not much,' Tony said. 'We're nearly there.'

CHAPTER FIFTY-ONE

'We're nearly there,' Duggan said, his breath short, the words clipped.

He straightened in the grave, pulled his T-shirt free from where it had been tucked in at his waist. 'Another few shovel loads will do us. You finish it; I'm going to find some large stones.'

'What for?' Tony asked. For a moment, he suspected Duggan wanted to place a marker on the grave, which would surely draw attention to its location.

'We need to put some on top of him to stop foxes and the like from digging him up,' Duggan explained as if speaking to a child. In terms of their levels of experience of such things, Tony reflected, Duggan's assessment wasn't far wrong.

Kelly lay on his side now, seemingly in a faint. His breathing had become quick and shallow. He whimpered where he lay, his body shivering involuntarily every few minutes. He seemed unable to lift his head from the ground and leaves and dirt were stuck to the side of his face. A leaf, attached to his lips, rippled and danced with each breath, but did not dislodge.

'What will we do?' Karen asked. She'd finished stripping him and had placed his clothes in the bag, which Duggan had given to her.

'Should we let him go?' Tony said, then realized that Duggan may not have gone too far away and might be wondering why the sound of digging had stopped. He took another shovel load of clay, deposited it to the side of the hole.

'I don't think he'd get very far,' Karen said. 'He's sweating, but his skin's cold.'

'He's in shock,' Tony said. 'See if you can rouse him.'

'I'm going to undo his hands,' Karen said.

She knelt behind him, working at the knots, but they were pulled tight by Kelly's having struggled against them. She got down on all fours, leaning down, as if to use her teeth to loosen them.

'Take his gag off,' Tony said. 'See if he's awake enough to run.'

Karen nodded and, reaching down, pulled the gag loose from his mouth. 'Martin,' she hissed. 'Martin?'

His eyes rolled towards her, his mouth lying open, his tongue moving uselessly.

'He must be thirsty,' she said. 'We've nothing to give him to drink.'

'Martin,' Tony said. 'Martin, can you hear us?'

Kelly's eyes swiveled back towards his direction, but he seemed for a moment to struggle to focus. He tried to speak, but the words, dry and rasping, made no sense.

'Martin, can you get up?' Tony hissed. 'Can you stand?'

In the middle distance, they heard something crash in the undergrowth and they both instinctively ducked. There was no further sound, and Tony guessed Duggan must have dropped some of the stones he was carrying. If they could hear him, he could hear them. He took another shovel load, deliberately clinking the metal edge against the side of a stone wedged about two foot down, the ringing carrying clear across the woodland floor. He deposited the spoil on the graveside, then hoisted himself up out of the hollow and scrabbled across to where Kelly and Karen were.

'Martin, you need to get up,' he said, shaking the man's shoulders. His skin was clammy, sticky to the touch. Closer to him now, Tony could tell that he had soiled himself at some stage, though Karen had not mentioned it. The wounds on his arms and shoulders were vivid, despite the relative murkiness of the woods, their eyes having long since adjusted to the dark in which they worked.

'Get up, Martin,' he repeated, putting his hand in under Kelly's trunk to try to help lift him. Kelly seemed to realize what he was doing, for Tony felt his weight shift as the injured man began using his legs to try to raise himself.

'You need to go, Martin,' Tony said. 'We'll say you ran when we weren't looking. You need to go.'

'I'm sorry,' Kelly rasped. 'I'm so sorry.'

They heard another crash, closer this time, and the hissed cursing of Duggan.

'You need to go,' Tony said, pushing him, encouraging him to leave. 'Please, run.'

'I'm sorry,' Kelly repeated. 'I'm sorry.'

'Please, run,' Karen said. 'Please, Martin.'

For a moment, Tony thought he was going to do so. His legs tensed, as if in preparation to sprint, but as he moved his foot, his weight seemed to drop under him and he stumbled, forcing Tony to have to grip him tighter to hold him. Kelly winced in pain as Tony's grip encircled the bruises on his trunk.

'Sorry, Martin,' Tony said, hugging against the man to help him remain upright. He felt the weakness of Kelly's pulse, the shallow rising of his chest with each quick breath. 'Jesus,' he said, the realization of what was happening made concrete with the smell of blood, sweat and piss, which emanated from Kelly's skin. 'Jesus, I'm sorry, Martin. I'm sorry. It shouldn't be you, it should–'

'He's here,' Karen cried, and Tony could not be sure whether she had heard what he was saying.

Duggan appeared into the weak light the torch he'd left at the edge of the clearing. He bore a number of rocks, cradled in his two arms, like children. He came across to the grave and, opening his arms, dropped them at the side.

'You got him up,' he acknowledged. 'Good. Let's go.'

Tony straightened, felt Kelly attempt to stand beside him. 'Hugh, should we really do this?'

'I knew you'd be the one to have second thoughts,' Duggan said. 'I knew you'd not have the balls for it.'

'It's wrong,' Tony said.

'His touting was wrong,' Duggan said. 'That's the only thing that matters. How can you ever count on soldiers if they break the rules?'

'We're not soldiers,' Tony said.

'You're not, that's for sure,' Duggan spat.

Tony angled himself to better support Kelly. 'I don't want to be a part of this,' he said. 'I can't.'

'You're already a part of it,' Duggan spat. 'You got the mercury we used in a tilt switch. You helped watch the cop for weeks. You brought a car load of weapons and Semtex from Paisley into Glasgow. What do you think happened with those?'

'No one knows I did that?"

'Your fingerprints are on the car,' Duggan said. 'You couldn't help yourself but have a look inside. You touched the boot.'

Tony looked at Karen who blushed. Clearly, she had told Duggan this after their first drive together.

'I covered my hands with my sleeves,' he offered weakly.

'Catch yourself on,' Duggan said. 'You're in this up to your neck. And you're going to see this through with us, together. No one can talk if we're all involved. That's how it works. That's what you signed up for.'

'I didn't sign up for this,' Tony said, sullenly.

'Your brother would be ashamed of you,' Duggan said. 'Man up and get him into the grave.'

Tony looked from him to Karen. She had lowered her head, the bag of clothes twisted in her grip. There was no other choice, he realized. Even if he admitted now that he had been the one to tell the cop, what good would it do? He told himself Kelly deserved it, but he did not believe it. In his heart, he knew that he was afraid to face the consequences of what he had done, that he was a coward. He hid his face against Kelly's body, for shame, his hands touching a wound at the condemned man's side that made him think of spears and a place of skulls.

'Get him into his grave,' Duggan repeated, then pulled the package from his pocket and, unwrapping it, revealed a pistol, its metal shining dully in the torchlight. 'Let's get this over with,' he said.

CHAPTER FIFTY-TWO

'Let's get this over with,' Mullan said. 'Are we near?'

Tony stopped and surveyed the land ahead. A thick-trunked elm stood to one side, sycamores and beech ahead.

'It was a clearing,' Karen said. 'There were thinner trees to one side of it. They'd be bigger now.'

'Taller, but not much thicker,' Tony said. 'They were spruce, I think. I remember them, straight and thin. You burned the clothes just past them.'

Karen nodded, did not articulate her version of the memory.

'How much longer?'

'A few minutes,' Tony said.

Duggan followed behind, not speaking, though maintaining his distance from them. Tony wondered at his thoughts, whether he was attempting to apportion blame, attempting to decide whom best should answer for what they had done to Martin Kelly.

They trudged up the incline on the opposite bank of the stream, their steps wide and laboured. Tony couldn't remember if they had taken this path, though he had a memory of having taken Karen's hand at one stage, on their way back, as they had passed the stream.

'Over to the left a little,' Duggan said. 'We headed towards the sunset as we came up this way.'

Tony didn't remember that, thought indeed that the sun had set already as they first made their way through the woods. But Duggan seemed certain. Either way, they were close.

Sure enough, after ten minutes of walking, they broke out into a clear area. It stretched for several hundred yards down from where they stood. Looking now, Tony guessed that where they'd stopped was a liminal point in the woodland, the stage at which the original ancient forest gave way to newer growth.

'There was spruce on one side and an oak on the other,' Tony said.

He made his way along the line of trees until, over to his left, he could see the thin lines of spruce trunks appear through the gaps in the tree line.

'It's around here,' he called, moving on, scanning the edge of the original woodland as he did, looking for the oak tree, which he remembered. Forty yards further down, he found it.

'This looks about right,' Karen said. 'Somewhere around here.' Her eyes shone, her lip quivered a little as she brought her hand to her mouth and took a breath. 'This is it.'

They stood in silence for a moment, even Duggan, as he drew level with them, not speaking, simply looking around the clearing, nodding to himself, as if confirming some suspicion he had not shared.

'Mark it on your phone,' Mullan said to Barr. The youth took out a mobile phone and, opening the Maps app, dropped a pin on their current location. 'Thank you, all,' Mullan said, when that was done. Then he turned to Duggan. 'So, what now, Hugh?'

Duggan regarded him, sullenly. 'I trusted you,' he said.

'Trust? What would you know about trust?' Mullan said, scornfully.

'I gave everything,' Duggan shouted. 'Everything. Just like you. Except I'm not swanning about in chauffeured cars, joking with the enemy.'

'No, you were joking with the enemy from the start,' Mullan said. 'We knew what you were. You want to shoot a traitor, you need to start with yourself.'

Tony flinched as Duggan pulled his gun, held it, wavering, pointed at Mullan. 'That's a lie.'

'Hugh here was a Judas goat,' Mullan said, turning to look at Tony. 'That night you were lifted, he was in your cell, right? They'd seen us speaking to you at the funeral, wondered if we'd said something to you about what we were planning. They put him into the cell with you to encourage you to talk. I'll guess he befriended you. Shared his smokes, maybe?'

'His shirt,' Tony said, nodding.

'That was his role; convince the younger ones to say something they shouldn't. Incriminate themselves enough that the cops could recruit them as informants.'

'That's lies,' Duggan said, progressing now on Mullan, the gun pressing against the other man's temple.

'So now you're going to shoot me?' Mullan said, laughing. 'First it was Tony, then Karen, now me? I hope you've enough bullets in there.'

'I've plenty,' Duggan said, swinging the gun between the three of them. Only Barr stood, silent, cautious, off to the side. 'You're not going to spread lies about me.'

'You protecting your legacy, Hugh?' Mullan laughed. 'You don't have a legacy. Everyone knows you for what you are.'

'They lied,' Duggan said, the gun turning on Tony again. 'They set up Martin.'

'Do you know why Doherty came across that time? We were sure *you* were the tout. He was coming across to finish you off. It was a surprise to all of us when this one said she saw Kelly going into that house and not you.'

'Liar!' Duggan said, raising the gun and striking Mullan with it on the forehead, the butt tearing the skin.

Mullan staggered a little, then straightened, blood already tracing a line down his face. He smiled. 'Come on, Hugh. Do it. Protect your legacy before that cancer inside you eats you up completely.'

Tony stepped towards Karen, wary of Mullan, wondering why he was goading Duggan.

'The truth is, Hugh,' Mullan spat. 'I don't think you've the balls for it.'

Duggan looked from one face to the other, his eyes wild, his mind racing. Finally, the gun settled on Tony. His expression hardened, as his finger tightened.

He pulled the trigger and fired.

CHAPTER FIFTY-THREE

The gunshot scattered clouds of crows into the night sky, their screaming in contrast with the soft grunt that Kelly made as he fell sideways.

Tony watched in horror as he dropped against the side of the grave and lay there, his mouth hanging ajar, his eyes open wide, but unseeing. He glanced across to Karen who was standing with her back turned, her hands over her face, not looking at what had unfurled.

'Fuck,' Duggan muttered and walked the circumference of the grave until he reached the spot nearest Kelly. With the toe of his shoe, he pushed the body sideways, causing it to slide fully into the grave itself. He stood, gun held steady, and fired off three shots in quick succession, each one thudding into the body.

'Get the stones on top of him,' Duggan said. 'There shouldn't be anyone about, but the shots could be heard for miles; we need to hurry.'

Tony stared at the body, the blood pooling round the hollows of each rib, then trickling down the side. Kelly's face lay against the soil, his mouth open and pressed against the earth.

'Hurry up,' Duggan said. 'And you, girl, snap out of it. Get those clothes burned, then cover over the scorch marks. We'll all need to get rid of what we're wearing soon as we get home. A hot wash – everything, even your pants and shoes. Hot as you can get it.'

Tony stared at him, at the easy manner in which he had shifted into practicalities. He looked across at Karen, watched as she turned to look at Martin first, then at him. He saw something in her expression change, her features grow impassive, her eyes lose focus a little. She took the bag in one hand and lifted the petrol can with the other, then set off through the trees.

'Get moving,' Duggan said.

Tony followed him, lifting the stones Duggan had gathered earlier and dropping them down onto the body. He struggled with one of the more awkwardly shaped ones and dropped it into the grave only for it to strike Kelly's leg and fall onto the grave floor.

'Get that fixed up,' Duggan said.

Tony tried reaching down with his foot to move it, but the depth of the hole and the weight of the stone made it impossible. Reluctantly, he dropped down into the grave and lifting the stone, laid it across Kelly's legs. He inadvertently touched one limb and was surprised to find the flesh warm, mobile. He laid his hand on the dead man's muscles and felt he should say something, a prayer, some Last Rites. He muttered a Glory Be as he traced the sign of the cross with his thumb. Then he climbed out, as Duggan began piling the earth on top of Kelly.

It took them almost twenty minutes to fill the hole. The work became easier once the whiteness of Kelly's skin had vanished beneath the first layers of dirt and Tony no longer had to face directly the consequences of his actions.

Across to one side, the flickering light illuminated Karen's face as she went about the business of burning his clothes, the enterprise soundtracked by the crackling of branches, the hiss of spruce needles. Even at this distance, Tony could feel heat emanating from the flames, could smell the mix of petrol and fibres and sap, thick and acrid in his mouth and nose.

When they had finished, there was still a small mound of spoil left to one side. Duggan and Tony spread it as best they could, dragging the dirt in all directions with the edge of their shovels.

'Gather handfuls of leaves now and scatter them about,' Duggan instructed. By now, Karen had returned and the three of them moved in different directions, scooping up armfuls of rotting ground cover which they then scattered across the area where the grave lay.

When they had finished, Tony stood in silence and looked at the area where they had buried Martin. He could hear Karen and Duggan already trudging their way back towards the car. Duggan had claimed he knew the way; this was not his first time having to do this, he said.

Tony stared at the spot before him, struggling to know what to say. An apology was too little, that he knew. But he also felt relief: that he had survived, that Alice had survived and that with Kelly's death, this was all over.

In the end, he said nothing, simply bowing his head with the weight of his guilt and moving away, following the bobbing light that wove its way through the trees ahead, leaving the grave to its silence.

CHAPTER FIFTY-FOUR

Silence.

Tony stared at Duggan, then looked down, his hands already searching his trunk, looking for the wound that must surely have been there. But there was nothing. Just silence.

Duggan himself seemed confused, aiming a second time and pulling the trigger again. A click. Then silence once more.

'What's wrong, Hugh?' Mullan asked. 'I thought you had enough bullets.'

Duggan gripped the gun in fury, opening the barrel, then yelled, an animalistic roar. 'Fucker!' he snarled, moving on Mullan, but Barr stepped in, grabbing his arm and shoving him back, twisting his wrist enough to dislodge the gun, which dropped solidly to the earth. The youth bent and picked up the weapon, then stepped back, away from Duggan.

'Where are they?' Duggan asked, looking at Mullan, who simply nodded back at his nephew.

Barr put his hands in his pocket and pulled out a handful of bullets. Tony noticed that, at some stage, Barr had put on a pair of clear latex gloves.

'Let me help you with your bag, Mr Duggan,' Barr said, smiling.

The deferential attitude, the carrying of the bag to the boot of the car, had all been a ruse, the last double-crossing of an old comrade, Tony realized.

'Did you think I was stupid, Hugh?' Mullan said. 'Did you think I'd not have seen what you were at? Looking to settle some scores before you bow out. Going in a blaze of glory.'

'That's not true,' Duggan said, sullenly, backing up from where Barr stood.

'That is, Hugh, and you know it. Richard here checked your bag in the car. Nothing in it but that gun and your flag and gloves. You weren't planning on ever leaving here, were you?'

Duggan stared at him, his mouth moving wordlessly, his lips dry, save for a speck of white spittle balled at one corner. 'Martin was my friend,' he said. 'And you made me kill him. Not you or Doherty. Me.'

Mullan nodded. 'Like I said, we thought you were the tout. Even after she said she saw Kelly, we thought maybe you were still pulling the strings. I wanted to see if we could trust you. If you would shoot your own friend.'

'I did it.'

Mullan nodded. 'You did indeed.'

Barr coughed lightly, to get Mullan's attention, tapped the face of his watch lightly. The exchange brought Duggan to his senses.

'How will I be remembered?' he asked, his head bowed a little, looking up at Mullan.

'As a good comrade who never got over the loss of his friend.'

'What are you doing?' Tony asked.

Duggan looked at him, then back to Mullan. 'I'm not ready.'

Mullan nodded. 'You wanted answers, Hugh. That's why you came here. You got them. We made a mistake. The boy here wasn't selling us out, he was protecting a kid and she was protecting him. Martin was a mistake. Our mistake. But it's done now.'

Tony moved over to Mullan. 'What are you doing?'

'We're leaving the past behind,' Mullan said. 'It's a new beginning. We have to go, Hugh.'

Duggan nodded.

Mullan walked past him, laid a hand on his shoulder. 'Safe travels, Hugh. Let's go, you two.'

Duggan stared at him blankly, watching him leave, but made no attempt to follow.

Barr loaded two bullets in the gun, slowly, carefully. He caught Tony's eye, indicated with a nod of his head that they should leave.

Karen walked across and stopped next to Duggan, her face flushed. She pressed her cheek against his, whispered something that only Duggan could hear. He nodded, but did not speak.

Tony approached him, trying to find something to say, something to adequately express thirty years of conflicting feelings. 'Are you… I don't…'

Duggan looked through him, nodded, his mind elsewhere, his lips still moving soundlessly.

'Do you want us to stay with you?'

'I'm trying to remember something,' the man muttered.

'What is it?' Tony asked. 'Is it about Martin?'

Duggan looked at him, clearly now. He raised his chin a little. 'J.B. Books. That was his name.'

'Let's go, Tony,' Barr said.

Tony felt he should do something for Duggan, embrace him, pray with him, shake his hand, but the man's mind was elsewhere once more and he simply repeated over and over a mantra of 'J.B. Books.'

The ground ahead splintered into tears as Tony moved away from Duggan, past the ancient oak to join Karen and Mullan, who were waiting. Behind him, he could hear Barr moving, his progress marked by the rustling of the leaves coating the ground beneath the oak.

They moved through the trees in silence, waiting. Waiting. Waiting.

The shot echoed through the woods this time, rolling down the incline towards them. Tony glanced around, briefly, to see Duggan slump to the ground, Barr standing to his left, his gun hand still raised. The youth knelt lightly beside Duggan, lifting his dead hand and, placing the gun in it, fired off the second shot, into the air, ensuring Duggan would have gunshot residue on his skin. He realized he had misjudged the youth, the eagerness and efficiency with which he had killed Hugh Duggan, the skill with which he had made himself appear innocuous all through their journey.

'Jesus,' Karen said, beginning to weep. Tony moved across to her and put his arms around her, felt the wracking of her sobs, joining with his own quieter tears.

'Well, that's Hugh, God rest him,' Mullan said, turning to Karen and Tony. 'Now, what do we do with you two?'

CHAPTER FIFTY-FIVE

'You two are going to need to keep your mouths shut,' Duggan said.

He was sitting behind them, leaning forward so his arms rested on the backs of their seats. Tony suspected he had chosen the seat so that he could keep an eye on them both.

'We're not going to say anything,' Tony said.

'We're all in this together,' Duggan said. 'You know that. If they find Martin, we'll all be implicated.'

'We're not going to say anything,' Karen repeated, flatly.

As the drive went on and the woods retreated further and further away from then, Duggan seemed to resign himself to what they had done. 'At least we know who we can trust, eh?'

His question elicited no enthusiasm from either Tony or Karen.

'For our next target,' he explained.

'Our next target?' Tony asked, incredulous that Duggan could be thinking of such a thing after what they had just done.

'There's always a next target,' Duggan said. 'And we're a team.'

'What about what they did to us? In the bar?' Karen asked. 'That hardly felt like being part of the team.'

Duggan shrugged. 'These things happen. We all have to make sacrifices. And what we did tonight will make a difference.'

He sat, his chin resting on his arms, waiting for a response, but got none. After a moment he straightened and laid a hand on each of their shoulders in front of him.

'Look, I know that was hard. Martin was one of us. If you want my advice, you do what I'm going to do when I get home: don't sit and mope about it, don't think it over to see what we could have done differently. Go to the offie and buy a bottle of something strong and forget about the whole thing. He's in his grave now and that's where he'll stay. We're soldiers and soldiers do as they're told. We followed orders and did our duty. We did the right thing.'

'I didn't,' Tony muttered.

They reached the station where Duggan asked to be dropped, so he could take the late train home.

'I'll be in touch,' he said as he left them. 'Go home and forget about the whole bloody business.'

They watched him shuffle his way into the station, sticking a hand in his pocket and pawing out a few coins to pass to the young fella squatted at the station entrance, a paper coffee cup his begging bowl.

Tony watched him go, watched him turn the corner and vanish from sight. He silently prayed it would be the last time he would ever see Hugh Duggan. If he was in touch, Tony knew he would not answer, could not conceive of himself being involved in anything like this again.

He looked at Karen to see if she was likewise watching Duggan go, but her head was bowed, her gaze fixed on her hands, nested in her lap. She looked up at him, as if aware of his watching her, but she did not say a word.

CHAPTER FIFTY-SIX

'We're not going to say a word,' Karen said.

'I know that,' Mullan said. 'After all, I saved your lives. If Richard here hadn't taken the bullets out of Hugh's gun, you'd both be dead.'

'As would you,' Tony pointed out.

'Ah!' Mullan swatted the claim away with a wave of his hand, as if it were of no consequence. 'You get cautious in my position. We did need to get Kelly's body back, but I suspected Hugh might try something if he had the chance; Kelly was always a sore point for him. And with his illness, he was a dog gone rabid. And there's only one thing you can do with a mad dog, and that's put him to sleep.'

He moved across to Barr and patted his arm. 'Good job, son.'

Barr took the compliment, with just a hint of a smile.

Tony dropped heavily to the ground, sat with his arms resting on his knees, exhausted from the constant buzz of adrenaline he'd fed himself all day.

'Why did we have to be here? To see this?'

Mullan inclined his head. 'He'd never have come without you. We wanted Kelly back; Hugh wanted to get answers on what happened back then. He couldn't get those unless all of you were here.'

'You used us?' Tony said. 'Again.'

'You're never out,' Mullan joked, mirthlessly.

'So, what now?' Karen asked, daubing her eyes with her sleeve. 'What happens to us?'

Mullan considered the question. Behind him, his hands clasped before him, stood Barr, waiting, like a well-trained dog.

'What about you?'

'I have kids. A husband. What we did happened thirty years ago, no one got hurt.'

'Martin Kelly would disagree,' Mullan said. 'As would his family.'

'Martin Kelly sold drugs to children,' Karen said. 'He sold stuff that caused a kid to overdose. He gave me a date-rape drug as a joke. Martin wasn't innocent. What we did was wrong, and we've all had to deal with that in our own ways, but, Jesus, we were only kids ourselves, Sean.'

She looked wildly round at Tony, who still sat on the woodland floor, pleading with him to say something. But he was too tired to argue for himself.

'Karen did nothing wrong,' he managed. 'If someone needs to be held accountable, it should be me. I went to the cop, Hamilton. I warned him what was planned. I took cold feet. And I should have spoken when Martin was brought here. I was a coward, from first to last. Karen just did what she thought was the right thing, for me. But ultimately, I did this. I was wrong.'

He sat for a second, lost in thought, picked up a stone that lay beside him and tossed it into the undergrowth. 'My father warned me why I shouldn't have looked for revenge for Danny. He told me it would spiral, a perpetual reciprocity of grief. He was right.'

He struggled to his feet, using the tree behind him for support. 'I've no family, no one left to cry for me. So if someone needs to pay for what happened, it should be me. There would be no more grief.'

He looked at Karen and, for a moment, was pained to see tears rise in her eyes for him. But she had a husband, kids, a life to go back to that did not, and would not, include him.

Mullan nodded. 'Someone needed to pay for the cop, Hamilton, getting away. Martin Kelly did that. Someone needed to pay for Martin Kelly; Hugh has done that. The way I see it, the sheet looks balanced. It's all about optics, right?'

He looked over his shoulder at Barr who shrugged and nodded.

'Now, I've to go back to Glasgow. Richard is coming with me. We can leave you in Glasgow.'

'I want to go home,' Tony said.

'He can run you both back to the ferry first,' Mullan offered, glancing at his watch. 'If we're quick out of here, you could still make the last crossing.'

Barr took out his phone and looked at it. 'I dropped a pin at the car park too,' he said. 'There's a more direct way back; it'll take about 25 minutes.'

'I'm visiting family in Glasgow,' Karen said. 'I'll go on in with you.'

'He'll drop you off, sure,' Mullan said, then turned to Tony. 'What about you?'

'I'm taking the ferry back,' Tony said. 'But I can take the train if you can drop me at the nearest stop.'

'The late crossing doesn't take foot passengers. But I can phone ahead, get it sorted for you.'

Tony felt drained, his chest heavy and dull, his arms hanging like pendula by his sides, aching. 'What about Hugh?'

'We'll take care of it,' Mullan said, moving across and kicking a scattering of leaves over the spot where Tony had sat. He turned, ushering Barr ahead of him. 'Lead on, Macduff,' he said, mimicking a Scottish lilt.

And so they set off, back through the woods. Tony turned, as he had done before, and regarded the scene: Duggan's body lying above the ground, Kelly's lying somewhere below, a strange marriage consummated with blood. But this time, he felt no urge to apologize. He'd told the truth, made his confession, and done his penance, he decided.

He turned his back on that place for a final time, and set off behind the others, the woods ahead of him full of colour and sound, though seemingly separate from him, as if perceived through a pane of glass, or by one who dreams.

THE LAST CROSSING

CHAPTER FIFTY-SEVEN

He dreamt of Martin Kelly that night, woke gratefully the following morning only to find the bed already empty. For a moment, he thought Karen had left, but then he heard rattling coming from the bathroom, the clatter of her toothbrush falling back into the cracked ceramic mug she used to hold it.

He climbed out of her bed and padded his way across to where she stood, putting on her make-up, her work shirt already on, hanging loose over her pants, her skirt still hanging on the radiator.

He moved behind her, placed his hands on her hips, moved them up beneath her shirt, cupping her breasts as he ground himself against her behind.

'Do you have to leave?' he asked, nuzzling into her.

But she shifted from him, wriggling her body to indicate she wanted him to move away. 'I'm getting ready for work,' she said.

Tony regarded her in the mirror, but she would not hold his eye, glancing fleetingly at him, then back to the mirror, rolling her eyes upwards as she applied her mascara.

'Is something wrong?' he asked.

'Nothing,' she said, moving to the other eye. 'I have to go. Can you let yourself out?'

Tony nodded, hurt by her coldness to him. His stomach ached from the day before, his leg and back causing him to wince whenever he moved. He did not want to face the reality of the new day, the reality of what they had done. In Karen's arms, in Karen's bed, he'd been able to escape that, pretend that what had happened in the woods was just a bad dream. Her indifference now brought reality, that they had watched someone be killed, crushing back to him. 'Are you annoyed at me?' he asked.

She shook her head, finishing her make-up and squeezing past him to retrieve her skirt. She pulled it on, balancing herself by placed one hand against the wall, despite his outstretched offer of his hand, then moved past him again and out into the bedroom.

'There's tea and stuff in the kitchen,' she said. 'If you need breakfast.'

Tony followed her out to the room.

'What's wrong?'

'Nothing!' she snapped. 'Just leave it, OK?'

Tony sat heavily at the edge of the bed. Had he said something he shouldn't? Done something? Or was he unnecessarily personalizing it? Surely it must be her reaction to what had happened the previous night. Perhaps reality had crashed down on her? She was pragmatic, business-like. Maybe this was how she was dealing with what had happened.

She went into the living area of her flat and appeared a moment later, her coat across her arm.

'I'm away,' she said.

Tony moved over towards the door and leaned down to kiss her. She turned her head a little, her lips pursed, and pecked the side of his mouth.

'Goodbye, Tony,' she said.

He watched her as she left, pulling the door behind her, not looking back at him, watched through the window showing nothing but empty streets until the echoing of her footfalls along the pavement had died away.

Rubbing at the bruises on his stomach, breathing in the faint scent of her perfume, which misted the room where he stood, he could not dispel the feeling that he would never see her again.

CHAPTER FIFTY-EIGHT

'We'll see you again,' Mullan said, as Tony climbed out of the car.

They'd driven him back to Ayr to get the final train there that would take him onwards to the ferry. Mullan had left his car parked in Howwood, knowing that they would have to come back that way anyway and he could pick it up then. In truth, Tony suspected he was keeping an eye on them, controlling the narrative, until they all went their separate ways.

Tony had sat in the back with Karen, in silence, while Barr and Mullan sat up front. The older man had spent most of the time on his phone while his nephew drove. Only one call had held Tony's interest.

'Richard's sent you on the map link,' he'd said. 'Duggan's there... Suicide... He's not been well, to be honest. Maybe he just couldn't live with the guilt anymore and went back to find the grave for the family, then took the easy way out... The guy was riddled with cancer. He... he told me himself... he told me himself that he couldn't face the treatment, the pain... Well, that's how you frame it... If you want to recover any of the others, you'd best not look too much into it... He brought his flag and gloves... Well, that's the story you're getting... That's not my job... Bye.'

He hung up the phone and glanced in the mirror of the sun visor, catching Tony's eye a moment, then turning his attention back to the road again.

'Who is J.B. Books?' Tony asked.

'Who?' Mullan said, looking back at him.

'J.B. Books?' Tony repeated. 'Hugh said his name before he... before we left him.'

He looked at Karen who shook her head. Mullan shrugged, then took up his phone and started typing on it.

'John Bernard Books,' he read from the screen. 'He was played by John Wayne in *The Shootist*. It was his final film.'

Mullan looked back at Tony again to see if this provided sufficient information, his face a pantomime of confusion.

Tony nodded. 'That makes sense,' he said, lapsing once more into silence. Karen sat next to him, took his hand in hers, held it for the rest of their journey together.

They dropped him at the railway station in Ayr.

'See you,' Mullan said, offering his hand, as Tony was getting out of the car. He took it and shook once, briefly, because he had no reason not to.

Barr got out of the car with him and, opening the boot, lifted out Tony's bag and handed it to him. 'I've searched it, so you're good to go,' the youth said, and laughed, though Tony could not be sure whether it was a joke or not.

'Thanks for the lift,' he said, feeling a little absurd in so doing.

He moved towards the station as the passenger door opened and Karen got out. She moved across to him and they stood, waiting for Barr to get back into the car.

'It was good to see you, Tony,' she said, her hand on his arm.

He looked at her, the softness of her face, the clarity of her eyes, their two differing colours still bright, the invitation of her mouth and, in that moment, he loved her as intensely as he ever had.

'I'm sorry how things worked out,' she said. 'How...'

'How life worked out?'

She nodded, smiled sadly. She hugged him then, embraced him tightly. He returned the gesture, felt instantly the comfort of her familiar shape and smell and touch.

'I still love you,' he whispered to her.

'I know,' she said. 'And I still love you, too.' she said. 'But I have a different life now. And so do you.'

They parted, and she stood in front of him, her eyes, like his, glistening with tears, both hands on his shoulders as if she was studying him, wanting to remember every detail of his face.

'And so do you,' she repeated, trying to laugh, her voice cracking a little. 'And so you should. Go. Live. Be happy.'

She moved forward and kissed him on the side of the mouth, their lips touching for the briefest moment, and he felt her tears against his cheek, his mouth and nose filling with her scent.

But she wore a different perfume now, her old scent at once as familiar and irrecoverable as the past.

CHAPTER FIFTY-NINE

As they passed Lady Bay, Tony watched Scotland slip away from him.

It was three weeks since he'd last seen Karen, that morning she had gone to work. She had not answered his calls, did not answer the door when he'd called. At first he'd been hurt, then angry. Now he was resigned. The place had changed for him after Martin Kelly. The country held his bones and, to Tony's mind, that infected everything that Scotland might hold for him.

He'd phoned his father and explained that he wanted to come home. He wasn't going to get involved in anything, he promised him. Nothing could bring Danny back, but he missed home and was ready to return.

His landlord had allowed him to leave a week early on his lease on condition he forfeited his deposit. The school hadn't been pleased about his leaving at such short notice, but he'd lied, said his father was sick and he needed to go back to look after him. They'd accepted the excuse, albeit reluctantly. After all, if he left the country, what else could they do?

He stood on deck, the wind whipping his coat, his hands gripping the rail, his face feeling stiff with the wash of salt spray and looked forward, towards where home lay. He felt in his breast an undercurrent of dread, but above that, the small still voice of Hope that said everything would work out OK.

He realized now, as he watched the same coastline recede from view, that perhaps the voice had been true. He'd gone home and, indeed, his father had become sick and he'd been there with him until the end. His mother had followed not long after. He'd met Ann in school one day when she was in as a visiting speaker. She might not have had the passion of Karen, but then, by that stage, his own passion had waned.

They'd been happy, he decided; happier than he deserved to be. And she'd been loyal to him, and funny, and silly at times, and balanced, and calm and insightful. And he missed her, he realized. Karen had been right; they had their own lives now and they owed it to the dead to live them as best they could.

He took a deep breath, holding the sea air in his lungs. His chest hurt, a heaviness sitting on his breastbone and with the inhalation, a sharpness ran up his neckline and across his jaw. He felt a cold sweat break on his brow and decided he'd best move indoors again.

It was quiet inside, most people content to sit on their phones, or dozing before the final drive home. The lounge at the front was busy, but subdued, save for the raucousness of that same group of old women in the corner he'd seen earlier on the morning crossing over. They'd been there all day, laughing, drinking, living as they crossed between Ireland and Scotland over and over. This was the last crossing of the day, and they seemed determined to make the most of it. Even the man behind the bar was laughing at their abandon.

Tony thought for a moment of Duggan, sitting here this morning, drinking his whiskey. And then in the pub in Howwood, his savouring of each mouthful. Duggan had never intended leaving those woods. He'd known all along that he would not be returning, had chosen that ending to his story, had known even this morning that that early ferry was his last crossing.

Tony went to the bar and ordered a Southern Comfort and Coke. Handing over a £10 note to pay, he waited for the change as he emptied the cola into the spirit and returned the bottle to the bar man. He picked a coin from his change and palmed it to the man, who took it with a quizzical 'Thank you.'

'Just paying the ferryman,' Tony joked.

He moved back down through the ship again, taking a seat at one of the tables, on the starboard side. He rested his head against the window, staring out into the gloom. Somewhere, a lighthouse flashed, guiding the ferry past the ragged coastline.

He took a sip of the drink, the first time he'd tasted it since that last night with Karen and, with that, felt, once more, her mouth on his, the ache, the longing for the touch of her skin, the heat of her.

A sudden tiredness washed through him.

He yawned, felt again the pain in his neck that accompanied the deep inhalation, considered that he should see the doctor when he got home. Perhaps it was a muscle pain, he decided, sitting up, craning his neck from side to side to relieve the ache.

The table next to him was empty, but the one beyond that seated a family of a mother, father and two children. They'd brought sandwiches and bottles of juice with them, which they now shared in a late supper. The younger child, a girl, was obviously tired and lay across the seat, her head resting on her father's lap, the man sitting with his back to Tony. Opposite them, her face obscured by her partner, sat the mother. Next to her, a son, older than his sister, was begging to be taken to the shop, unhappy with the food on the table in front of him.

Tony thought of his own mother, then. They'd gone to Scotland several times when he was young, to visit his relatives. They'd taken the ferry together; Danny would sit with his mother, he beside his father, as they'd play cards, eating their packed lunch of ham and tomato sandwiches, the bread made soggy and stained pink from the tomato. The flask of tea always had a distinctive flavour and he could taste it now, stronger almost than the taste of the drink he'd just been sipping.

Of a sudden, as they reached deeper waters, Tony felt the surge of the ship moving forward and, with it, a commensurate feeling, as if he were floating, as if he had been freed, himself, from the shallow waters through which he had been navigating.

The pain in his chest bloomed once more, sharp and sudden, and then was gone.

Beyond him, the mother finally gave in and stood, taking her son's hand to bring him to the shop. Tony studied her features and, in that moment, imagined that he recognized her. She was slim, slight, her dirty blonde hair pulled back in a ponytail. Despite the demands of her child, she smiled at her husband as he spoke, asking her to bring him something nice.

Tony felt his eyes droop, leaden, felt a tiredness born of the day's exertions lie heavily on him. He rested his head against the window as he watched the girl come closer, her son's hand in hers, both their faces alight with some joke they shared.

She was happy. And with that, he believed he knew her now.

'Alice?' he whispered.

As she drew level with him, she glanced at him, quizzically.

'Are you OK, sir?' she asked, leaning over and touching his shoulder.

Tony smiled as he felt the ferry move further out. He knew he should be afraid, this far from shore, but the crossing was warm and gentle and brought with it, not silence and darkness, but the sweet taste of flasked tea, the smell of Karen's perfume, the sound of Ann's laugh, the tenderness of Alice's hand on his shoulder, and the sight, not of Martin Kelly as he'd feared, but of his father and mother and Danny, and Ann and his son, all somehow together at the table with him.

Joining him on this last crossing.

'Sir?' the girl repeated.

Beside her, the child called to his mother.

ACKNOWLEDGEMENTS

I owe a huge debt of gratitude to many people who helped me bring this book to fruition. Since I first wrote *Borderlands*, in 2003, I've been incredibly fortunate to have been supported by two Davids. Dave Torrans has always been such a champion of my writing and this book simply would not have been finished without his advice and encouragement; likewise, Dave Headley has been such an advocate for my work from day one and continues to be a source of huge encouragement and guidance now as my agent. I'm very grateful to them both.

The book also benefited from the insight and encouragement of Adrian McKinty, Steve Cavanagh, Ann Cleeves, Claire Allan and Gerard Brennan. I'm grateful to them, and to so many other members of the crime-writing community for their friendship and collegial support.

I'm immensely grateful to the team at The Dome Press – in particular, my editor Rebecca Lloyd – for taking a chance on *The Last Crossing*.

Thanks also to my many teaching colleagues and students who have been so supportive of my writing over the past decade or more. Special thanks to the members of The Magic Conch for their insights: Jamie,

Niamh, Franki, Maya, Michelle, Shonagh, Megan, Tara, Sara, Alannah, and Saoirse.

Thanks to Emily Hickman for her continued support and good advice and to Jenny Hewson, Emma Warnock, Susan McGilloway and Patricia Devine for their help with various aspects of this book.

Special thanks to the McGilloways, Dohertys, O'Neills and Kerlins for their support, and most especially Carmel, Joe, Dermot and my mum, Katrina.

My continued love and thanks to Tanya, Ben, Tom, David and Lucy who bring me more joy than I can ever fully express.

Finally, this book is dedicated to the memory of my father, Laurence, the finest, the kindest and the gentlest man I have ever known.